Praise for *Active Defense*

"*Active Defense* by Lynette Eason is a riveting romance, full of character development and edge-of-your-seat moments. . . . *Active Defense* has it all."

Life Is Story

"*Active Defense* by Lynette Eason proves once again that she is at the top of her game in Christian romantic suspense."

More Than a Review

Praise for *Acceptable Risk*

"Readers will be kept on the edge of their seats."

Booklist

"*Acceptable Risk* by Lynette Eason is another can't-put-down suspense thriller. Eason never disappoints me and *Acceptable Risk* is no exception. . . . You won't want to miss this one."

More Than a Review

"Buckle up, folks, because you are going on a wild roller-coaster ride, and you'll probably not put this book down until you are done."

Interviews and Reviews

HOSTILE INTENT

Books by Lynette Eason

WOMEN OF JUSTICE
Too Close to Home
Don't Look Back
A Killer Among Us

DEADLY REUNIONS
When the Smoke Clears
When a Heart Stops
When a Secret Kills

HIDDEN IDENTITY
No One to Trust
Nowhere to Turn
No Place to Hide

ELITE GUARDIANS
Always Watching
Without Warning
Moving Target
Chasing Secrets

BLUE JUSTICE
Oath of Honor
Called to Protect
Code of Valor
Vow of Justice

Protecting Tanner Hollow

DANGER NEVER SLEEPS
Collateral Damage
Acceptable Risk
Active Defense
Hostile Intent

DANGER NEVER SLEEPS ④

HOSTILE INTENT

LYNETTE EASON

Revell

a division of Baker Publishing Group
Grand Rapids, Michigan

Published by Revell
a division of Baker Publishing Group
PO Box 6287, Grand Rapids, MI 49516-6287
www.revellbooks.com

Library of Congress Cataloging-in-Publication Data
Names: Eason, Lynette, author.
Title: Hostile intent / Lynette Eason.
Description: Grand Rapids, Michigan : Revell, 2021. | Series: Danger never sleeps ; #4
Identifiers: LCCN 2020049184 | ISBN 9780800729370 (paperback) | ISBN 9780800739966 (casebound) | ISBN 9781493430369 (ebook)
Subjects: GSAFD: Mystery fiction. | Suspense fiction.
Classification: LCC PS3605.A79 H67 2021 | DDC 813/.6—dc23
LC record available at https://lccn.loc.gov/2020049184

21 22 23 24 25 26 27   7 6 5 4 3 2 1

Then you will know the truth,
and the truth will set you free.

John 8:32

ONE

BEGINNING OF APRIL
NEW MEXICO

Today, the watching ended and the killing started. Anticipation arced through him. The man in the ski mask turned his gaze from the front door of the luxury home to the end of the street. For ten days, he'd hidden and observed—and learned—the routine of the household and even the neighborhood.

Right on time, the mail truck turned onto the street and began its stop, deliver, go. Stop, deliver, go.

As soon as the vehicle moved on to the house next door, the man's gaze swung back to the front door once more. And there she was. In her midsixties, the woman of the house took care of herself. She ate healthy with the occasional sweet indulgence, used her gym membership daily, and jogged two miles every morning. On Wednesdays, she volunteered at the local elementary school.

He could have snatched her off the street during one of her runs, but he couldn't take the chance that a doorbell camera would catch him. No, this was better. They had an alarm system, but no cameras.

She slipped out onto the porch, down the walkway, and to the mailbox. She'd done the same thing every day at approximately the same time. Other than the Wednesday break in routine, it was like she had nothing else to do but work out, jog, and wait for the mail. What a sad, sorry life. But that wasn't his problem.

On the wraparound porch, the planter with the seven-foot piece of lush greenery to the left side of the door hid him well. Adrenaline sent his heart thudding, and his right hand curled around the grip of his weapon. He'd had fifteen years of preparation and training, research and planning. The time was now and he was ready.

She was on the first step, then the second, then walking to the door.

As she twisted the knob, he stepped from behind the tree and clapped a gloved hand over her mouth. A muted scream slipped from her, and he brought the weapon up to the base of her skull. Whimpers escaped through his fingers. She shook so hard, he thought he might lose his grip. He shoved her through the door and kicked it closed behind him.

"Where's your husband?" He kept his voice low.

A sob ripped from her throat and harsh breaths gushed from her nose. He released his grip to hear her say, "He's not here."

"He is, because I know you're supposed to be leaving in an hour for your holiday in Turks and Caicos. The suitcases next to the door tell me he's getting ready to load the car. So, if you want to live to enjoy your trip, you'll get him in here."

"He's—"

"Darling?" The voice came from the balcony overlooking the foyer. "I'm almost ready. Was there any mail? I'm expecting—" He stopped, gasped. His hands gripped the railing and his gaze met the man's. "What do you want?"

A smile curved beneath his mask. "Hello, Maksim. Come on down."

"Don't hurt her." The husky baritone held fear—and . . . something else . . . resignation?

"Well, now, that depends on you, doesn't it?"

"I'm coming." The man hurried down the winding staircase, stopping at the bottom. "Please. Let her go. I'll do whatever you want. Do you need money? I have ten grand in the safe."

Money? He almost snorted. Money was the last thing he needed. He kept the weapon on the woman's head. "Turn slowly," he told her without taking his eyes from her husband, "and reach into my left-hand pocket. Pull out the object." She didn't move and he narrowed his gaze on the man at the bottom of the steps. "You might want to convince her to do as I ask."

"Darling, do as he says, and it will be all right."

The woman whimpered and turned, her eyes downcast. She reached for his right pocket.

"My left," he snapped.

She jerked her hand away and then slid it into the left pocket of his blazer. "Good. Pull out the photo."

With shaking fingers, she did so.

He nodded to the husband. "Come get it."

The man's brows dipped farther over the bridge of his nose, but he did as ordered without having to be told twice. When he held the picture between his thumb and forefinger, he looked at it—and swayed. "I see."

"I'm sure you're starting to."

"Max? Make him let me go." The woman mewled and the intruder tightened his grip.

"Who are you?" Maksim whispered.

"I think you know that answer."

What little color the man had in his face drained away as his suspicions were confirmed. "You're Nicolai, aren't you?"

11

"I am."

"How did you find me?"

"It's a long story. And not one I have time to tell. I have one question, and if you know the answer, you will live."

Maksim's eyes lifted to meet his. "Let me guess, you want to know who the man is."

"No. I know who he is. I want to know who the child is."

The woman had gone completely still, with only an occasional tremor shuddering through her.

Maksim stood still, studying the picture. When he looked up, his fear was written in his blue eyes. "Why?"

"It doesn't matter why," Nicolai snapped. "Who is it?" He dug the suppressor harder into the woman's head. She shrieked, the sound grating against his eardrums.

Her husband stepped forward, hand outstretched. "Please!"

"Who. Is. The. Child?" Nicolai asked, his voice low. Calm, controlled. "Don't make me ask again."

"His daughter."

A daughter.

A thrill like nothing he'd ever experienced lit up everything inside him. His enemy had a daughter.

"Well, well," he murmured.

His original plan immediately shifted. He had a lot of thinking to do, but he'd stick with the beginning of it. It was the end that would change.

In the end, the daughter would be the last to die. "What's her name?"

"I don't know and that's the truth." He held up a hand. "I don't know. He never mentioned her. Ever. The only reason I know he has a daughter is because I overheard him say something to his boss about protecting her."

The desperation in Maksim's eyes said that he was telling the truth. That was okay. He'd find out who she was.

Nicolai fired the first shot and the woman slumped, dead before she hit the floor.

The husband screamed. "You promised!"

"Exactly. I made a promise, and now, I'm keeping it." He aimed the weapon at Maksim.

"How did you find me?"

The wobble in his voice did much for Nicolai's disposition.

"Some people just can't throw anything away."

Maksim swallowed. "The files?"

"The files, the pictures, copies of those old floppy disks with your handiwork on them. Everything. Now, it's just you and me, and we have a lot to talk about before you die."

"A death that will be slow and painful, no doubt?"

"The slowest and the most painful." He quirked a smile at the man. "I learned from the videos on those disks."

Maksim bolted into the hallway.

Nicolai blinked. Okay, he hadn't expected that, but he knew this house as well as its owners, thanks to the blueprints he'd acquired. He followed his target to the closed office door. He might try to call for help, but no calls would go through. He'd made sure of that.

Nicolai didn't bother trying the knob. He simply lifted his foot and kicked the door in on the first attempt.

Maksim sat behind his desk, pistol to his chin, blue eyes teary, yet determined. And resigned.

"No! Don't you dare!" He lunged.

Maksim pulled the trigger. A red mist coated the window behind him. Nicolai screamed his fury before he grabbed the nearest bookcase and shoved it to the floor. Then the next and the next and the next.

Until he slumped to the floor amidst the chaos to catch his breath and reconfigure the plan. Visions of torturing the man now staring at the ceiling with sightless eyes were shattered, and his blood pounded from the rage of being robbed of that dream. But—he drew in a steadying breath, ordering his pulse to slow—there was the daughter. That fact brought him a peace he'd not known since his childhood.

He had a new target. He'd find her and make sure she suffered greatly before she died.

o o o

Six weeks later
Sunday morning, May 15
Greenville, South Carolina

FBI Special Agent Caden Denning stood outside the home in the upper-middle-class neighborhood with his phone pressed to his ear. "There's a security system, Annie. This is a very nice neighborhood with a lot of cameras, but first see if you can get anything on the home system." Annie's skills at the Bureau were legendary. Hacking into an alarm system that recorded footage would be child's play for her. Sheriff Jay Nichols had called the Bureau when he recognized the similarities of the case to the killing of the Bailey family in Houston, Texas. "Officers are going house to house asking for footage," he said to Annie, "but I want inside the home cameras now. I don't want to have to wait for the alarm system powers that be to give it to me."

"Of course," she said. "And I know it's early and missing a lot of data since you haven't even seen the crime scene yet, but I'll run this murder through ViCAP and see if it matches any other murders of entire families—including the one in Houston. Depending on what shows up, we can add the other information as we get it."

"Perfect."

Caden shoved his phone into his pocket, pulled the little blue booties over his shoes, and signed the crime scene log just as a black Jeep Wrangler pulled to the curb. His partner, Zane Pierce, joined him on the porch, coughing into a tissue. The man's nose was red, his lips chapped, his hazel eyes bloodshot with dark circles beneath them. Morning stubble graced his face and his dark hair looked finger combed.

"Dude, are you on some undercover assignment I don't know about?" Caden asked him. "That's one heck of a disguise."

"I wish. I think I'm officially sick."

"Sorry, man. I can take this if you need to go home."

"I'll be fine, just don't get too close."

"You don't have to worry about that." The last thing he needed was a cold—or whatever affliction the man had.

The foyer held a set of stairs to the second floor. From his position in front of the door, Caden could see straight ahead into the den. The living room was to the left, the dining room to the right. From his vantage point, he could see the kitchen, with a large island, connected to the dining room. "Who found them?" Caden asked.

The officer looked up from the log. "The neighbor. She and the wife—"

"Angelica," Caden said, his voice low. He'd studied what little notes the responding officer had gleaned. "Staff Sergeant Michael Fields, his wife, Angelica, and their two youngest children, Brian and Ellen, ages eight and ten."

"Right. Angelica. They go walking every Sunday morning. When the woman—Angelica—didn't show up at their usual meeting spot on the curb, the neighbor came looking for her. The front door was open, so she walked in."

Caden groaned. "Walked in to see—"

"Yeah. She ran screaming to her husband, who called us. Paramedics almost had to sedate her, she was so hysterical. They finally got her calmed down."

15

"Poor woman." Bracing himself, Caden forced his covered feet forward and entered the den.

He spotted the victims and let his chin drop to his chest while sorrow slammed him. Kids. He'd almost quit the job more than once because of the children. But they had to have someone fighting for them, to see they received justice.

Zane blew out a harsh sigh, coughed, and pinched the bridge of his nose. "Man."

"Yeah . . ." Caden shook his head. For a brief moment, he squeezed his eyes tight. He didn't want to see any more. He finally opened his eyes and studied the family huddled together on the couch. Each had one bullet to the forehead. The nausea swept him and he fought it to focus on the building rage. He could manage the anger. "Where's Mickey?"

"Who?"

"Their oldest son. According to the notes I read on the way over here, he's fourteen or fifteen. His name is Michael Jr., but he goes by Mickey."

"I'll get someone looking for him." Zane turned to the nearest officer and requested he ask the neighbor about the teen.

"Who would do this?" Caden didn't expect an answer. The question wasn't so much disbelief that someone could actually kill them, but him fathoming who would *want* to do it—or why.

"Robbery doesn't appear to be a motive," Zane said. He nodded to the elaborate media system nestled into the wall unit. "That would bring in a lot of cash."

"So, why?" Caden muttered. Another rhetorical question. Until they took apart this family's lives, they wouldn't speculate.

Zane continued to frown and turned his eyes from the scene. "Adults are bad enough," he muttered, "but kids . . . they get to me. I'm going to be seeing them in my nightmares for months."

16

"I know. Same here." It would probably be more like years. Caden's phone rang. Annie. He swiped the screen. "That was fast."

"I had an almost immediate hit in ViCAP. There are two other murders that I can say initially match yours."

"Tell me."

"The information received was that the entire family was murdered with one gunshot each to the head. They were all seated on the sofa, kind of huddled together. The scenes were middle- to upper-middle-class neighborhoods."

"Where?"

"First one was the Holden family in San Diego, California, last month. Second one was two weeks ago—like the observant sheriff noted. Carl Bailey and his family in Houston, Texas."

"So, this is the third," Caden said.

"Yes. I've pulled the photos and other information from those two scenes and sent them to you. Family members also reported missing photos."

"Of what?"

"Family pictures. Mostly older photos. No one seems to know why."

He was stealing pictures of the families he killed? For a souvenir? To relive the killings? "Okay, I've made note of that. Thanks. What else?"

"That's all for—" A pause. "Hold on, Caden, we might have something more for you."

We?

In a short minute, she came back. "Okay, Daria's got more information for you." Daria Nevsky, another analyst with mad skills in all things technical. "And as of twenty seconds ago, she'll be your go-to on this one. Gary's handed me something else to work on." Gary Smith was Annie's supervisor.

Caden went still. Daria had worked on other cases with him,

but . . . "This is a big one, Annie. Probably a serial killer. You think she can handle this?"

"Without question."

Her complete lack of hesitation settled his momentary twinge of anxiety. "Fine."

"Truly, Caden, she's better than I am. I'm putting you through to her. Hold on."

Better than Annie? Not likely. The line clicked. "Caden?"

Man, she sounded too young to be as good as Annie said. "Yeah." Not that age had *everything* to do with skills or being a good agent, but still . . .

". . . has a camera in the den facing the sofa, so I'm sending the footage to your phone. You can watch it yourself."

"Wait, you actually got something?"

"Yes. Our speech reader even got some of the words from Mr. Fields's lips before . . . well . . . before."

Before he'd been shot. He just prayed the father had been the last one to die and the kids hadn't seen—

"Caden?"

He blinked the images away. For now. "I'm here."

"Did you get the video?"

He checked. "I did." Along with everything Annie had sent him.

"I added the captions to it so you can see what the words are."

"Impressive."

"I aim to please. Unfortunately, the camera in the kitchen area wasn't working, so I'm not sure what happened after you see the gun fly back into the living area."

"What?"

"Just watch it. It's self-explanatory. Call me if you need anything else. I've also texted you my direct line."

"Thanks. I'll be in touch." She'd managed to reassure him

18

she was up to the tasks ahead of her with that one conversation. Caden hung up and filled Zane in.

His partner rubbed his head. "Three?"

"Yeah. And at the moment, it looks like they could all be connected. Too many similarities not to be, even without the full workup of this scene."

"Then it's got to be the same person or persons doing this." Zane's hoarse, flat words pierced Caden's carefully constructed emotional barrier. "I hate to say it," Zane said, "but . . . I think we've got a serial killer running loose in this country."

"Probably." Caden kept his voice calm, detached, even as his heart thudded hard enough to hurt. *Focus.* "Serial killers don't usually have a territory this wide. Three different states? And opposite ends of the country?"

"True. Not that it's impossible, but what's the connection that made them targets?"

"That's the question of the day, isn't it?"

"So, once again, we circle back to motive," Zane said. "When we find out the connection, we'll figure out the motive. Or vice versa. You know what I mean."

"Exactly." Caden rubbed a hand over his chin. "So, this is it. We don't leave here until we know what we're dealing with."

"Yeah, because if we don't, what you wanna bet there's going to be a fourth?"

"I agree." He looked up as the officer Zane had assigned to find Mickey stepped next to him.

"No one seems to know where the teen is," the man said. "The neighbor had the kid's number. I've called it, but it went straight to voice mail." He handed Caden a piece of paper with the number on it.

"Thanks." He texted the number to Daria and asked her to find the phone. He looked at Zane. "We're going to need to set up a task force."

"I was thinking the same thing." His partner coughed and pulled a pack of tissues from his pocket. "Be right back."

Caden let his gaze scan the room, ignoring the chatter of the other officers coming from the open front door. He stopped at the mantel. Pictures lined it. Mostly of the children. Some of the family.

"Hey, Caden?"

He turned at an agent's voice.

"Yeah?"

"You're going to want to see this." She handed him a box. "Found it in the attic behind a wall."

Caden opened the box and sifted through the pictures and other items. At first, he didn't see anything that caught his attention. They were just things that someone had stuck in a keepsake box. But the closer he looked, the more intrigued he became—especially of the one with two people he knew. Ava Jackson as a child sitting in a swing and her father pushing her. What in the—

"Sorry." Zane returned with a bottle of water. "Had to find some Motrin and blow my nose. Seriously, how can your nose feel stuffed completely full and when you blow it, noth—"

"I don't need the details, dude." Caden nodded to the tablet Zane still held in his other hand. The box could wait for now. "Let me see those pictures from the Houston crime scene again, will you?"

Zane pulled them up. "Why?" He popped a cough drop.

"Scroll through them. I'm looking for something in particular."

His partner swiped one picture after another.

"There," Caden said. "Stop."

"What do you see?"

"The same picture on that end table in the Baileys' home that's over there on the mantel." He pointed, then enlarged the

20

photo for details. "There." A do-it-yourself Christmas photo in a small black frame sat on the stone mantel next to others like it. An antique clock behind the pictures ticked away the minutes. He stepped forward. "But look, there's a space next to it like another picture is missing. Now, look back at the picture Daria sent us. Same space next to that one?"

Zane raised a brow. "Yes. Exactly. You and that memory of yours," he muttered. "Okay, then. It's possible family number one and family number three knew each other and had the same photo that the killer took. Could family number two know one and three? But how? Or is that a stretch? Is there any evidence in family number two's home to suggest a connection? Did they have the same pictures? Or were they pictures that the killer just liked and have no connection at all?"

The questions came rapid-fire, Zane not necessarily expecting immediate answers, but Caden said, "If family number two had the same picture, they didn't have it out." He scrolled through the crime scene photos from family number two. No spaces between pictures to suggest one was missing. "It could be any kind of a connection," he said. "Could be a college fraternity or sorority. We also have to look at both spouses' connections to each other."

"Let's watch the footage. Maybe that'll help."

Caden tapped the link to the footage. Zane watched over his shoulder as it began to play.

The picture was clear.

As was the barrel of the weapon aimed at the family.

Unfortunately, the killer's face was not.

Beyond the gun, seated on the couch, were the staff sergeant, his wife, and the two younger children. All four of them looked terrified. Mingled with Michael Fields's terror was fury. He appeared to hold himself still only out of fear for his family.

"That's freaky," Zane said. "I feel like I'm watching this from his point of view."

Caden paused the video, turned, and pointed to the wall behind them. "That camera up there in the corner near the molding. It almost blends right into the wall. The killer might not have realized it was there."

"I don't know. He keeps his back to it."

"You think he wanted us to see the footage?"

"Who knows, man. Let's get this over with and watch to the end."

Caden ignored his anxiety at what he knew was coming and pressed Play. Daria's captions popped up on the screen.

"I'll give you whatever you want, just let them go," Fields said. He stopped speaking and seemed to be listening. Then his lips moved once more. "You want me to say what?"

The tip of the gun turned on his wife. She cowered over Brian and Fields held up a hand, yelling, "Stop! I'll say it. 'Trusting a liar will only get you killed.' There. I said it. Now, let them go."

The gun jerked. Four times. And it was over.

But no. It wasn't.

The gun flew back into the room and landed on the floor just within range of the camera. A foot appeared in the frame for a brief second before disappearing. For the next ninety seconds, the footage simply revealed the family on the sofa. Then the killer returned. He walked from the foyer, his back still to the camera, and went to the mantel to snag the now missing picture.

Caden blinked, swallowing hard. "Mickey must have made it home," he said, his voice low. "He walked in the front door as the man was killing his family and he acted."

"Kicked the gun out of the guy's hand?"

"Yeah."

"Then what?"

"I don't know." Caden's mind played out several scenarios of what could have happened next. None of them good. All of them stomach-turning. He drew in a shuddering breath. "But the man wanted that picture. He came back to get it for a reason."

Caden swallowed twice and sighed. He handed the iPad to Zane, walked outside, and lost his breakfast in the nearest bush.

TWO

It hadn't taken long for them to be discovered.

Nicolai, dressed in a gray T-shirt, blue jeans, baseball cap, and sunglasses, ignored his throbbing knee and watched from across the street. This was the second time something had gone wrong with his plans, but it wasn't irreparable.

Just annoying and frustrating.

Thankfully, no one paid him any attention as he blended in with the other neighbors who'd stopped their Sunday morning routine to gawk at the unfolding scene.

The cell phones were out in force, no one wanting to miss a moment of the excitement in their otherwise boring routine. Nicolai made sure to stay out of the line of sight of those cameras. Positioned toward the back of the crowd, he leaned against the nearest tree, pulled the ball cap lower, and crossed his arms. He also had a good view of the busybody neighbor who'd found the family. She'd disappeared when the paramedics had arrived, then two officers had joined her in the back of the ambulance. No doubt grilling her about what she'd seen. He wasn't worried. She hadn't seen him. A short time later, she'd rejoined the neighbors, her face pale, the horror of what she'd seen written in every line, but still watching the action.

She spoke to each person she knew, and he prepared to duck away if she came at him. For now, she seemed content to speak to the older gentleman on the other side of the tree.

Law enforcement had been in the house for a while, wondering who the monster was who'd kill an entire family. Especially kids. He frowned. He could understand their horror. He'd admit the kids were the hardest, but they were part of the promise.

I'll kill them, I'll kill them all. I promise.

Just two more families and his mission would be complete, his promise kept. His grandmother was wrong. Vengeance didn't belong to God. It belonged to *him*. And it tasted sweet.

"Terrible shame, isn't it?"

He almost came out of his skin when the man to his right spoke and he realized the words were directed at him. He cleared his throat. "Uh . . . yeah."

"So, who are you? I know everyone who lives around here, but don't think I've seen you before."

"Oh, I was looking at that house for sale on the corner, saw all the excitement, and thought I'd stick around to see what was going on."

Thank goodness he'd spent some time coming up with a plausible story, should something like this happen.

"Oh, well, it's a great neighborhood. Don't let this keep you away. We've never had any trouble like this before."

"Of course, of course. Thank you for letting me know." He paused. "So, you've lived here a while?"

"Yep, me and the missus built one of the first houses back here."

"And you know the family, of course?"

"Yeah. I'm just glad the older boy wasn't home when it happened."

"Heard someone mention that. He'll probably head somewhere he feels safe."

"Probably."

"Can't believe he just ran off. Guess shock can make you do things out of character."

"Of course it can," a familiar voice butted in. Nicolai stiffened when he recognized it belonged to the nosy neighbor. "That poor boy," she said. "I just pray he turns up soon. Or heads straight to the nearest police station." She sighed. "Knowing him, though, he'll head to that dojo. I think he'd move in there if he could."

"Naw," the other man said, "my guess is he'll head to his grandparents' house. They're close."

Nicolai shoved his hands into his pockets and clenched his fists while pasting a smile on his lips. He doubted the kid would go to either place since he'd ensured the teen knew the consequences of such actions, but . . . the neighbors might be right. Kids wanted to feel safe. If he had to put money on one or the other, he'd guess the dojo. Wouldn't hurt to check there first. "Well, I guess I'll be on my way. I have a realtor to talk to about a house."

He slipped away with the woman's comments floating behind him. He wasn't quite ready to leave yet, he simply wanted to get away from the two chatterboxes. It wasn't hard to find another spot in the crowd to blend into. Officers questioned the neighbors and took their names and contact information. Each time an officer got close to him, he moved behind someone else.

For the next two hours, he watched, careful to stay out of the way of the panning phone cameras. With his position at the rear of the crowd, he wasn't worried one bit about being caught on video.

Nicolai sighed and worked his jaw with a wince. That kid had taken him completely by surprise. He'd known he took karate at the dojo, but he'd severely underestimated the youngster's skills. He wouldn't let that happen again. He could admire him even as he killed him.

He wished there was a way he could let the cops know that it would all be over soon. As soon as he fulfilled his promise. Because, if he didn't keep his promise, what kind of man did that make him?

When the FBI agent had puked into the bushes, it bothered him. He had no agenda with the officers. They were just doing their jobs.

And he'd done his. Part of it anyway.

It was time to go.

He turned on his heel and winced at the shooting pain in his right knee. That was one complication he didn't need, but it wouldn't keep him from doing what he'd come to do. He limped across the front yard to the stolen car he'd parked at the neighborhood pool. He was ready for all of this unpleasantness to be finished. He missed his home, the peaceful lull of the water lapping against the sides of his boat. But . . . a promise was a promise.

Unfortunately, the oldest son of Michael Fields was still alive and that had to be rectified as soon as possible.

THREE

SEVENTEEN YEARS EARLIER
OCTOBER
GREENVILLE

Fifteen-year-old Ava Jackson woke with a start, her heart pounding like a runaway stallion. For a moment, she lay in the double bed, listening to the rain lashing her home as though punishing it for merely existing. The vinyl-sided structure shuddered at the strength of the whipping wind. Thunder boomed and she bit back a shriek while jerking the covers to her chin.

Lightning flashed in the not-so-distant sky, illuminating her room for a brief second.

She glanced at the clock and noted the blank area where muted red numbers should glow.

No power.

The door to her room slammed open and she gasped. Then wilted in relief. Seven-year-old Nathan ran and vaulted into her bed to clasp his arms around her neck. "There's a monster who keeps trying to come through my window!"

"Shh . . . it's okay. It's just a storm."

Another crash of thunder sent shudders through his small frame. "It's too loud."

"I know. Come on, climb under the covers. You can stay with me."

"Good, 'cuz I wasn't leaving."

Laughter bubbled up and suddenly the night didn't seem so scary. Her little brother had brought her nothing but joy—okay, and maybe a few headaches since his surprise appearance seven years ago—and she'd do anything to make sure he felt safe and secure. The thunder boomed once more and he clutched her.

She kissed his head. "Hey, think about this."

"What?"

"Remember that Bible verse you had to memorize in Bible school?"

"I memorized a lot. Which one?"

"The one from Psalms . . . about when you're afraid, you'll trust. Come on. I know you can quote it."

For a moment he was silent, then his small voice said, "'When I am afraid, I will trust in you. In God, whose word I praise, in God I trust; I will not be afraid.' That one?"

"Yeah. That one." She repeated it silently in her own mind. "We don't need to be afraid."

"Jesus calmed the ocean one time too."

"He did?"

"Uh-huh. The disciples in the boat were afraid and Jesus was sleeping. They woke him up and he stopped the storm."

"Just like that?"

"Yep. Maybe he'll calm . . . this . . . one . . . too . . ." His words slowed, slurred, and finally stopped.

Soon his even breathing whispered past her ear and her own eyes grew heavy once again. She was simply going to trust that God could stop this storm too. She kissed Nathan's forehead and had just closed her eyes when a dull thud sounded from somewhere at the other end of the house.

She stiffened. That wasn't thunder.

Ava eased away from her brother's relaxed warmth, grabbed her robe from the end of the bed, and pulled it on as she stepped into the hallway. The ranch-style house had a simple layout. Ava's bedroom was at the very back, across from the master. She peered inside and saw her mother stretched diagonally across the bed, sleeping soundly. Ava spotted the empty wine bottle on the end table. A sigh escaped her. It would take more than a thunderstorm to wake her.

Another *thunk* sent her heart hammering in her chest. Had someone broken in? No, wait. Her father must be home. He was supposed to have arrived last night but had been delayed due to the bad weather. She continued down the hall, passing Nathan's room and the full bath she shared with him. At the end of the hall, she walked into the den and paused. Glanced at the antique clock on the mantel, just as another flash of lightning lit up the room. Ten minutes past two. She'd wound and set it yesterday. The pendulum continued its rhythmic swing in stark contrast to the chaos outside.

More noise from the office off the kitchen sent her scurrying toward it. It was probably her father, but she had to know for sure.

A loud crash. A shout.

"Dad!" She raced to his office in time to see him throw a punch at another man's face. The intruder stumbled backward into the wingback chair in front of her father's desk. The chair fell sideways. Her father grabbed the man by the collar of his shirt and slammed him into the built-in bookcases along the wall.

Ava could only watch, open-mouthed and terrified for her father. A hard punch to her dad's gut sent him reeling back, even as the attacker aimed his other fist for a head hit. Before Ava could screech a warning, her father ducked. Then retaliated. He went through a series of punches and kicks that left the invader groaning on the floor and Ava gaping.

Just as Ava thought she might be able to breathe again, a knife appeared in the man's hand.

"Dad! Look out!" She grabbed the lamp from the end table, stepped forward, and slammed the heavy base down on the man's wrist.

He screamed and turned to glare at her, giving her father a few precious seconds to act. He snagged the knife and had it to the attacker's exposed throat before she could blink. Her dad's gaze locked on hers, the glint of admiration there thrilling her despite the panic pulsing her adrenaline into overdrive.

"I've got this," he said. "Go check on your mom and Nathan."

"Leave you alone with him? I don't think so. I'll call 911, though."

"Ava . . ."

She froze. Whenever he used that tone, she knew better than to argue with him.

"I'll take care of him. I don't want to wake up the whole neighborhood with lights and sirens. I'm going to take him to the police station, and when I get back, we'll talk."

He was going to take the intruder to the— "Are you crazy?"

He huffed a short laugh, a sound she'd never heard from him before. "Quite possibly, but I'm serious. Don't argue with me, please."

Ava studied him a moment, then nodded. "All right."

"That's my girl. Go on."

Still not sure about the wisdom of his decision, she backed out of the office, rounded the doorjamb, and paused to listen. Words in a language she couldn't understand filtered to her.

Her father's voice. Sounding like he spoke fluent . . . Russian? The man answered in a guttural tone filled with hate—and something else? A shiver slid up her spine and she tried to commit the sounds to memory.

More soft-voiced, yet intense arguing, then footsteps aimed at the door. She fled back to her room and climbed into the bed next to her still-sleeping brother.

But her mind wouldn't click off. Her father was not the mild-mannered, soft-spoken, nerdy travel writer she'd known all her life. Tonight, she'd seen a whole different side of him—and she determined to figure out exactly who he was.

□ □ □

Present Day
Sunday evening in May
Greenville

Ava sat up with a gasp, inhaling the scent of bleach, pine, and rubbing alcohol. She'd fallen asleep in the chair next to her mother's bed. Her phone buzzed once more, and the dream faded, even as she wondered what had triggered it.

She snagged the phone. Nathan. Finally. She tapped the screen. "Hi, little brother."

"Hi, big sis."

She'd been trying to get ahold of him about his credit card bill and he'd been ignoring her. "I guess you got my message."

"All five thousand of them."

She'd left four. Her threat to withhold his monthly allowance until he called her back must have scared him.

"I'll take care of the bill, Ava," he said. "I needed new tires. I've been putting it off, but after I hydroplaned and almost hit a tree the last time it rained, I decided it might be smart to stop procrastinating."

Oh. She shuddered at the mental picture he painted. "Well,

that was important. Of course you needed new tires. You did the right thing." She hadn't recognized the name of the tire place on the bill and hadn't known what the charge was for.

"I know I did. I do occasionally make good decisions. You don't have to constantly be watching out for me." He paused. "It's time to close that account and get one in just my name. There's no reason for you to have access to it. I'm twenty-five years old. Old enough to weather my own storms, pay my own bills, and more. So, you can quit helicoptering and just be my sister, all right?"

Helicoptering? Was she really doing that? Probably. "Well, you're still little bro to me," she said, "and you're not quite on your own yet, so please excuse me for checking to make sure you're all right." And not racking up credit card debt that would take him forever to pay off. But the tires were necessary. She also paid his tuition and rent for the small house he lived in near the hospital, but she refused to hold that over his head. "Regardless, what's most important is that I need you to answer your phone in case something happens with Mom."

He went silent for a few seconds. "How is she?" he finally asked, sounding subdued. "I figured you'd leave a message if it was something really bad." Before Ava could groan at the thought of leaving bad news in a message, he said, "I can come sit with her this weekend if you need me to."

"She's the same, Nate. There's no point in you coming unless you just want to see her, but I know you have that big exam on Monday. I recommend you stay there and study."

A sigh filtered through the line. "I'm sorry, Ava. I know I'm not helping you like I should."

"You're doing exactly what you're supposed to be doing." She hoped. "Answer your phone when I call or text me a certain time that would be better to call, but don't ignore me, please."

His audible sigh made her wince. "Will do. I've gotta go now."

"I love you, kiddo."

"Love you too." The phone clicked off and she let out her own sigh.

She prayed he was focusing on his studies. He was in his last year of medical school in North Carolina. With a prayer winged to the one she had entrusted him to, she turned back to her mother.

The woman was in the final stages of dementia and didn't know Ava was on the planet, but Ava found herself spending as much time as possible with her. She grieved the loss of the strong, vibrant woman her mother had finally become once she'd kicked the alcohol addiction. She took comfort in the good memories simply sitting with her invoked.

A knock on the door made her smile. "Come in, Caden."

"It's just me, Ava." One of her mother's nurses, Petra Cortez, stepped through the door.

"Oh, sorry," Ava said. "I was expecting Caden. He'd texted he might stop by."

The dark-skinned nurse winked at her. "If I was a few years younger, I'd look for him too."

Ava ignored the heat climbing into her cheeks and chuckled. "Now, Petra, you know Caden's just a friend, no matter how much you'd like to play matchmaker. Some things just aren't meant to be."

"You had dinner last night, thanks to me, didn't you?"

"Because you told him I'd been here for six hours and hadn't eaten and if he didn't feed me, you were going to call the cops because that was a crime."

"And he fed you, didn't he?"

"You do know he *is* the cops, right?"

Petra shrugged and walked to the bed, checked her patient's vitals, and turned back to the door. "He'll be here soon, I'm sure. I'll send him on in when I see him. He might even ask you out on another date."

"It wasn't a date."

"Uh-huh."

Ava couldn't help laughing once again as Petra disappeared into the hallway. The sweet nurse always managed to brighten her day. And she had to admit, Caden Denning had somehow captured her attention like no other man had ever been able to do. But—

Her mother moaned and Ava turned to grip the woman's cold fingers. "It's okay, Mom, I'm here." Ava smoothed strands of gray away from her mom's forehead. "I'm here. Just relax. I love you."

She couldn't believe the disease had struck her young mother, but it had started creeping in two years ago at the age of fifty-six. And now, she probably had mere weeks to live.

"Rest, Mom," she whispered. "Everything's okay."

She never knew if her words penetrated the diseased mind, but her mother's restlessness eased and her breathing settled. A lump formed in Ava's throat and she glanced at the clock. If Caden was coming, he would have been there by now. She checked her phone. No text or call from him. "Hmm. Wonder what that's about?" she muttered. Must be a case he was working. She sent up a brief prayer for his safety and kissed her mother's cheek. "I've got to go now, Mom. I'll be back to see you tomorrow."

Ava stood and left the room, making her way to the exit. She waved to those she knew, glad she'd allowed her best friend, Sarah Denning, to talk her into moving her mother into this facility while she relocated into an apartment two miles away. Getting out of the Navy hadn't been the original plan, but after her mother's diagnosis, when the opportunity had arisen, she'd taken it.

Now that she was in Greenville, Caden—and a few of her other friends—had been regular visitors over the past three months, joining her in the evenings when they could, talking, playing cards, keeping her from going crazy while her mother continued her decline. But it had mostly been Caden. Or Caden and Sarah. Ava had grown up with the two siblings and readily admitted she didn't know what she'd do without them at this stage in her life.

She pushed through the glass doors into the evening. Mid-May, and the weather was warm enough to take a dip in a pool. Her friend Brooke James wouldn't mind if Ava came over and used hers, but for now, Ava simply wanted to go home where she could think. Mostly about what she was going to do with her suddenly wide-open future. After ten years in the military, this was a rather daunting topic. And, of course, she needed to think about Caden's obvious interest in her. But she knew what she was going to do about that last one.

Absolutely nothing.

Streetlights cast long shadows as her footsteps led her to the parking lot, while a light breeze played with her ponytail.

A car started backing out of its space and she stopped to let it finish and drive away before resuming her walk to her own vehicle. Past a Mercedes-Benz, a minivan, and a green truck.

From around the side of the next vehicle, a white truck, stepped a figure dressed in jeans, a black T-shirt—and a ski mask.

Ava gasped and stumbled back, letting her purse fall to the ground as he lifted his hand. She kicked out, her foot slamming against his forearm. The object in his gloved fist clattered to the ground. A yell escaped him, and he lunged.

"Ava!"

Ava heard her name as she dodged her attacker's attempt to grab her. She lashed out with the heel of her palm and caught the attacker's chin beneath the mask. He roared his displeasure and staggered back. Ava spun to run, but a hand closed over her wrist, jerking her off-balance.

She hit the ground hard on her back, the breath whooshing from her lungs. She lay stunned, while her mind screamed at her to move. He loomed over her, wrapped a hand around the material of her shirt at the base of her throat, and drew back a fist. Fear wanted to smother her, but anger slid past the initial shock, even as pounding footsteps grabbed her attention.

"Hey! Let her go! Get away from her!"

Her attacker halted, released his hold, and whirled to run. Ava lurched forward, snagged his pants leg, and yanked. He went down on his right shoulder and rolled. When he came up, he held a knife in his right hand. She scrambled to her feet, lifted her hands, and bent her knees into a defensive fighting position, determined not to let him get away, while equally resolved not to get hurt.

Then he was on the ground with Caden on top of him. Panting, Ava ran toward the duo. A glint of metal flashed in the parking lot light.

"Knife! Caden, duck!"

Caden dropped as though they'd practiced the move a hundred times. The knife went over his head. She hollered again and kicked out, catching the man's wrist and sending the weapon spinning through the air. It hit the side of a car, then bounced off the asphalt.

The man screamed, swung a fist, and caught Caden in the temple. Caden reared back and crashed to the asphalt, giving the attacker time to roll to his feet. He fled, racing across the parking lot, dodging vehicles. Caden lunged to his feet and shot after him, then pulled up short, spun, and raced back to Ava. Still stunned, she watched the running man hop the wrought iron fence and disappear from sight.

Caden jogged toward her, one hand rubbing his temple. He stopped in front of her, eyes narrowed in concern. "Are you okay?"

"Yes." She dragged in a ragged breath. "I think so. You?"

"Yeah. Just going to have a headache."

She frowned. "You could have caught him."

"As much as it pains me to admit it, there was no way. He was too fast. Really fast. Like track-star fast." He paused. "And I didn't want to leave you alone, just in case."

Which meant he probably could have caught him if he hadn't been worried about her. "In case he managed to double back?"

"Or had an accomplice." He pulled out his phone and called it in while she caught her breath. "Officers are on the way." He bent down and picked up her purse.

She took it from him. "Thanks."

"You just saved my life, Ava. I didn't see the knife."

"And you saved me from being hauled off by him. We're even."

His left brow rose. "I don't know. You seemed to be doing okay defending yourself." Something flickered in his gaze. Surprise that she could defend herself? Probably. "What was that all about?" he asked.

"I have no idea. He never said a word, just tried to grab me." A shudder went through her and he placed a hand on her upper arm. "Any kidnappers on the loose in this city right now?"

"Not that I can think of."

That meant there weren't. Caden remembered everything.

"That was some serious fighting you did," he said.

She gave a low laugh. "I wasn't going with him. Not alive anyway." She let her eyes scan the asphalt. "He dropped something when I kicked him the first time."

"The first time?"

"Yes." She knelt down and, using the flashlight on her phone, scanned under the vehicle to her left. Then her right. And there it was. "I don't suppose you have an evidence bag on you." He raised that brow again and she shrugged. "I've been around you long enough to know these things."

"I suppose you have. And yeah, I have one in my trunk." He glanced around. "But I don't want to leave you here alone to get it."

She nodded to the patrol car that had just turned into the parking lot and was heading toward them. "You don't have to."

"Fine." When the officer pulled up next to them and rolled his window down, Caden flashed his badge. "I'll be right back to give you my statement. I need to grab an evidence bag from my car."

The officer's eyes went wide. "FBI? What in the world happened here to get you called in?"

Caden gave a short, humorless chuckle. "I'm not here in an official capacity. I just happened to be in the right place at the right time to help out a friend. This is Ava Jackson. Someone attacked her."

The officer climbed out of the vehicle. "I'm Harry Ward." He shot a concerned look at Ava. "Did you call an ambulance?"

Ava swallowed a grimace. "I don't need one. I'm a little banged up, but nothing that requires medical attention." No doubt she looked rough after rolling on the asphalt. She fingered the tear in her jeans and noted she was starting to feel the bumps and bruises too. Her back, her shoulder, her hips . . . basically everywhere.

"And he left something behind?" Officer Ward asked.

"Yeah. I was just going to grab an evidence bag," Caden said.

"I've got one. What size?"

Caden told him. Officer Ward popped his trunk, found the bag, and handed it to Caden, along with a pair of gloves. "I'll let you do the honors."

Ava rubbed her eyes and stepped aside while Caden knelt down and snagged the item from the ground, then stood.

"What is it?" she asked.

"Looks like a can of mace or pepper spray. There's no label, so might be something else in there." He dropped it into the bag.

"He wore gloves," she said, her mind flashing to the moment he'd gripped the front of her shirt. "There won't be any prints."

"Maybe not, but I'll have someone run it anyway. It's possible he touched it before he put the gloves on. I'm sure he wasn't planning on leaving it behind."

"Of course." She nodded.

A half hour later, after they'd both told the officer everything they could remember, Caden wrapped an arm around her shoulders. "Come on, I'll follow you home. I need to talk to you about something when we get there."

"What?"

"A murder that you may be somehow mixed up in."

FOUR

Ava stared at him for a good three seconds before giving a nod. "Fine. I'll meet you at my place. Lakeside Apartments on Wellington. Apartment 1102A. First building, first floor, just off the parking lot when you turn in." She climbed into her car.

Caden moved quickly to his own vehicle and followed her out of the parking lot. Funny. He'd never been to her place. He'd always just met her at the care facility, since that's where she spent most of her time.

As he kept her taillights in view, he pondered the way she'd defended herself—and him—against her attacker. He'd always thought Ava to be quiet and unassuming. Definitely smart, probably even genius-level intelligent, but . . . reserved and a little shy. And maybe she *was* all that, but she'd also had some training, which had served her well today.

How had he not noticed this side of her before?

Of course, he'd known her since she was a kid when she and Sarah were inseparable, but he hadn't really been around her that much after he left for school, then Quantico.

Sarah had told him her group of friends had convinced her to move closer to them in order for her to have help with her mother, so Caden had only started to get to know the adult Ava. And he was thoroughly enjoying doing so. Even wanted to ask her out on a date. Unfortunately, he felt like he'd hit a wall with her.

And now he had to ask her how she was involved in the murder of the Fields family. His phone rang and he hit the car's Bluetooth button to run the call through the speakers. "Zane? How are you doing?"

"The same."

"Ouch. You sound rough."

"Yeah. So, let me talk while I have a voice. Daria just called and said she tracked the teen's phone to the backyard. Officers found it, so it's not going to give us anything on his present location, obviously. But they're working on getting into it to get a picture of his movements, names of friends he might be with, et cetera."

"Excellent."

"Also, I've been talking to neighbors. Mickey spent the night with a buddy of his, Evan West. Evan said they hung out and went to bed at a decent hour because Mickey had to be at the dojo at 9:00 a.m. for a karate competition thing. Mickey left Evan's house around 8:15 to run home and grab his gi, but everything was still in his room, so we know he didn't make it up there."

"No, just inside the front door to confront the man killing his family," Caden said. "It's Sunday and a beautiful spring day. Lots of people outside. No one's said anything about seeing him walking home. But finding his phone in the backyard says he made it there." He paused. "What if they fought, Mickey managed to get away, and then ran out of the back door, losing his phone in the process?"

"Sounds feasible."

"If by some chance he's alive, we need to find him."

"We've got a BOLO out," Zane said. "I'll let you know if anything pops up."

"Thanks. Go home, Zane. Take some medicine and sleep."

"I'm planning on it. Soon."

"I'm almost to Ava's place, getting ready to talk to her. I'll let you know what I know when I know it."

"Good. I got clearance for her from the SAC. Her high level of security with the Navy let him fast-track everything so you can talk to her about the case. She's considered a contract consultant at this point. He said he had a feeling we were going to need her help to figure this out—especially the part her father plays in all of this."

"Well, that'll make things easier. Thanks."

"Sure thing. Talk to you later."

Caden hung up and pulled into Ava's apartment complex, found a visitor's parking spot, then joined her at the door just as she unlocked it.

Once they were inside, he shut the door behind him and looked around. "Nice place."

"Thanks. I was relieved to find something near Mom that I would be happy living in. Temporarily anyway. I'd love to get a small house somewhere so I could plant a little garden and some flowers. Maybe get a dog." She shrugged. "All in good time."

The front door opened into the kitchen area. To the right, she had a round table that seated four. A puzzle in progress took up most of the surface. He walked over to study it. They'd done a few puzzles while he sat with her at the nursing facility. "You always have one going, don't you?"

She smiled. "Of course. That was my dad's thing that quickly became my thing too. Something we could share when he was around. He got me addicted when I was around three years old. Between puzzles and his silly scavenger hunts, I was never bored. I tried to pass that on to Nate, but he wasn't interested. Science experiments that blew up and spewed something everywhere? Yes. Snakes and bugs and everything 'ew'? Also, yes. Puzzles? No, they were too tame."

He laughed. "I remember that about him." To the left was the kitchen with a bar area and two more chairs. The living area was straight ahead.

She gestured to the couch. "Have a seat. Would you like something to drink?"

"Water or coffee would be great."

She made a left into the kitchen, started the coffeepot, then grabbed the waters and joined him on the couch with a long sigh. "Coffee will be ready in a few minutes." She swiped strands of dark hair from her eyes and sipped the water. "I have to admit I'm glad I didn't have to walk into an empty apartment by myself. Thank you for being here."

Her soft words reached him and he shifted toward her. "I'm thankful I showed up when I did."

"So am I. You had perfect timing. As usual." She took a deep breath. "Now, tell me what's going on. You said something about a murder."

"Yes, it's a highly sensitive case, but I have permission to read you in on it."

Her brows rose. "Okay."

"Do you know a man by the name of Michael Fields? He was Army."

She frowned. "No. I've never heard of him. Why?"

"He and his wife had three kids. Staff Sergeant Fields and his wife and their two younger children were shot and killed this morning. A neighbor found their bodies shortly after it happened. Their teen son, Mickey, is nowhere to be found right now. We're still looking for him. And the killer. That's why I was late coming to the nursing home."

She gaped. "Children?"

He nodded and tightened his jaw on the tears that wanted to rise. "Yes." He cleared his throat.

"Caden, I'm so sorry. That's . . . awful. Beyond awful, really, but . . . and you still came intending to sit with me? I don't know what to say."

He shrugged. "Unfortunately, I had another reason for coming, but I'll get to that in a minute." He paused. "Although I will say that every other time besides tonight, coming to sit with you has been more selfish than anything."

"How so?"

He laughed. A sound without much humor. "This is probably going to come across pathetic, but I needed the routine of it. The normalcy of doing something that . . ." A sigh slipped out and he shook his head. "I don't know how to explain it."

She covered his hand with hers. "It's okay. You don't have to. I get it."

He looked into her eyes. Compassionate, guileless. Honest. He should be just as honest and tell her that *she* was the big draw. That simply being with her lowered his stress level and let him relax. "Thank you." He cleared his throat, going with his gut that she wasn't ready to hear that. "Back to the case. As we searched the home, we came across a box in the attic."

"Okay."

A muscle jumped in his jaw. "We have special equipment that helps us find things most people would miss. Anyway, tucked away into a little hidden corner, behind the wall, was this box, and it had some interesting stuff in it."

"Like what?"

"Clippings from a Russian newspaper. We're not sure of the date yet, as the headline wasn't included, but it looks like it was from the mid-1990s. A floppy drive that can only be used on an ancient computer, and some pictures."

She waited, her eyes steady on his, not rushing him, and he appreciated that.

"This was one of the pictures we found." He tapped the screen of his phone and turned it to face her.

She gasped. "What? That's my dad and me!"

"I know. I remembered what you looked like at that age. And, of course, I remember your dad."

"I could only have been three or four in that picture." She took the phone from him and zoomed in. "It's the park behind our house. My dad always used to take me there whenever he was home from . . . his trips, remember?"

"Of course. The four of us had some good times in that park." He, Sarah, and their younger brother, Dustin, had often swung by Ava's home to grab her before racing through their backyards to the park.

"At least until Mom decided Nathan was old enough to come along and I was old enough to watch him," she said. "I used to be so frustrated that I had to chase a toddler instead of trying to flirt with you."

He laughed, then scoffed. "You never flirted with me."

She rolled her eyes at him. "Trust me, I did. I was just really bad at it."

Caden clenched his jaw to keep it from dropping open. He had no idea what she was talking about. "Or maybe I was just a clueless dork."

"Or that." She smirked.

She'd had a crush on him back then. Maybe there was hope for him yet. Just one more thing to investigate when he had the chance. He cleared his throat and swiped again. "What about this one?"

"My father again," she whispered, "when he was in his early thirties, I would guess." She blinked and cleared her throat. "About thirty years ago. He was quite a bit older than my mom. And he seemed a lot older by the time Nathan was born. Obviously."

"I remember that. You used to get so mad when people thought he was your grandfather."

She grimaced. "Yeah. When I looked at him, I didn't see him as old. He was just . . . my dad. But he was a health nut. Always making sure he ate healthy and stayed in shape, so thankfully he aged well—in spite of the grandfather appearance."

Caden studied the picture over her shoulder. "Do you recognize that place?"

"No, but the sign is in Russian. It's the White Rabbit Café."

"You read Russian?" Yet one more thing he hadn't known. He was starting to wonder if he knew her at all.

"Fluently." She smiled. "My father taught me. Who's the man he's shaking hands with?"

"From family pictures, we've discerned that it's Michael Fields's father, Jesse."

"Interesting. So Jesse Fields was in Russia the same time my father was, and they were photographed outside a restaurant together. And this picture was in Michael Fields's attic. It makes absolutely no sense. Except my father obviously knew this man." She shook her head. "I don't understand. Who was he and how did he wind up here in the same city?"

"I was hoping you'd be able to answer those questions."

"I'm sorry. I have no idea." She paused. "Could I get these two pictures? I have so few of my father . . ."

He hesitated. "I can't give them to you right now since they're part of this investigation, but I can make sure you get them when we're done."

"Sure." She handed the phone back to Caden. "My dad hated having his picture taken—and he pretty much instilled that in Nathan and me. Do you know who took these?"

"No, and I'm guessing your dad didn't know the pictures were being taken. Mostly, I'm just curious about how they came to be in the Fields's house."

"Can you ask his father?"

"We're planning on it. They're cutting short their vacation in Florida. I expect they'll be home in the next couple of hours."

Ava rubbed a hand across her eyes and stood. She paced the distance to the front door and back. "Those poor people. I can't imagine."

"It looks like this is the third family to be killed."

She jerked her gaze to his. "Third?"

He told her about the other two, along with the missing pictures, and she paled. "And," he said, "there's some kind of connection to the first family. They appeared to know one another, as the Fields family had a Christmas picture of the first family on their mantel."

"Huh."

"What are you thinking?"

"I'm . . . not sure." She paced while she rubbed her chin. "I mean, I don't know *what* to think, to be honest. Because this is all very weird."

Caden watched her. "Okay. You think about it and call me if you figure it out."

She blinked. "Okay, I will. I promise. I just need to sort through some things before I can put it into words. I think."

Caden walked to the door and hesitated. When she looked up, her eyes two big question marks, he sighed and leaned over to press a kiss to her forehead. "I'll be in touch." He stepped out of the apartment and shut the door behind him. Then waited for the deadbolt to shoot home. Only then did he walk down the steps and head for his car.

□ □ □

Mickey Fields huddled against the trunk of the tree and pulled his hoodie strings until the fabric encased his head, chin, and eyes. Everything except his nose. He lowered his forehead to his knees and rocked as the images from the morning flashed in his mind.

He'd been almost to the door when he'd heard the first odd noise come from the living room. A weird sound that had sounded almost like a muffled balloon pop. His hand was on the knob when he heard it again. He opened the door on the third burst and watched as the fourth bullet entered his father's head.

He couldn't scream, couldn't move, couldn't breathe.

But he must have made a noise, because the killer had whirled and turned his gun on Mickey.

And Mickey reacted.

He kicked out, connecting with the killer's arm, sending the weapon flying.

With a scream, the man lunged and grabbed Mickey by the upper arm. "You're dead, kid." He jerked him around, blocking his escape out the front door.

Acting on years of training, Mickey had gone into autopilot and done exactly what he'd been programmed to do—using skills that had made him the champion fighter at the dojo four years in a row.

With his free hand, he jammed his palm against the man's chin, heard his teeth click together when his head snapped back. The grip on his right arm loosened and Mickey kicked out, slamming his heel against the guy's kneecap. With a scream, his attacker went down and Mickey was free. He scrambled backward, trying desperately not to fall. If he could make it to the back door—

"I'm going to kill you! If you go to your grandparents, I'll kill them! And your dojo sensei and your little buddy down the street. If you go to the cops, I'll kill them all!"

Mickey made it to the back door and bolted out onto the deck. He'd launched himself over the railing, then scrambled over the chain-link fence, managing to disappear before the killer made it to the door.

Mickey had run until he couldn't run anymore. He now found himself in a small homeless community that had set up in the woods behind a large superstore. Tents surrounded an open fire that people used to cook whatever food they managed to find. Some had scooters or a motorcycle. No one had a car. All of these things he noticed absently while his mind spun and his heart raced out of control.

Oh God, what do I do? Please help me.

He brushed away the tears that wouldn't stop. His family was gone. Dead. All of them. With the killer's words echoing in his ears, he knew he couldn't call his grandparents or the cops. That guy would know. He might even be watching to see if Mickey showed up. How had he known all that stuff anyway?

He must have been watching. Studying them. And had struck at a time when his family was home. When Mickey was supposed to be there. His overnighter with his friend had been a last-minute decision. If he'd stayed home, he had no doubt he'd have been dead on that sofa as well. And maybe that would be better than living. His heart cramped and more tears flowed, despite his brain ordering him to stop crying. He needed to think. To figure out what to do.

He shuddered and drew in a breath, just now noticing the odors wafting around him. Body odor, unwashed blankets—and food cooking. Flies buzzed around him and he waved a hand at them. No one else seemed to notice them.

A little boy no older than Brian peered at him from behind the woman cooking the food over the open flame. He thought it might be chicken a wasn't going to get close enough to find out.

He had to go. But where?

The little one must have decided Mickey wasn't a threat,

because he finally left his mother's side and ventured closer. "Who are you?"

Should he use his real name? He settled for, "I'm Mike."

"I'm Rocky. Why you cryin'?"

"I'm not." Not anymore anyway.

Rocky shot him a knowing look. "You ain't got no home either?"

Mickey dropped his face into his hands. "No," he murmured. "I don't have a home." He didn't recognize the hoarse voice that came from his throat.

"You hungry? We went to the grocery store today and got some chicken. Today is special 'cuz it's my birthday. I just wanted some chicken to eat, but you can have some too. I'll share."

There was no way Mickey was taking this kid's food. He swallowed hard and looked around, noticing the attention he was attracting. He stood, dug in his pocket, and found the ten-dollar bill his mom had given him just before he'd left for Evan's house.

Making sure no one saw him, he slipped it into Rocky's small hand. "Don't let anyone see that, okay? Thanks for the invite, but I've gotta go. Happy birthday, Rocky." He shuddered. He didn't want to think about birthdays and what his would look like in three months. If he managed to live that long.

Rocky's fist closed over the bill and his eyes went wide. "Thanks," he said, his voice soft. "But where you goin'?"

"I have no idea."

FIVE

After Caden had left, Ava had paced and thought, tapped those thoughts into the notes app on her phone, then paced some more. Now, night had fallen, and she stood in her den, staring out the window at the well-lit parking lot.

Tonight, she didn't care about the lousy view. She finally drew in a steadying breath and dialed a number she'd known by heart since she was fifteen. She waited for the secure call to go through and pressed the fingers of her right hand to her throbbing temples. When the line clicked, she waited again.

"Ava?"

"Hello, John, how are you?"

"I'm doing well. Surprised to hear from you, but glad of it. I heard you've left the Navy."

"I have." It didn't even bother her that he led with that. She almost laughed, he was so predictable.

He paused. "How's your mother?"

"The same. I . . ." Deep breath. "Unfortunately, I don't expect her to live much longer."

"I'm sorry. I never met her, but your father spoke very highly of her. Always had a funny tale about her and her sense of humor."

"He never talked bad about her alcoholism, did he?"

John paused, as though taken aback by her question. "No. Never."

"He blamed himself, didn't he?" It was a realization that had hit her late one night when she had been pacing and remembering.

"He did."

"I thought so." And yet it hadn't been enough to make him change jobs and stay home. "I'd still love to hear those funny stories one day."

"Happy to share." She could hear the smile in his voice. "What's going on?" he asked. "You never call for small talk with me, so what can I do to help?"

A pang of guilt hit her. He was right. She actually went out of her way to avoid talking to him, annoyed with his unceasing push for her to join the organization. "It's about my father."

"All right."

"I can't tell you everything, but I've recently discovered two pictures of him."

He was silent.

"John, you know how my father was about being in any pictures. The only ones he'd allow me to have are the ones of his and Mom's wedding, in the safe-deposit box. And he was adamant that they stay there—at least until after his and her deaths." Which meant she might be able to take them out soon. The thought was depressing. "He was so careful. How would someone manage to get those two?"

"I need to see them."

"A friend has them. I asked for them, but he can't give them to me right now."

"Because something's happened and there's an ongoing investigation and he's ethical."

Ava stopped. Blinked. "Well. Yes. He only showed them to me due to special circumstances."

"Who's the friend?"

"Caden Denning. He's with the FBI."

"I'll get them and get back to you after I take a look." He paused. "So . . . you're not in the Navy anymore."

She stifled a sigh. "I think we clarified that at the beginning of the conversation."

He chuckled and she grimaced. "You know," he said, "I have the paperwork all ready here at the agency. All you have to do is sign your name."

"I know, but I need to be here to take care of Mom, and I don't want to live in Washington—or overseas."

"You just moved your mother to South Carolina. You could just as easily move her here."

What part of "I don't want to live in Washington" had she mumbled? "I'm not interested in living the life my father did." A life that was a lie and ended much too soon. "Thanks, but no thanks."

"I'm going to keep asking."

"I know. Hence the reason I don't call for small talk."

He laughed. "I miss your wit too. Julie misses you terribly, you know. You'd be able to see her more if you moved here."

Julie. His wife. A woman who'd been a mother to Ava when her own mom couldn't be. "I miss her too, but guilt trips never worked with me in the past. They won't work now. Give her my love and tell her I'll come *visit* soon."

He laughed. "Bye, Ava."

"Goodbye, John." She hung up and realized she hadn't said a word about the attack in the parking lot. Not that she should, but the more she thought about it, the more she couldn't help believing the murder of the family and the attack on her tonight were related.

She had no idea *how*, but the thought wouldn't leave her alone. But how had the person known to find her at the assisted living home? A chill skittered up her spine as the only answer was that he'd been watching her.

If it hadn't been some random encounter.

Without the pictures to tie her to the murders, she wouldn't have given the attack another thought—other than to be glad she'd escaped relatively unscathed and to pray he was caught before he could find someone else to terrorize. But Caden's revelations shed a different light on everything. So she kept circling back to, What if the attack hadn't been random? Why had he targeted her?

Her phone rang and she jumped. Sarah Denning. She swiped the screen. "Hi, there."

"Hi. I'm just calling to see what you're doing for lunch tomorrow."

"Um . . . eating with you?"

"And Brooke and Heather. Heather will be back from that conference thing late tonight, so she's ready for some girl time. You in?"

Was she? "As of right now, I can be in. My schedule may change, but if it does, I'll let you know."

"Of course." She paused. "Everything all right? Besides your mom, I mean. I know that's not all right."

"Mom is about the same, but . . . someone attacked me in the parking lot of the nursing home and I—"

"What! Are you okay? Do I need to come over there? Do you—"

"Sarah, Sarah, I'm okay. It's okay."

"You just said you were attacked! How is that okay? Tell me the details."

Ava filled her in on the attack and Caden arriving at just the right time. She didn't mention the investigation or the pictures. "Anyway, I'm not sure what tomorrow holds."

"Wanna come stay with me tonight?"

The offer made her smile. "No, that's okay. I'm sure you're planning that wedding. Gavin's there, isn't he?"

Sarah laughed. "He is, but he's headed out the door in ten minutes. I'd love to have you."

It was tempting. But she needed to think. "No, I'm fine staying here, but thanks."

"Okay then, if you change your mind, you know where to find me. See you tomorrow. Maybe."

"I'll text."

"Bye."

Ava hung up and pressed fingers to her eyes. Aching muscles, a sore hip, and a scraped elbow all chimed in with a pain level that required a good dose of ibuprofen. She made her way into the kitchen and popped the pills.

She placed her hands on the counter, drew in a deep breath, and thought about the boxes lining her bedroom wall. She could unpack more or she could get on her father's old laptop and see what she could find.

The boxes could wait.

She returned to her bedroom and opened her closet door. On the back wall of the small area, she pressed on the top left corner and a portion sprung open. She reached into the small storage area and pulled out a laptop. Then hesitated. The puzzle that had arrived three days after she'd learned of her father's death rested patiently inside the hiding place, waiting for her to put it together without him.

Her throat tightened. Not yet. Maybe not ever. She shut the door and it clicked into place.

When her father had died eight months ago, she'd gone to

his home in Falls Church, Virginia, and grabbed everything he'd told her to get in the event of his death. She'd brought the items home, and there they'd sat, hidden away in her closet, while she dealt with her loss in the only way she knew how—pretend it wasn't there. She still hadn't even put his house on the market, just paid someone to keep the exterior looking nice and the interior cleaned once a month.

Now there was no more pretending. No more telling herself they'd never found his body, so he wasn't really dead. She was going to have to come to terms with the fact that he was gone and pull herself out of her denial.

Soon. But maybe not today.

She carried the laptop to the kitchen table. After shoving aside some of the puzzle pieces, she opened the computer as grief swept over her. When she opened her eyes, a picture of her mother and father stared back at her. She blinked, wondering if profound sadness could cause hallucinations, but the picture was still there. "What were you thinking, Dad?" If the wrong person had gotten their hands on the laptop and saw—

She shook her head. It didn't matter now. He was gone. Her mother didn't have much longer, and it would just be her and Nathan. No cousins, no aunts and uncles, no one. Once more shoving the depressing thoughts aside, she typed in the password.

And froze. "What? What do you mean it's not a valid password?" She asked the question aloud as if the computer could answer her. It remained silent, of course, but her father had left specific instructions on what she was to do upon receiving word of his death, and that had included how to access his laptop.

Only the password didn't work.

Had it expired? She rubbed a hand across her forehead while she debated what to do. "Why'd you change the password, Dad? And what would you change it to?"

She sighed and pushed away from the table.

A creaking noise came from her French doors and she froze. She always pulled the curtains at night for privacy and had done so upon arriving home from the visit with her mother. She'd also set the alarm so if the doors actually opened, the whole apartment complex would know. Her heart thudded and she stood.

Calm down. It could be a cat or a raccoon.

Or it could be that the person who'd attacked her in the parking lot had somehow managed to follow her home. Or already knew where she lived?

She grabbed her phone and checked the security cameras. A dark figure showed up, his head down, his hand on the doorknob. Ava's adrenaline kicked up a notch and she dialed 911.

"911. What's your emergency?"

"Someone's trying to break into my apartment." She gave the address and hung up. She had a few questions for the would-be intruder. Forewarned was forearmed, right? She shoved the phone into her pocket and darted from the table and into her bedroom to slip the gun from her nightstand. Her father had rarely carried a weapon, but he'd taught her how to use one. Holding it at her side, pointed toward the floor, she stepped back out of her room, walked past the laundry area, and buttonhooked around the corner and into the den. She faced the glass doors.

And felt her phone buzz.

□ □ □

When Ava answered, Caden's short spurt of relief that she was okay fizzled. She was still in danger. "There's someone sneaking around your apartment."

"I know." Her hushed voice came through the Bluetooth earpiece. "I heard him. By the French doors?"

"Yeah." He opened the door to his truck and stepped out, eyes scanning the area.

"Are you outside?"

"I am."

"Dumb question, sorry. Do you still see him?"

"No. He slipped around the side of the building, heading toward the back area."

"Should have taken that second-floor apartment when I had the chance," she muttered. "I'm coming out the door. If you'll walk to the north side, I'll go south."

She would? What did she think she was going to do if she came upon the guy? Then again, she'd done a really good job of defending herself in the parking lot.

"Stay put, Ava. Please. You're safer inside at the moment." She didn't answer. "Ava?"

A car engine roared to life, tires squealed on the asphalt, and the vehicle sped toward the exit. Ava ran toward him, her hands wrapped around the grip of her weapon. The sight of her holding the gun completely discombobulated him. It was so . . . un-Ava-like. She stopped next to him. "Was that him?"

"I think so. He probably circled the building and came back on the opposite side. We missed him."

A long sigh slipped from her. "Okay, I have to admit, I'm starting to think someone is out to get me."

"Is it bad that I'm not even tempted to tell you that I think you're overreacting and paranoid?"

"I was kind of hoping you would." She could hear the sirens heading their way.

Two cars pulled into the parking area and she tucked the weapon into the waistband of her jogging pants while Caden slipped his into the holster at his side.

When the police arrived, they spent the next thirty minutes filing their report, and Ava printed off a picture of the man her camera had caught. Which showed absolutely nothing but a hoodie-covered head.

When the officers left, she shook her head. "I seriously doubt they're going to find the guy, but at least it's on record." She turned away from him and walked back toward the door of her apartment. Caden followed, his mind spinning at what he'd just witnessed. When he stepped inside for the second time that night, he shut the door behind him and watched her pace from the foyer into the kitchen and back, thumb and forefinger pressed against the bridge of her nose. Finally, she stopped and looked at him. "How did you know to come back?"

"I never left."

"What?"

He shrugged. "I was worried about you after the attack in the parking lot. It didn't feel right leaving, so I sat in my truck and kept an eye on your place."

"Oh. Thank you. I didn't expect you to do that, but I appreciate it." She walked to the couch to drop onto it. "It's been a long night."

"No kidding." He made himself at home in the chair positioned next to the couch. "I have a question for you."

"Okay."

"Who *are* you?"

She blinked at him. Frowned. Seemed to search for something to say. "Caden, you've known me my entire life," she finally said. "What do you mean, 'who are you?' Why would you ask that? You know who I am."

He leaned forward, keeping his eyes locked on hers. "No, the Ava I've known is a very different woman than the one I saw—am seeing—tonight."

"Why? Because I know how to defend myself? I was in the Navy, remember?"

"And you spent your days fighting our country's bad guys on a computer, not engaging in hand-to-hand combat."

A small smile tugged at the corner of her lips. "I still trained."

"But . . ."

She sighed. "My father taught me too, all right? We didn't just work puzzles. He made sure I could defend myself if I had to."

"Your father, huh?" He crossed his arms and studied her.

"Yes." She pulled in a deep breath and rubbed her eyes. "Yes. It was one of the things we did together when he was around."

"I remember him being gone most of the time. He was a travel writer, wasn't he?"

"Yes, he—" She stopped and groaned.

"Ava? What is it?"

"I hate lies." She met his gaze and he frowned at the torment in her eyes. "I honestly can't tell you how tired I am of lying about him—and . . . everything."

SIX

And now that her father was dead, did it matter if she told Caden . . . some? Although, she was so used to keeping the truth buried, would she actually be able to get the words out?

"Ava? Hello? Earth to Ava." He waved a hand in front of her face and she shook her head.

"Sorry," she said.

"What do you mean, you're tired of lying about him?"

Well, it was now or never. "As you know, my dad had a job that sent him all over the world. Sometimes for months at a time. Other times, he was gone a few days to a week. Mom and I never knew when he'd show up or how soon he'd have to leave again."

Caden's gaze held hers. "The life of a travel writer, right?"

"That's what he told everyone. And that's what it looked like if anyone were to investigate him."

"Investigate him? But . . . ?"

"That was simply his cover. He was actually an . . . officer."

Caden went still. His brows rose. "With the CIA, I'm guessing?"

The breath whooshed from her lungs. "Why is that the first officer that comes to mind for you?"

"It just made sense with everything else added in—but mostly the pictures found in the Fields's home and the Russian connection."

"I've never told a soul," she whispered, "knowing it could mean his life if I let it slip."

For several moments, he didn't move. Instead, he studied his hands clasped between his knees. Finally, he lifted his head. "Ava, you do realize this puts a whole new spin on my case."

"I know. Ever since you showed me the photographs, I've been thinking and thinking. Could it all be connected? Your case, the attack on me in the parking lot, and then someone trying to break into my home?"

"I'd say it's connected, all right."

"But how? I've never heard of the Fields before today. Then again, if this has to do with my father, I wouldn't have." She stood. "So we need to start with that. What's the connection between that poor family and my father?"

Caden nodded, then rubbed a hand over his chin. "How did you know your father was CIA? I can't see him just coming out and telling you."

"He didn't. I found out by accident."

"How so?"

"An intruder broke into our house one night." She paused. "Do you remember the night of that horrible storm with the thunder so loud it would make your teeth rattle?" He frowned. "I know, I know. We had a bunch of storms growing up, but this one was different."

The light dawned in his eyes. "You're talking about the night that the whole city practically flooded? And the lightning was nonstop? And the tornados were everywhere?"

"Yes. That's the one."

"It was awful."

"And the next day the neighborhood was in shambles."

He nodded. "I was a little shook when I learned the tornado had swept through our neighborhood and missed our houses by mere feet."

"Same here. Anyway, during the storm, Nathan was terrified and had come to join me. It didn't take him long to fall asleep, and just as I started to go back to sleep, there was a break in the noise. I heard somebody in the house making a racket. So I went looking for the source. My mother, who liked her nightly three or four glasses of wine, had apparently decided to drink the whole bottle and passed out cold. I knew my father was supposed to be coming home and figured it was him. The closer I got to his office, the more noise I heard. Dad and someone else were fighting."

Caden's brows drew together over the bridge of his nose. "Fighting? Who?"

"I don't know. Dad subdued the guy and I was going to call 911, but he told me not to. He said he'd take care of everything. I was stunned. I thought my dad was more like Clark Kent, but that night, he was Superman."

Caden huffed a small laugh. "Bet that was a bit of a shock."

"I can't even really describe how stunned I was. I slipped out of his office but stayed close enough in case he needed help. In the end, they were both speaking Russian."

"You know what they said?"

"Not at the time, but I managed to figure it out after a couple of weeks."

He raised a brow. "Really? How'd you manage that?"

"I wrote down what I heard phonetically and asked a friend at school—who was a Russian exchange student—to translate for me. My father said, 'How did you find me?' The other guy said, 'You're too arrogant for your own good.'"

Caden blinked at her. "You remembered what was said . . . phonetically?"

"Yes." She smiled. "I have a good memory."

"I can relate." He paused. "Okay, so what did he mean by that?"

She shrugged. "When I asked my dad about it later, he got really agitated and shut me down. Even after he took me into his confidence about his real job, there were things he never told me. One of those things was the details related to that night and who the guy was that broke in. And trust me, I've thought about it. I've finally decided that on one of my father's overseas trips, he didn't cover his tracks well enough and someone followed him home."

"What happened to the man?"

"I don't know." She paused. "I was good friends with the resource officer's daughter at my school. She and I shared several classes. I told her about what happened, in spite of my dad asking me not to." She held up a finger. "Keep in mind, I didn't know my dad's involvement with the CIA at that point and I was scared to death the guy would come back when he got out on bail or whatever. She told her dad and he asked me about it the next day. I told him that my dad had turned the guy over to the authorities and had told me not to worry about it any longer."

"But?"

"But I don't think he did."

"Why not?"

"Because when my father wouldn't talk to me, I called the police station a few days later and asked about him. I was told no one had been brought in with that description. And definitely no civilian had brought anyone in with a story about capturing an intruder in their home. And, last, no one with a Russian accent."

"I see. What do you think happened to the guy?"

"I think my dad either let him go for whatever reason or . . ."

"Or . . ."

"Or he killed him."

□ □ □

Caden hid his internal flinch. "*Killed him?* You mean *killed him*—killed him? When did you come to that conclusion?"

"Not until after I figured out what my dad did for a living."

"Yeah, you haven't really said how you discovered that."

"I asked him the next day how he learned to fight like that. He made up some stupid story about taking karate as a kid and it all came back to him when he needed it." She scoffed. "But I knew anyone who fought like that practiced on a regular basis." She rubbed a hand over her eyes. "And even at the age of fifteen, I was really good with a computer. I followed the digital footprints my dad thought he'd erased and came across some interesting files. But I also followed him whenever he left the house."

"Followed him?"

She nodded. "He did most of his work overseas, but he had some kind of meeting one afternoon, and I followed him to a little café not too far from our house. I took pictures of him handing over a manila envelope in exchange for something else. I hacked into the local police department's facial recognition software and ran the guy's face. He was on the FBI's most wanted list, with terrorist ties in Russia and China. When I took the information to my father, I thought he was going to either kill me or have a coronary. He did neither, fortunately. Instead, we had a long talk about what he did and how I had to keep my mouth shut if I didn't want him to wind up dead."

Caden let out a low breath. "You hacked int—" He stared. "And you were fifteen?"

"Yes." She shrugged. "I had skills and a vivid imagination. Not necessarily a good combination. Looking back now, I can't believe I wasn't caught. But I wasn't. Probably would be today, thanks to all of the technology improvements, but back then . . ." She offered him a small shrug. "Anyway, I was fascinated with law enforcement and was always reading true crime stories, CIA and FBI thrillers."

"I remember you always with a nose in a book," Caden said.

"It was a good tool to use to shield the fact that I was watching you."

He blinked. "What?"

"When I was trying to figure out how to flirt with you." She grinned.

He really had been a clueless dork.

"So," she said, pulling his scrambled brain back on topic, "when my mind went where it did, turning my beloved fiction stories into real life, I let it. Although, to be honest, I was surprised that it wound up being true. Fiction come to life. Now, how often does that happen?"

"Like . . . never?"

"Well. At least once. For me anyway. The night we had our little talk, before he came clean, my dad tried to tell me he was undercover FBI. I didn't buy it because of what I'd already seen on his computer. I flat out asked him if he was CIA. He finally admitted it was true." She gave him a tight smile. "He showed me some very graphic pictures of former officers who'd been discovered. Needless to say, I understood the gravity of the situation and swore I'd never tell a soul—or press him about what he was doing when he was gone. And I didn't. I wasn't going to be the reason my father wound up in the hands of people who'd see him dead." She ran a hand over her hair and shrugged. "He said he'd made the difficult choice to keep his true profession from his family because he didn't want to burden us with his job. He told me something I'll never forget. He said, 'When you speak falsely because of an ignorance not of your own making, it is very different than having to tell a lie every day of your life. Especially when you're a truthful person in general.'" She shrugged. "He was right. Having to lie to my friends, my family, everyone, was hard. I wound up hating talking about my dad, because I didn't want to lie to the people I loved."

That made sense. No wonder she hated lies so much. "And he taught you Russian."

She laughed, her sadness fading somewhat. "Yes—along with Chinese, Pashto, and Spanish. And a working knowledge of Farsi and Arabic."

His jaw dropped.

"I have an ear for languages," she said.

"Apparently."

She sobered. "I think having me know relieved some of the burden for him. It was like he was lighter when it was just the two of us. He taught me how to fight and shoot a gun, and encouraged my language and technical skills. I went along with it because he seemed to take such joy in teaching me."

"Of course he did. And I'm sure you enjoyed the time you spent with him."

"More than anything." She dropped her gaze and frowned. "Until I realized he was grooming me to follow in his footsteps."

Caden paused. "Oh. And how did that go over with you?"

"Not very well at first. I'd already planned to go into the military as soon as I graduated high school. He backed off and figured when I was twenty-one, I could transition to the CIA." She smirked and shook her head. "He bugged me about it almost every day up until his death eight months ago. Used to drive me crazy." She bit her lip and looked away from him. Caden watched her swallow her emotion before she turned back. "I'd give anything to have him call me and bug me one more time."

"I'm sorry, Ava," he said, his voice soft.

"Thanks."

"So, did you ever find out who the man was in your dad's office?"

"No."

Silence fell between them for a moment. Then Caden leaned forward. "Did your mom know about your dad? Did your brother?"

"No. Dad said Mom wouldn't be able to handle it, and he was right. She was already drinking a bottle of wine a night whenever he was gone. The truth might have sent her right over the edge. And Nathan . . . well, no. I thought about telling him after Dad died. I mean, he was just devastated, but I didn't see the point in saying anything." She shook her head. "It doesn't really matter now, does it?"

Caden propped his chin in his hand. "You realize all of this sounds way too far-fetched to be true, right? No one would believe any of it."

"But you do." She shot him a knowing look.

"Yeah, I do." He hesitated and scrubbed a hand down his cheek. "And after tonight, I think your father's past has caught up with you."

"The thought has crossed my mind a few times."

"Then we need to ensure your safety until we can find whoever's started causing problems. You have security cameras here. It's a good system."

"It is. I even activated it after you left. I watched the camera near the French doors and saw some movement, but never a face or anything. Whoever was out there kept his head down. I turned the system off to go outside."

Which wasn't the brightest idea he'd ever heard of, but then again, she was obviously confident that her skills were good enough to deal with an intruder.

Caden was inclined to agree. "All right," he said, "it's getting late. I need to consult with Zane on where we are on the Fields case, then get some rest before my meeting at eight in the morning." He glanced at her, noting the tension in her shoulders and the tight jaw. "Do you want to call Sarah, Heather, or Brooke and stay with one of them?"

"Are you crazy?"

He blinked. "Not last I checked, but it's been a while."

She snickered and he was glad to see the brief flash of mirth. The sadness in her eyes when she had talked about her father was hard on his heart. "Let me bring you up-to-date on their lives," she said. "Brooke is pregnant—"

"I'm aware."

"—ready to give birth at any moment."

"Actually, I think she's got a few more weeks."

"Regardless, the last thing I need to do is add stress to her life or pull her into whatever problems I've acquired. Sarah—your sister, by the way—"

"Yep. Familiar with her."

"—is planning a wedding that's supposed to take place in six weeks. And Heather is on her way back from a medical conference."

He frowned. "Oh. Right. Travis told me about that." Travis Walker was Heather's fiancé and was doing his best to help keep his parents' ranch operating smoothly while directing his security business. On top of that, he was taking care of a young man working his way through med school. "All right, then . . ." He held his hands up. "I guess I camp out in your parking lot."

"What? No. You need your rest. Go home. I have the alarm system and my gun. I'll be fine."

"But I won't sleep a wink."

She groaned. "Ugh, seriously?"

Man, she was . . . cute. Fierce and feisty. And very, very capable. His admiration for her had been high to begin with. Now it was off the charts. But that didn't mean he was leaving.

"Unfortunately, yes. And it's not that I don't think you can take care of yourself. It's the fact that we all need someone to have our back sometimes."

She sighed, and he thought he might have seen a tear before she blinked. "Okay, okay. I can't be responsible for your lack of sleep. You can have the guest room, but no snoring."

"I don't snore."

She laughed. A real, full belly laugh. "Have you forgotten I used to spend many nights at your house when we were kids? Sarah and I used to stuff toilet paper into our ears to block out the sound of your snoring. Trust me, you snored as a teenager, I'm sure you snore now."

"I don't believe it." He thought of the many times he'd awakened in the morning to find his bedroom door shut. Had that been Sarah shutting out the sound of his snores? He'd always just assumed someone had done that in order not to wake him up.

"You drool too," Ava said.

He gaped. "Now you're just being mean."

"The truth hurts sometimes." Her smile faded and she stood. "Everything you might need is in the bathroom off the guest room. I have some of Dad's clothes in a box in that closet. Ones I just couldn't bear to get rid of. Feel free to help yourself to some sweats and a T-shirt."

"I have a go-bag in my truck. I'll be fine." He paused. "One more question."

"Sure."

"How'd your father die?"

◻ ◻ ◻

Eight months ago

Ava opened the door to her apartment to see John Sparks standing on her doorstep. She studied him and the expression on his face shattered her, although she refused to let it show. "He's dead, isn't he?"

"Yes."

She bit her lip and nodded, forcing the grief to someplace manageable. For now. "Come in."

John stepped inside, and she shut the door, motioning for him to have a seat on the couch. He ducked his head. "I can't stay long, Ava."

"All right. Tell me what happened. The real truth, not the story the world will know."

"You don't work for the Navy anymore. I came to recruit you."

"I'm not interested in working for the CIA, you know that."

"It was Paul's dying wish."

"No, it wasn't, and it's crass and manipulative of you to say so." She crossed her arms and walked to the mantel that held an antique clock, a picture of her mother and brother, and one of Ava with her childhood best friends, Sarah and Caden Denning. No pictures of her father, though.

"How can you say that? He's been training you since the day you were born. You just didn't know it until you were fifteen. We need you, Ava. We need your skills."

"Those were his choices, not mine. By the time I realized what he was doing, I simply went along with him because it meant spending time with him. But I never planned to join the CIA. Still don't."

"Your country needs you."

She whirled. "I served my country!" She stopped, gained control, and composed her features. "And I served it well. My mother needs me now and I'll appreciate it if you don't bring this up again. Now, how did he die?"

"The official version is a car wreck."

"And the real version?"

"He was on the Donghae-Vladivostok ferry. The water was rough and he was swept overboard into the sea."

Oh, Daddy, no . . . "You found his body?"

He sighed. "No, not yet. They will. They found his coat and a shoe."

Her head snapped up. "Then he might not be dead. You know that as well as I do. He's resourceful and—"

"There's video. He went into the Sea of Japan, Ava. He didn't survive."

Ava pressed a fist to her lips and sucked in a breath through her nose. "Okay. Well, if he did, he'll be in touch."

"Ava—"

"Thanks for letting me know, John."

"Ava! He's not going to be in touch. It was a long fall. The water isn't freezing, but it's definitely too cold to survive for long. And land was a long way away. He went down, probably got knocked unconscious—and never came back up."

Tears pressed against her lids and she fought to keep them from falling.

"I'm sorry, hon," he said, his voice softening. "I'll show you the video footage from the ferry's security camera if it will help convince you."

She sniffed and swiped her hands over her eyes. "Yes, okay, fine. Show me the footage."

Twenty minutes later, he was gone—at her insistence—and she sat on her couch, replaying the images in her mind. John was right. There was no way he'd survived that fall.

She released the tears.

CHAPTER
SEVEN

Ava stood in front of her dresser mirror, sucking in breaths to calm her racing heart and battered emotions. When she'd finished telling Caden the details of her father's death, she'd had to leave the room. She understood his need to know, but revisiting memories that hadn't had time to even scab over was brutal.

Caden's knock on the door sent her pulse skyrocketing once more. Okay, she could do this. When she'd excused herself, he said he was going to check in with Zane. She suspected he knew she needed a few minutes to herself, but he must need something if he was knocking.

She crossed the room and opened the door.

"You okay?" he asked.

"I'm . . . managing. Sorry. I just needed to . . ." She waved a hand as though to push aside the thought.

"I understand. Come on back in here whenever you're ready and we'll see if we can figure some things out. Zane said they're still running tests on Michael's laptop—and they're looking into your father's history, trying to find the link between him and Michael's father."

She scoffed. "You know as well as I do, they're not going to find a thing."

"I know. Which is why we need you to do the finding." He nodded to the laptop on her table. "Your father's?"

"How did you know?"

"I'm assuming that's yours on your desk."

She shot him a tight smile. "Observant."

"Occupational hazard."

"I guess so." She walked out to the table and sat down in front of the computer. "I was trying to get into it, but he changed the password." She raked a hand over her ponytail and sighed. "About five years ago, he gave me strict instructions what to do should I receive word of his death—such as how to clean out his secret residence. He had more IDs and money stashed in different places than you could imagine. Anyway, I did that and, of course, grabbed his laptop. I haven't looked at it since. But when you showed me the pictures, I pulled it out and got nowhere."

"You're a genius with computers. I have a hard time believing you can't get in."

She smiled. "I don't know about genius, but yes, I should be able to get into it at some point, although it would definitely be a lot faster if I had the password." Her smile flipped and she shook her head. "When I figured out his password at the age of fifteen, he upped the difficulty level. But later, he explained how to get into the laptop. He said I was the only one he trusted to destroy the information on there." A groan slipped from her. "I don't understand. Why make sure I had the password memorized—and the exact changes he would make each time he had to change it on the date he planned to do so—and then deviate from that?" The only answer she could come up with was because he planned to come back. But that was impossible, because he was dead—which only meant he'd been planning to come back, not die.

"Could it be he was afraid someone else would know his system?"

"Maybe." She mentally ran through all of the calculations and still came up with what she'd entered earlier. But . . . She typed it again. And again, got a Password Denied notification. "Ugh."

"Are you sure he didn't tell you and you just didn't know he was telling you?"

"Caden, my father and I spoke often. Sometimes via secure email, other times over a secure phone line. There was nothing in any of those communications about him changing the system for his password."

"Maybe it wasn't anything he said. Your father was always into games and surprises, puzzles and whatnot. Maybe there was something special about a scavenger hunt or—"

She laughed. "Do you know how many of those he did? How many word games—head games, really—and other stuff we did over the years?"

He sighed. "All right, then, I can get Daria to get into the computer."

"Excuse me," Ava said, indignant, "I can get into it, thank you very much. I just have to figure out—" She stopped and swiveled her attention on her bedroom. "Wait a minute. Puzzles."

"What?"

"It couldn't be that easy." She gave a short laugh.

"What are you talking about?"

"The puzzle he sent me. Oh, you've got to be kidding me. Of course he would do that."

"Puzzle?"

Ava darted to the bedroom and into her closet. She could hear Caden behind her. It only took her a second to extract the puzzle from its hiding place and rip the plastic off the plain box.

"Ava?"

"My father sent me this. It arrived three days after I learned of his death." She shot him a tight smile. "Like I told you before, puzzles were our thing. Something we could do while we talked about whatever, but mostly while he taught me whichever language we were focusing on."

"Okay. And?"

"I don't know. And maybe nothing." She hugged the box to herself. "I couldn't handle doing the puzzle without him, so I stashed it for later." She shrugged and sighed. "I guess now is later." She cleared the table of her unfinished puzzle and dumped the new pieces onto the surface.

"You think he left you the password in this puzzle?"

"I have no idea, but I wouldn't put it past him." She shook her head. "You know as well as anyone Paul Jackson's love of scavenger hunts, treasure hunts. *Any* kind of hunts. But mostly puzzles. And not just the ones with interlocking pieces. All kinds of puzzles and mind games." She started separating the pieces, looking for the straight edges. "One thousand pieces, Dad?" she muttered. "Seriously? Why a thousand? Why not a hundred? Or five hundred? A thousand takes *forever*." The grumbling helped keep her focus off the fact that her father wouldn't be here to help her put together the puzzle.

"Maybe he wanted to make sure someone didn't put it together too fast."

"Maybe. And there's an awful lot of white in here. With black writing. And some color, blues and reds we can group together. Looks like it might be a picture of something—or several somethings."

His hand covered hers. "We don't have to do this tonight. You've had a bad scare and you're exhausted."

She stilled. "I am. But my adrenaline is racing too. I'm probably fine for a couple of hours at least. I want to get this done so we can find that connection." She paused. "Assuming I'm even right about this puzzle. It may just be . . . a puzzle. A gift that he planned to be here to share with me. But . . ." A groan slipped from her. "Why didn't I open this before? How could I have not realized—"

He gripped her fingers. "Stop, Ava. Just stop. You were grieving. Still are."

She let out a slow breath. "Yes, I was grieving, but I was . . . in denial too." She rubbed her eyes with her free hand. "It's just between everything going on with my mother, trying to figure out what I want to do with the rest of my life, trying to make sure Nathan makes the right choices and doesn't fall into . . ." She stopped. Pulled herself together one more time. "Sorry."

"You have nothing to apologize for." He frowned. "What's going on with Nathan?"

Ava pursed her lips, her out-of-character outburst sending waves of heat into her cheeks. "Nothing."

"Tell me."

His shrewd eyes studied her, and she withdrew her hand from his grasp and dropped her face into her palms. What would it feel like to share her burdens? If there was anyone she could trust, it would be Sarah and Caden. When she lifted her head, he hadn't moved. "I just worry about him. He's young, possibly a little stupid. I just want him to make wise decisions."

"Any reason in particular that makes you feel that way?"

"No. It's just a feeling." Ava let her gaze fall back to the puzzle and she separated another edge piece. "I could find out, of course, very easily by simply hacking into his computer." She shot him a tight smile. "His would be much easier than Dad's. But I don't want to invade his privacy like that. I'm just hoping that by talking to him every other day, at some point, he'll confide in me if there are any issues." She paused. "But don't think for one minute that I won't do it if I think there's a real need for it."

"You're a good sister."

She smiled. "I try. For now, though, let's see what we can do with this puzzle. You ready?"

"Ready."

□ □ □

Two hours after they started, with not even a third of it put together, Ava had taken some more ibuprofen and, at his urging, stretched out on the couch for a short break.

He'd popped some of the little orange pills himself, grateful when they kicked in to douse the throbbing in his head. He shot another glance at Ava and smiled, then pressed another puzzle piece into the correct spot. That short break had turned into four hours while Caden drank a pot of coffee and kept going.

If Ava thought this puzzle could somehow lead them to answers, lost sleep was the least of his worries. Zane had texted thirty minutes ago to tell him that Mickey was still missing, but someone had reported seeing him near a homeless community in the woods behind the highway. They would continue looking.

Zane
And now, I'm getting a few hours of sleep. I'll text when I'm conscious again.

Caden thought the man should sleep for more than a few hours. He should stay in bed until he was ready to get back to work full speed ahead. But Zane was Zane. He probably had pneumonia—and he wouldn't let a little case of something like that keep him from tracking down a killer.

A group text from Daria, sent to him and Zane, popped up on his screen.

Sending this now on the off chance you're awake. If you're asleep, I don't want to disturb you by calling. First . . . I talked to the local

authority's lab about that can of mace. They
tested it and found no prints. Not even on the
little piece you push to squirt it. The interesting
thing is the contents. It's chloroform. So,
whoever was planning to use it wasn't planning
to kill anyone, just knock them out. It's kind of
a dead end. For now anyway. Unfortunately,
speaking of dead ends, so is Ava's dad. The man
exists. His DMV photo matches the man in the
pictures you sent me, but the Bureau's facial
recognition software came up empty. Which
is not unheard of, but kind of surprising. What
little I do know is this: Paul Jackson was a travel
writer. His articles appeared in many magazines,
newspapers, etc. His byline says Paul Jackson.
But . . . honestly, if this guy's real name is Paul
Jackson, mine is Ada Lovelace.

Caden blinked. Who the heck was Ada Lovelace? Another text
popped up:

And before you ask, she's the first known
computer programmer—because women rock.
We celebrate her contributions to math and
science every fifteenth of October.

Good to know. Before he could tap a response to get her off
the short rabbit trail, she was back on track.

There are no other pictures of Paul
Jackson—or whoever the man is in the two
pictures you sent me. His author photo has him
bent over a keyboard, but you can't see his face.
Seriously, I can't find anything. And because
I knew you'd question my abilities due to my
newness, I consulted with Annie. She came up
with exactly what I did. If I had to take a guess,
I'd say he was CIA, but I don't have anything to
base that on, although I'm working with some
sources to find that out.

Okay, that stopped him. He finally tapped out his own message.

> I'm awake. Working on this case. And no need to check with Annie any longer. If she says you can do the job, you can do it. I'll ask Ava if she knows of any other names her father might have gone by and get back to you.

Perfect.

Her response came swift, like she'd already typed the next message and went back to fill in the one word in answer to his statement before hitting send. She was probably texting from her laptop.

> One other thing. I've run the floppy disk—do you know how hard it was to locate that kind of antique computer??—and it's all code. And the few words that are on there are in Russian. I've sent it to CRRU—with my translation of the Russian words—to see what they can do with them. The newspaper clippings—also in Russian—seem innocent enough until you notice the little marks on certain letters. CRRU also has the clippings because, again, I think it's a code. I've been tinkering with it off and on myself and think I've figured that code out, but I'm still playing with it. Hopefully, CRRU will figure it out faster than I do. I'll let you know when I have something more. Until then, I'm headed to bed for a few hours. I'll text when I'm back online.

> Thanks, Daria. You're killing it.

A heart emoji flashed at him and he smothered a laugh. She might be a genius, but she was still a very young one. He'd done a little investigating on his own and was surprised to learn that

Daria had been taken in by Linc and Allie St. John. When she was just shy of eighteen years old, she'd helped them put her organized crime boss of a father out of commission. Linc was in a field office in Columbia and they'd worked together on several cases in the past.

Zane hadn't responded, so hopefully that meant he was sleeping.

Caden pressed his thumb and forefinger to his suddenly gritty eyes. Sleep would be nice, but—

But why not? The puzzle pieces were starting to blur and his mind was fogging. He'd be no help to anyone in his current fatigued state. With a sigh, he set the alarm on his watch and lowered his head to his forearms.

Two hours later, the buzzing on his watch woke him. Or maybe it was the tantalizing smells of coffee and cinnamon. Instantly awake, he sat up and spotted Ava across from him, bent over the puzzle. She'd managed to finish a good bit of it, which told him she'd been awake about as long as he'd been asleep. A coffee cup and a plate containing a few crumbs sat to her left. How had she managed to do that without waking him?

She glanced up. "Hey."

"Hey." The word came out on a croak and he cleared his throat. "How are you feeling?"

"Like a truck ran over me, but at least a little rested. How about yourself?"

"Like I could use another six hours or so, but grateful for the two I got. I must have been really gone."

"Yep. You were snoring."

He chuckled. "At least I didn't drool." He checked to make sure and Ava let out a short laugh. He picked up a puzzle piece and fit it into its spot. "Any idea what it is?" The section he'd just added to was still a good-sized hole.

"There's a lot of black and white, but it's still missing too much to figure out what that part is. I see a few words, some animals, which is where the color comes in, part of a blueprint—which gives us some blue lines to match up." She frowned. "I think it's a collection of different things."

"But no password?"

She sighed. "Not yet, but I decided it was time to bring out the big guns." She pointed to her desk and he noticed she had the laptops hooked up to each other. "I tried a lot of different combinations with no luck, so I'm putting my hacking skills to work."

He covered his ears. "I didn't hear that."

A laugh bubbled from her and she shook her head. "Not to worry, Mr. Agent Man. It's all legal. I have some software on my laptop that can scan for passwords on his computer and—" She shrugged. "Anyway, when it finds the right combination, it'll beep. Unless . . ."

"Unless?"

"Unless it doesn't. There's no telling what he used or how long it is. It could be a fifty-letter phrase or something. But I figured I'd let it run while I worked on the puzzle and thought. Puzzles always help me think." She ran her fingers over a portion they'd finished. "And I've been thinking how special this one is. He had to have had this made shortly before he died."

"I'm honored I get to be the one to put it together with you," he said, his voice soft.

She smiled once more. "Thanks."

"Could I ask you a question?" he asked. "A personal one?"

Wariness flashed in her eyes, but she shrugged. "Sure."

"Whatever happened to that guy you were seeing?"

A blank expression replaced the wariness. "What guy?"

"I don't know. I was over at Brooke and Asher's house a few weeks ago and they mentioned you had a date." The announcement had sparked something in him. Since that night, he'd made it to the memory care home as often as possible.

Her brow furrowed and she shook her head. "I have no idea."

"They said you met him at some coffee shop?"

A light flickered in her gaze. "Oh, Ryan." She laughed, a short burst of sound that died quickly. "He was a nice guy, but not for me."

Relief crashed over him like a tidal wave. "Okay, well. Huh."

"What made you ask about him?"

"I was just curious. Wondered if you were still seeing him."

"You know I'm not."

"Well, you hadn't mentioned him to Sarah, so—"

"You asked Sarah about him?" Her brow arched on the question.

Busted. He hesitated. "Yes. She said she didn't know what I was talking about."

She studied him a moment. "I don't talk about my . . . dating life. Mostly because I don't have one. I didn't say anything to Sarah because there wasn't anything worth saying. The only reason Brooke knew about it was because she was in the room with me when I took the call and accepted the date."

"Oh."

She eyed him, her gaze making him want to squirm and very sorry he'd brought up the topic.

"Caden?"

"Yeah."

"I don't really date much."

Well, that was good news. For the most part. Or was it terrible news? "Okay." He was ready to put the awkward topic to rest.

"My father's job pretty much ruined dating for me."

Caden blinked. "What do you—?"

"Never mind. It's not important. I shouldn't have said that." A sigh slipped from her. "Did you hear anything from Zane while I was sleeping? We still don't know what those newspaper clippings were or what was on the floppy disks."

Should he let it go or push his agenda? Letting it go seemed to be the better idea. "I had a text conversation with Daria, one of our analysts," he finally said. "She's still working on that and has others doing the same. They finally dug up an old computer to see if they can read the disks." He picked up his phone and tapped the screen. "Zane was supposed to be getting a few hours of sleep, but he texted that he's up, so I'll call him and see what the plan is for him today."

"Don't you have an eight o'clock meeting?"

"It was supposed to be with the task force, but I'm going to request we postpone it—or that they meet without me and fill me in later. I have an idea I'd like to chase down first."

"What idea?"

"I'm still working on it. Which is why I need to talk to Zane."

She stood. "You do that and I'm going to go get ready for the day." She paused. "Wait. Today is Monday, isn't it?"

"I think so. Yeah."

"I'm supposed to eat lunch with Sarah and Brooke today. I'm going to back out. This needs to take priority right now, I think."

He nodded. "Probably a good idea."

She grabbed her phone. "There's fresh coffee in the pot and cinnamon rolls on the stove. Help yourself."

"Gladly. Thank you."

She disappeared down the hall, and Caden loaded a plate with two of the large pastries. He refilled his coffee cup and returned to his seat at the table. After allowing himself one bite of the sugary sweetness, he dialed Zane's number.

EIGHT

Ava's mind was too busy to bother enjoying the hot shower. After letting her friends know she wouldn't be able to join them, she simply went through the motions required for getting ready for the day. When she'd awakened to see Caden asleep at her kitchen table, her heart had done some weird flip-flop thing that knocked her a bit sideways. Fortunately, he'd continued to snooze and hadn't been witness to her struggle to ignore the sensation.

But it had been there and she didn't like it. Okay, she did, but she . . . couldn't. Romance had never been very high on her priority list—as an adult, not a starry-eyed teen—but she had to admit, Caden made her consider rearranging the items on the list. And want to put on mascara.

And that was just weird.

Swiping the black liquid over her lashes, she sighed. "Quit it. Stop thinking so much."

The muttered words simply served to shift her thoughts to her father. And that blasted password. Why would he change it? The only thing she could come up with was . . . he didn't want her to have access.

She lowered the tube of makeup. All righty, then. That possibility changed the question. Why would he make sure she had the password—and all the timed variations—memorized, only to completely change it *so she couldn't get in*? Easily anyway.

She'd figure out a way around the password eventually—especially with the help of the software—but it could take a very long time to do so. The fact that the software was still running didn't bode well.

So . . . going with the thought that he didn't want her to access the laptop only added another why to the list. What was the point in keeping her out of the laptop . . .

. . . unless—as she'd thought more than once—he wasn't dead? And planned to come back for it.

The hope that sprouted terrified her. If she allowed herself to believe and it turned out she was wrong and he was really dead, it would shatter her.

She could hear Caden on the phone on the other side of her closed door and took a steadying breath. First things first. She'd call John. Maybe he would know what her father had been thinking.

Ava stepped back into the living area just as Caden hung up. "You look a little more awake," he said.

She smiled. "Thanks."

"Do you mind if I . . ." He pointed to the guest room.

"Of course. Help yourself."

"Great. I'll fill you in on my plans for the day when I'm done. They involve you if you have the time."

She raised a brow. "I have the time. Other than my daily visit with Mom, I'm still trying to figure out what I want to do with my life."

"Perfect. I'll be back in a few minutes."

He disappeared into the guest room, and Ava walked into

the kitchen with the intention of cleaning it up and found it already spotless. She eyed the foil-covered plate, then the empty sink.

She opened the dishwasher to confirm their two plates were in there and let out a low chuckle. "My, my, Mr. Agent Man," she murmured, "you really know how to impress a girl, don't you?" Then again, she'd always been impressed with him. She shut the dishwasher and walked back to the puzzle.

Twenty minutes and four measly pieces later, Caden appeared in the doorway of the guest room, dressed in clean clothes and his hair still wet from the shower.

And, boy, did he look good. Ava swallowed and looked away. Her suddenly dry throat had her swigging her cold coffee. With a grimace, she pushed it away. She didn't date. Ever. Especially not after Ryan. Remember? For some reason, it was getting harder and harder to hold to that rule.

He dropped his go-bag on the floor next to the chair opposite her and sat. "Zane said there were no real leads in this case, but the lab has all the evidence and will be going through it."

"What about the relatives of the family?" She hoped her question was coherent. She was still reminding herself she was no longer a teen with a crush on Caden Denning. No, it looked like she was an adult with one. Great. Just fabulous. *You don't do relationships or dating.* Maybe if she repeated it enough times, she'd get it through her head. And heart.

His lips quirked. "Are you sure you're not an investigator?"

She blinked, his question slapping her back to the here and now. "Quite."

"Before I headed to see you, we were talking to Michael's parents via a Facetime call. We had them pull off into a rest area so we could question them. I know that sounds cold, but we had to push forward with the investigation. The more time that passes . . ."

"You don't have to explain that to me. I understand."

"We're going to talk to them again. In person this time." He rubbed his chin and narrowed his eyes. "I've got to say that when we questioned them the first time, something was off."

"Off how?"

"I'm not sure. He was definitely grieving. So broken up he could barely talk. His wife finally just gave up and wept. It was truly awful."

"But?"

Caden sighed. "I've questioned enough people in my career to know when something doesn't feel right. When we showed him the pictures, he held the phone close enough to see his microexpressions. He was studying them and . . ."

"And?"

"Remembering? He was especially interested in the newspaper clippings, but when we got to the pictures of you and your dad, it was subtle, but I think he was stunned, freaked. I'm not sure of the word, but I definitely got the impression that Jesse Fields wasn't being completely straight with me from that point on."

Ava leaned forward. "But that doesn't even make sense. What would he have to hide about his son's family's murders?"

"That's just it. I don't know. Daria did backgrounds on the family and everything checks out. No hidden bank accounts, no consorting with organized crime. Everyone at his office had nothing but good things to say about him and the whole family. The same with the other two families as well. Perfectly normal people with no run-ins with the law or . . . anything. Like there's nothing that should be setting off any alarm bells for me about this particular family."

But something was, and Ava wanted to know what, almost as bad as he did. "So you want me to go with you?"

He sighed. "This case has something to do with your father.

It's possible Jesse Fields might say something that has meaning only to you." He paused. Frowned. "Wait a minute. That's it."

"What's it?"

"What's been bothering me. It wasn't Jesse Fields's reaction to your father's *name*, it was his reaction to the *pictures*."

"So he might not be hiding anything about Michael and his family, he might be hiding something about my father?"

"Yeah. I think that's a real possibility. I want you there this time, because I'm going to ask him about your father again. I want you to see his reaction, hear what he says. If there's something that only you would notice, then I don't want to take a chance on missing that."

Ava gave a slow nod. "Makes sense." She paused. "If he knew my father when Dad was in Moscow, my father wouldn't have been using his real name."

"Of course not. He would have been using an alias."

"Yes. The question is, which one?" She glanced at her room, then back to Caden. "Hold on a second."

"What is it?"

"If my father was using an alias, then I probably have it." She walked toward her bedroom. "When I cleaned out his safe house after he was . . . killed . . . I brought all of his passports home with me." In the closet, she opened the compartment once more and pulled out the stack of little booklets. She carried them into the kitchen and called the names out to Caden while he typed them into the notes app on his phone.

"Twelve names. Twelve different identities." He shook his head. "That's impressive. I've done some undercover stuff and it was hard enough keeping one made-up name and background straight. I can't imagine this."

"He was very good at his job." She drew in a deep breath. "All right, then. When do we leave?"

"In fifteen minutes."

She glanced back at the puzzle. "Fine. I bet I can find more pieces than you before we have to walk out the door."

"You're on."

□ □ □

Caden appreciated Ava's willingness to ride with him to the senior Fields's home, then allow him to take her back to her apartment when they were finished. He didn't come out and say it, but after the two weird incidents yesterday, he wasn't comfortable leaving her alone. The fact that she didn't put up any kind of argument could mean she felt the same. Or not. He wasn't sure, but he wasn't going to ask, either.

"How's your father doing?" she asked. "I haven't had a chance to ask in all of the craziness."

Her question came out of the blue, but he rolled with it. "He's doing all right. Sarah doesn't keep you updated?"

"She does, but she said he hadn't been feeling well over the past couple of months."

Caden frowned. "No, he hasn't. The doctors aren't sure what's going on with him. He has another appointment the day after tomorrow. Sarah's going with him, so we'll know more then."

She didn't respond, and he could tell she was mentally chewing on something. "What is it?" he asked.

"What do you mean?"

"You're thinking. I can almost hear the wheels turning in your brain."

"I'm thinking about something that's none of my business."

"Now you have to tell me."

She shot him a tight smile and shrugged. "I guess I was just curious about your relationship with your father. I know things were rough going there for a while, but that he and Sarah patched up their differences and are doing well. However, when we were all together a few weeks ago for dinner, you hardly spoke to him. Actually, it looked like you went out of your way to avoid him."

Caden didn't want to talk about his father. His mother had died when he was a teen, and thanks to his father's treatment of Sarah, she'd gone off the emotional deep end. Granted, all was well between them now, but it had taken years for her to get to that point. "I'm glad for Sarah's sake that they've found their peace with one another."

"And you? Have you found your peace with him?"

He wanted to give a flippant answer, but this was Ava. She wouldn't let him brush her off. "I'm working on it. You know as well as I do, he treated Sarah very badly and I had to be the mediator, the go-between. I tried my best to be a buffer and keep him from doing irreparable damage to her, but . . ." He shrugged. "Frankly, I resented the need for it. Then again, part of me knows he didn't realize what he was doing, that he was, in actuality, trying in his own way to protect her. But his way is usually just that. *His way* or the highway. Sarah took the highway and I almost lost her because of it. Most of the time I'm okay, but only because Sarah's okay. It's when I think about what might have happened that the old anger wants to rear its head, and I have to let it go all over again. And then there's Dustin—"

"Yes. I know." Dustin Denning, Caden and Sarah's younger brother, had been a victim of a drug scam a few short months ago. He'd taken medication he'd been hopeful would help with his PTSD. Instead, one missed dose sent him spiraling into depression and he jumped off a building. His suicide had rocked them all. "Do you blame him for Dustin's death too?"

"No. Not consciously, at least. I've seen what the grief of knowing he funded that drug trial is doing to him. But it's still hard to be in the same room with him on occasion."

Ava took his hand in hers. "You're a good man, Caden Denning. A good brother and a good son. You'll get there."

"We'll see." He paused. "It's a trust issue. And I may be a tad cynical since I grew up with the man, but he's always had hidden motives—some kind of self-serving agenda. I'm not sure he still doesn't."

"So, you're watching and waiting?"

"Something like that. Unfortunately, it seems like I have a weakness for that kind of personality. I'm trying to change that."

"Weakness how?"

"Never mind. It doesn't matter."

"Seriously? Does this have anything to do with Wendy?"

He grimaced. Why had he said anything? He hadn't thought about her in months. Why now?

"Caden?"

"Yes, it has to do with Wendy."

She glanced at the GPS on the dash. "We have seven minutes. Give me the abridged version. Sarah was surprisingly tight-lipped about her."

Well, that was good to know, but still he hesitated. Then gave a slight shrug. "She and I met at a baseball game. She seemed nice and she gave me her number. I ended up calling her one night"—the night he'd heard Ava was dating someone else—"and we went out a few times. I learned the reason she went out with me was because her brother was in prison for drugs and she thought I could pull some strings to get him out."

Ava gasped. "She did *not*."

"She did. I told her I didn't have the power to do that—nor would I use it if I did—and she couldn't get away from me fast enough."

"I'm so sorry. What a jerk."

"Girls can be jerks?" She raised a brow and he nodded in

answer to his own question. "Never mind. They sure can." He glanced at the clock on the dash. "And that didn't even take seven minutes. That's pretty sad."

Three minutes later, Caden pulled to the curb in front of the million-dollar home and cut the engine. He'd already pushed Wendy from his thoughts and circled back around to his father. Ava seemed to think he'd "get there" in forgiving the man? Would he? Maybe. As long as his father continued to support Sarah and didn't revert back to his old ways, then yeah, he might be able to let the resentment go for good in the future. He just wasn't sure he could trust the man yet—or ever.

Ava swept an appreciative glance over the brick house. "Where'd the money come from?"

Grateful for the change in topic, Caden let his shoulders relax a fraction. "The senior Mr. Fields is a retired cardiologist, but still does some consulting work. She's a high-end realtor."

"A power couple, huh?"

He laughed. "Appears that way, doesn't it?" His smile slid from his lips. "Michael and his family appeared to live comfortably, but simply. You'd never know he came from all of this. Privileged and lacking nothing."

"Not a bad way to grow up."

"No. I have nothing against living well. As long as you don't shirk the responsibility of using your position to help others." Caden's phone buzzed and he swiped the screen. "Hey, Zane, what's up?"

"Something very bad and very . . . weird."

"Like your voice?"

"Not now, dude."

The seriousness in his partner's hoarse voice flipped Caden's smile into a frown. "All right. Sorry. Tell me."

"Daria just called. Another family was murdered."

Caden's heart dropped and he swallowed hard. No wonder his partner didn't feel like joking around. "Who? Where?"

"Portland, Oregon. But get this. It was the sister of the guy who was killed in Texas. Her name is Bridgette O'Reilly."

"What!" Okay, that was beyond weird. As well as heartbreaking and soul-shattering. "How many in the family?"

"Her and her three kids. There's no husband. She's a single mom."

He could feel Ava watching him. "Where are the parents? What do they have to say?"

"I'm not sure yet. The crime scene is only a couple of hours old. We'll know more in a bit."

Caden pressed fingers to his eyes. "Fine. Where are you?"

"Just pulled in behind you." His cough came through the line.

A glance in the rearview mirror confirmed his partner's words. "Ready to do this?"

"Yeah. I'm going to keep my distance, though. I don't need to be getting anyone sick."

"I'm okay with that." Caden hung up and summarized the conversation.

She shook her head and sorrow darkened her eyes. "How awful. We need to find this person, Caden."

"I'm not arguing." He squeezed her hand. "You ready?"

"Waiting on you."

They climbed out and all three walked to the front door together.

Caden noted Ava's relaxed composure. "How do you do that?" he whispered in her ear.

She frowned. "Do what?"

"Maintain such a serene outer façade?"

"Serene?" She scoffed. "I'm a bundle of nerves."

Zane rang the bell and stepped back.

"That's my point. You don't look it. Remind me never to play poker with you."

She wrinkled her nose at him but had no time to respond as the door opened and Jesse Fields stood in the doorway.

"I'm sorry to bother you again, Mr. Fields," Zane said. "However, we've thought of a few more questions, if you don't mind. We've also had some new developments that we'd like to discuss with you."

Grief flashed. "You found out who did it?"

"No, sir, not yet. But . . . could we come in?"

The man sighed. "Sure."

He pushed open the storm door, and Zane stepped inside. Caden placed a hand at the small of Ava's back and guided her in behind Zane.

Once they were all seated in the formal living area just off the massive foyer—with Zane keeping his distance by standing near the fireplace—Caden cleared his throat. "Mr. Fields, first question. Do you have any other children besides Michael?"

The man winced and shook his head. "No. He was an only child."

"Okay, that's what I thought, but wanted to clarify. Thank you."

"Why?"

"Some other information has come up, but if you don't have any other children, it doesn't pertain to you or the case." No reason to tell him another family had been murdered. "Do you remember the pictures I showed you yesterday? The man named Paul Jackson and you?"

"Of course."

"I don't suppose you've remembered the name he went by when you knew him?"

Mr. Fields's gaze held steady. "No. Sorry. I told you yesterday, it was a very long time ago. We met briefly at that café in

Moscow. I think he was a salesperson or worked for a magazine or something. We struck up a conversation and . . . I had no idea someone was taking pictures or how they came to be in my son's home. I'm sorry, I just don't know."

Caden still wasn't sure he believed him. "All right. This is Ava Jackson, Paul's daughter. She's the little girl in the other picture."

Mr. Fields paled and his blue gaze swung to Ava. She offered a sympathetic smile. "Mr. Fields, I'm so sorry about the circumstances of our meeting, but I wanted to come hear the details myself."

He took a moment to gather his composure and Caden wondered why the reaction to Ava. Finally, the man shook his head. "There aren't any more details than what I've already told these two."

"All right," Caden said. "We have a list of names that Ava's father used as aliases when he was working in Moscow. Maybe you'd recognize one of them?"

"I doubt it."

"Do you mind if I read them to you?"

Another heavy sigh. "If you insist."

Caden read from the list on his phone. For each name, he'd mentally figure out how to say it, then look up and voice it aloud, watching for any kind of reaction. When he said Dimitri Golubev, he thought he got a slight blink. Caden lowered his phone after the last name. Either the man didn't recognize any of the names or he was very good at hiding his emotions—except when it came to his son and family. Caden waited. "Nothing?"

"No. Sorry."

"One more question. The picture that was taken from your son's home, on the mantel. The killer made a point to come back and get it. You said you would try to remember which picture it was. Have you had any success?"

Another blink. Similar to the one he'd gotten when he mentioned Dimitri Golubev. A frown creased the man's forehead. "I think it may have been a picture of the children when they went waterskiing last summer."

"Actually, it looks like it might be a picture of five men. We just can't make out their faces. And the photo was black and white. Does that help?"

The man's face never changed and he shook his head. "No, sorry."

Caden wanted to sigh. Instead, he looked at Ava, who was studying Jesse Fields.

"Your American accent is very clean," she said. "How long did it take you to lose the Russian one?"

Mr. Fields froze. Then stood and pointed toward the door. "It's time for you to leave."

Caden's heart picked up speed a fraction. "Mr. Fields, what's wrong?"

"I'm done talking. I can't—" He raked a hand over his graying head. "I need you to leave."

This time, Caden heard the slight intonation Ava had referred to. If he hadn't been listening for it, he would have never noticed it. "Mr. Fields, if someone is threatening you, we can help."

The man pressed a hand to his forehead and drew in a breath. "No one is threatening us. Just please, find out who killed them."

"That's my point, sir. We need every tiny detail you might have in order to put all the pieces together. Whatever you're holding back could be the one thing we need."

"It's not!" Tears welled in his eyes. "I should never—"

"Jesse, I'm not feeling well." The voice from the kitchen doorway that led into the great room swung their attention to the woman Caden had met last night. Red, swollen eyes, blotchy cheeks, and hair that hadn't seen a brush, probably since she'd heard the majority of her family had been killed.

Mr. Fields rose and went to his wife. "Martha, honey, what is it?"

She pressed a hand to her chest. "I just don't feel well."

Ava stood. "Can I do something to help?"

He waved a hand toward the door. "You can leave. Now." He turned and gripped his wife's upper arm. "Come. Sit. Let me check your blood pressure."

Caden nodded to the door and Zane frowned but gave a quick dip of his head in response. "I hope you feel better, Mrs. Fields," he said. "Mr. Fields, please. If you can think of anything at all to help us find who did this, you know how to reach us."

"Yes, yes. Go. I will . . . think."

This time Caden didn't have to search for the accent. "Thank you, sir," he said. He led the way outside to the porch, and Zane pulled the door shut behind him.

"He's lying," Ava said. "And I think he's terrified."

Caden met her gaze, saw the concern there. "I know. What do you think he's so scared of?"

"I don't know, but he didn't want to admit he was Russian. And that's a big red flag in my book."

"None of the information Daria sent us says anything about any Russian connections," Zane said.

Caden shook his head. "But I heard it too, once Ava pointed it out. Let's ask Daria to do another search—this time adding in the possible Russian element."

Ava pulled her phone from her pocket. "You do that. I'm going to make a call too."

Caden's eyes narrowed. "You've thought of something?"

"Not something. *Someone.*"

NINE

Ava left Caden and Zane standing next to Caden's vehicle and walked far enough down the street that they wouldn't be able to overhear her conversation. She punched the programmed number on her phone with more force than necessary.

John answered on the second ring. "Ava, two calls in two days? To what do I owe the pleasure?"

"I need your help on something and I need it fast."

"Sounds serious."

"It is." She hesitated. "I can't betray a confidence, but I know you have friends in high places at the FBI. Can you find out everything there is to know about several cases the FBI is investigating and then call me back? Start with the murder of the Michael Fields family." That was in the news so nothing confidential there.

"All right." He drew the words out, but she knew John Sparks and was sure he was already typing a message to his Special Agent friend. "Now you've got me curious."

"I know. Call me back as soon as you're read in."

"It won't take long."

"I know that too." He hung up and Ava waited, pressing the phone to her forehead.

"Ava? You okay?"

She looked up. Caden eyed her with concern. "I'm fine. Just waiting on a call. Do you mind if we hang out for a few minutes until he gets back to me?" She supposed they could leave and she could take the call in the car, but for some reason, she wanted this to be a private conversation.

"Sure. Zane and I have a lot to discuss, so we'll just do it in the car." He mumbled something she thought sounded like, "With the windows down."

He turned back to Zane, and Ava did what she did best when she had to wait on something important. She paced.

Ten minutes later, her phone rang and she snatched the call. "John?"

"Yep. Okay, I know about the Fields murders, the most recent one in Oregon, and everything else."

"That was really fast."

"My friend was busy. He kept it short."

"Okay, so something's going on. There's a connection between all of these families, but more than that, there's a connection between at least one of those families and my father. I need to know what that is."

"I have the names of all the families. Is there anything else?"

"Yes. It has to do with Michael Fields. Caden found a picture with my father and Jesse Fields, who is Michael's father. But I suspect that Jesse Fields isn't his real name." She explained about the faint Russian accent and his reaction to her catching it. "He shut down, John. Like fast and furious. I think he's scared."

"Of what?"

"No idea. I was hoping you could help me out with that. Like how he and my father knew each other." She paused. "In addition to that, I need you to tell me. Is Paul Jackson my fa-ther's real name?"

Silence from the other end.

"Well, I guess that answers that question," she said.

"Come on, Ava. You, more than anyone, know what his job entailed. He went by any number of aliases."

She *did* know that, but . . . "Fine. What was the name he used in Russia?"

"That's classified information. I can't give you—"

"Someone is killing families, John. Entire families! And some-how my father is connected to it. He's in a picture with a murdered man's father. And they've got a picture of me too. On a swing when I was a child. I need his name. The FBI needs that name."

More silence.

Her head started to throb. "He's dead, John. What does it matter?"

He huffed a short laugh. "You know as well as I do why it matters. It's called the domino effect. I can't give you that." He ignored her groan of frustration. "But I'll look into this, and if I find anything that I can pass on to you, I'll do so."

"John—"

"I'm serious, Ava. Call me back when you're ready to join the organization. It would make answering your questions a lot easier." He hung up and she barely resisted tossing her phone. That would be stupid.

"Ava?" Caden asked, walking over to her. "You okay?"

She grimaced, realizing she'd expressed her frustration in the form of a low growl. No, she wasn't okay, but . . .

She and Caden returned to his truck as Zane pulled away from the curb with a wave. "Just a phone call that I thought might help things and wound up . . . not." She paused. "We need to know the name my father was going by when he met with Jesse Fields, right?"

"It's possible it could help. Or it could wind up being a dead end."

"But if we had his name, at least we'd know—one way or another."

"Yes. Maybe." He paused. "I think the aliases might work better in the connections search. I've sent Daria the names he used as aliases. There's no way he'd use his real name. I think I noticed a flicker of a reaction when I called off Dimitri, so I told Daria to focus on that one first."

"Okay."

"I was also thinking that while the aliases might reveal more, there's a slim chance he used his birth name for something. If we had it, Daria could still check for a connection between your father and the families who've been killed. If she's able to find that connection, it might lead us to the person who had a grudge against this family—or at least Michael—and the others as well."

"So, it's like it might be helpful or it might not, but if we don't have it, we might be missing something."

"I'd say that's an accurate summary."

"Then we're going to find out his name."

"How?"

She sighed. "There's really only one way I believe it can be done—at least done quickly—and you probably don't need to know the details."

"What do you mean?"

"Because it's not exactly the most *ethical* thing I've ever done."

"You've lost me."

She studied him. "I honestly don't even know if it'll work." She nodded to his car. "How do you feel about a road trip?"

"I'm okay with it. Why?"

"I'll explain on the way."

"On the way to where?"

"Give me your phone and I'll put the address in."

□ □ □

THIRTEEN YEARS AGO

Nineteen-year-old Ava opened the door to her father's safe house and stepped inside. "Dad? I'm here. Why wasn't your door locked?"

"Because I knew you were coming." His voice came from the kitchen. He walked toward her, wiping his hands on a towel. "I got you something."

"Let me guess," she said with a laugh.

He picked the puzzle box up from the table and waved it at her. "I got you a puzzle, Ava-girl." They said the line together like always.

"Come on, Dad," she said, "we both know the puzzles are for you." But she'd admit she loved them too. Mostly because of the time spent with him. She took the box from him and smiled at the picture on the front. "Cades Cove, huh?"

"You loved the bears."

"I was ten. Of course I loved the bears."

"That was nine years ago." His eyes flickered. "I always wanted to take you back there."

"I always wanted you to."

"Well"—he drew in a deep breath—"this will do for now. Come on, dump it out."

Two hours later, Ava looked up from the puzzle and frowned at her father. "Why does John keep asking me about my plans after I get out of the Navy? Is he trying to recruit me?"

Her father's eyes met hers. "Probably."

"Well, tell him to stop. I'm very happy doing what I'm doing, and he needs to leave me alone."

"I assume he figures if he keeps harassing you, you'll cave eventually."

She laughed. "Has he met me? He does realize I'm your daughter, right?"

"He does. And I know how stubborn you can be, so just let him talk. He'll give up eventually. Maybe."

"He's so predictable. Not the best thing for a CIA director. Before he opens his mouth, I know exactly what he's going to say."

"Yep." He chuckled. "He'd be mortified to hear you say that, but it's not just with you. He's that way in every aspect of his life. Predictable and hates change. Julie jokes that if she cooks the rice in a different pot, he knows it. And if the government didn't remind him to change his password, he wouldn't."

They shared a grin, and Ava placed the last puzzle piece into the empty spot. "Good work, Dad."

"Good work, Ava. Now use your Russian. I need to practice."

o o o

Mickey hurried across the street, pulling his hoodie farther down on his head. He'd spent the night back at the homeless community, tucked inside the cramped tent of the birthday boy. He'd waffled about going to the police. If he went, would the killer find out and kill his grandparents like he'd said?

Could the police protect what little family he had left?

The dojo was just ahead and Sensei would know what to do. And besides, he had to warn him that the killer knew about the dojo. Just like he had to find a phone to call his grandparents. Mickey had ditched his phone before he'd even left the yard, not knowing what the killer's skills were or the technology he had available. But if he could kill four people without blinking, he could probably find a way to track Mickey's phone.

Mickey's throat tightened at the thought of never seeing his family again. What was he going to do? The downtown side-walk wasn't busy, thanks to this being a Monday morning, and he was able to jog most of the way to the building. The man lived above the karate school. Odds were in Mickey's favor he'd be home.

Just as he was about to open the glass door that would take him up to the apartment, he froze. The man who'd killed his family was standing ten yards away, staring. When he caught Mickey's eye, he started walking toward him. No expression flickered across his face, but those black eyes sparked a malevo-lence that sent Mickey's pulse skittering and his heart thun-dering.

He spun and pounded down the sidewalk.

Something slammed into his back and burned a fiery path just below his right shoulder blade. He stumbled, got his bal-ance, and spotted a police officer sitting in the diner to his right. Weakness invaded his knees, but he pushed through the door. And fell to the floor, breathing hard.

Someone screamed. Then the officer was bending over him. "Hey, kid, what happened? You okay?"

"Don't let him kill me," Mickey whispered.

The diner faded, the officer's face blurred, and his voice—the voice yelling into the radio on his shoulder—echoed. He'd been shot. Really? That's what it felt like?

"Help's on the way, you're going to be okay." The officer's concerned gaze locked on Mickey's. "Just keep breathing."

Someone turned him over and put painful pressure on his wound. The world wobbled. Mickey blinked, trying to stay awake, not wanting to black out. "He shot me?"

"Yeah. He did. Who? Who shot you?"

"Killed my family," he whispered. "Gonna kill me."

"What's your name?"

"Mickey F—" Nausea hit him and he turned his head, looked

through the glass door, and straight into the eyes of the killer. The man turned and walked away.

And Mickey surrendered to the darkness.

□ □ □

Caden hadn't realized she'd meant an eight-hour road trip. "We'll need a place to spend the night."

"If you'd rather not go, I understand. I can drive myself."

He hesitated. "This has to do with the case? You think you know someone who can tell us your father's real name?"

"Yes."

"Then I might be able to get a chopper. Personally, I like three hours versus eight."

"Sure, if you can arrange it. That would be great. We'll also need a car once we land."

"Already thought about that." He opened the truck door. "Climb in and I'll get the ball rolling." He hesitated. "Do you want to call and let your mystery person know we're coming?"

"No."

"Then how do you know he'll be home?"

"She. And today's Monday. She'll be home. And if it's only three to four hours from now when we get there, she'll be either playing bridge with her ladies' group or working in her garden."

He gave a slow nod and lifted his phone to dial.

Ava waited in the front seat while Caden made his calls. It took some convincing, but he got what he wanted.

When he finished, he slipped into the driver's seat and placed his phone in the clip on the dash. "All right. I got approval. Grudging approval, but I got it."

"Grudging?"

"It's a slim lead to justify the chopper, but I convinced the SAC, so it's all water under the bridge."

She frowned. "I'm sorry. I can just drive, get what I need, and be back tomorrow."

He reached for her hand and held it. It surprised him how fragile it felt in his. She was so strong and capable, *fragile* wasn't a word he'd think to associate with her now. "It's all taken care of, Ava. I've even called Zane to let him know what's going on, and he's going to keep working the case from this end."

She released a slow breath and nodded. "All right."

"So, who is this person we're going to see?"

"A longtime family friend who's adored me since she met me when I was about fifteen years old, but she's known my father much longer. If anyone knows his name before he entered the CIA, it will be her."

"Childhood buddies? High school friends?"

"That is the million-dollar question. I'm not sure, but I think the high school angle is true. Neither of them has ever said, but I think my dad dated her before she married her husband." She shrugged. "They stayed good friends, and for whatever reason, she's taken an interest in me from day one."

"What does she do in Washington?"

"She refers to herself as arm candy, but I call her the wife of a friend. Her husband has a very visible job, and she thrives on her role of supporting him and making him look good."

"And her husband?"

She hesitated, then said, "He's also involved in the CIA and was best friends with my father."

"But they both dated the same woman?"

"I think so. Like I said, that was just me reading between the lines when we were all together—which was only on occasion until I was older." She paused. "And they didn't think I was listening. Or would understand what they were saying should I happen to overhear them." A sigh slipped from her. "It's hard to explain."

"Interesting."

"No kidding."

She fell silent while he drove to the airport, and Caden pondered the connection between the Fields family and Ava's father. He had a theory, but nothing he could prove. Had Jesse Fields also been involved in working with the CIA? It would explain why the man appeared to be hiding something and had refused to talk about it. But it did lead him to wonder if someone had discovered that and retaliated by killing his family.

Maybe they needed to look at the other families from that angle? He used voice commands to call Zane.

"What's up?" Zane asked, answering on the first ring. He sniffed and blew his nose.

"Dude . . ."

"I know. I know. What is it?"

"I have a theory."

"I'm glad someone does. Hit me with it."

While Ava listened, Caden laid out his thoughts. "So, if Jesse Fields is actually CIA, it would explain a whole lot."

"Yeah . . . and the wrong person found out?"

"That's what I'm wondering."

"What about the other families, though?"

"Again, it's just speculation, but the families killed are young. Are their parents still alive?"

"I don't have any idea," Zane said, "but I'll call Daria and get her working on finding that out—along with whether any of them were spies. I did find out that the parents of the family killed this morning are alive. They're devastated, of course, but like all the others, claim to have no idea who could have done such a thing. And truthfully, just a surface background check reveals nothing. However, we're digging deeper. We'll see if something turns up."

"Okay. Interesting." Caden spun the wheel into the small private airport parking lot. "We'll catch up in a few hours."

"Have a safe flight."

Caden hung up just as Ava's phone rang. She glanced at the screen. "It's your sister."

"You talk to her and I'll go sign the paperwork." He parked in front of the double glass doors.

She nodded. "I'll be there in just a few minutes." She swiped the screen. "Hello?"

Caden climbed out of the vehicle and shut the door. Ava chatted with Sarah while he let his gaze sweep the area. As far as he could tell, no one had followed them to the Fields home or to the airport, but he wasn't planning on relaxing his vigil any time soon. The more he thought about it, the more he felt certain someone had targeted Ava and it had to do with her father.

At least their visit to the Washington area would throw off anyone for the time being. Unless someone was able to get their hands on the FBI flight plan, they should be good.

Once he had the paperwork ready, he turned to find Ava standing behind him. "We're set."

She nodded. "Good."

"Sarah okay?"

"Just checking on me. She said to let Gavin know if you needed his help or any kind of backup." Gavin was Caden's soon-to-be brother-in-law and one of his best friends.

"I think we're all right for now."

"Yes. For now. Might be a different story in a few hours."

Caden was still debating whether or not he should ask her to clarify that statement, even while he followed her into the chopper.

CHAPTER

TEN

The flight seemed to take forever, but while they whipped through the air, Ava leaned her head back, closed her eyes, and plotted. Julie Sparks was John's wife. She was a woman he loved and trusted more than any other human in the world, and she adored Ava. Julie had become a second mother to Ava once her father had introduced them, and Ava fought with her conscience, even as she planned how to approach the woman in order to get what she needed.

At some point in her late teens, just before she'd shipped off to boot camp, she'd heard some banter between Julie, John, and her father. Ava and her father had gone to dinner at John and Julie's as they did every so often. When they could slip away from her mother and Nathan. Ava had been putting a puzzle together in the corner and the three adults were chatting.

"Your face was priceless," her father said. "When that box of confetti exploded all over you, I thought you were going to have a coronary right there."

Ava looked up, instantly intrigued at the rare glimpse into her father's past.

"And that is merely one of the many reasons why I broke up with you," Julie said, her tone frosty.

"Ah, love, it was for the best. John was the man for you."

Her expression morphed into tenderness as she glanced at John. "Yes, he was. And always will be."

Ava had decided right then and there she wouldn't settle for anything less than what John and Julie Sparks had. She'd never been completely sure her father loved her mother. He seemed to when they were all together on the rare occasions, but she always wondered.

Later, on the way home, she turned to her father. "Dad?"

"Yes?"

"Do you love Mom?"

He blinked, but otherwise didn't react. "Yes."

"Then why don't you quit what you do and get a real job? One that doesn't require you—and me—to keep your lies straight?"

He sighed. A heavy sigh that sounded so burdened, she wanted to take her questions back.

"I don't know how to explain it so that you'll completely understand, but I'll try. I've been doing what I do since I dropped out of college my sophomore year. I've done a lot for this country of ours, saved a lot of lives, and put a lot of bad guys out of commission."

"Killed them?" she asked. Hesitant, but wanting to know too.

For a long while, he didn't answer, then cleared his throat. "Yes."

Ava shuddered, then looked out the window. "Thank you."

"For what?"

"For not lying."

"Yeah. I'll admit it gets old."

"But you have to keep doing it."

"For now." He reached over and gripped her hand. "I hate

that you're burdened with this knowledge about me. If I could give you back your innocence, I would."

She shrugged.

"But I'll have to admit, knowing you know makes it easier to be with you because I don't have to constantly guard my words."

"I know." But she had to guard hers while he was gone. Day in and day out.

"Hey, guess what?"

"What?"

"I've got a puzzle for you, Ava-girl."

His sing-song words made her smile. "Great. I'm sure that's what I need to be doing during finals week."

"You're smart. You can study later. We'll see if Nate wants to join us tonight."

She laughed. "Right." Only if he could set it on fire or dissect it would Nathan be interested in doing it.

They fell silent until they were almost home and Ava said, "So, you and Julie dated in high school?"

"No way."

"But she said—"

"It was just a joke. Forget about it."

And she had, for the most part. Until today when the idea had hit her how she could find out for sure.

When they landed, she opened her eyes and realized she'd slept a good portion of the flight. She found Caden watching her and lifted a hand to her mouth. "Did I drool?"

"Not even a little bit."

"That's a relief."

"And unlike some people, I wouldn't tell you if you did. So, where are we going exactly?"

She half laughed at his add-on and covered a yawn. "I think the person we're going to see went to high school with my father. I'm not absolutely positive, and it's really just a hunch, but if she did, then she'd know his real name."

Caden nodded. "What high school?"

"Well, my father said he grew up in Texas and went to Fairmont High School. However, I went online and looked at their yearbooks and he wasn't in them. There were two Paul Jacksons, but neither was my father, so I'm not convinced that he actually went to that high school. And if he didn't, then I don't have a clue where he would have gone."

"And you couldn't just call this person and ask?"

"No."

A pause. Then he asked, "And you're not going to tell me why not?"

Ava sighed. "There are a lot of things involved in that answer. The first, she might just refuse outright because she knows what my father did for a living, and if it was his wish that she not tell anyone his real name, she'd honor that. If I'm there, it might be harder for her to say no to my face."

"Good point, and second?"

"Second, she might mention to her husband that I called to ask about my father, and he would then shut her—and me—down."

He tilted his head. "Why would he do that?"

"Because he worked with my father. He's the one person who knows everything there is to know about my dad and he's not talking. Trust me, I asked." She paused. "And if he knows that I've contacted Julie so soon after talking to him, he'll know I'm up to something and will make sure he's there to run interference."

"That's who you called back at the Fields's house?"

"Yes."

"What's he going to say when we show up out of the blue like this?"

She cut her eyes toward him. "I don't plan for him to know. It's three o'clock in the afternoon. He'll still be at work."

"And if he comes home early?"

She laughed. "He won't."

"What if she calls him? Or if he calls her to check in and you're there?"

"Then we're toast, but we'll worry about that if it happens."

He huffed a short laugh. "All right, then, the car's here. I'm ready when you are."

"I just have one call to make."

"What's that?"

"I'm going to see if Brooke, Heather, and Sarah will go over to my place and finish that puzzle. Heather has a key, so they can get in." She shrugged.

He frowned. "Are you sure you want them to do that? I know that puzzle is special for you because it's the last one that's connected to your dad."

She sighed and rubbed her eyes. "I'm sure. You have murders to solve, and if getting that puzzle done will help do that, then I can always take it apart and do it again later. But for now, we need it finished."

He reached out to grip her fingers. "Thanks, Ava."

"Sure, but you might want to hold on to that thanks. Things are probably about to get interesting."

o o o

Caden followed the GPS directions Ava had entered into the device and had to admit, he found her cryptic words a bit disconcerting. He'd also admit he had doubts about this whole venture, but there was something about Ava that made him want to trust her—in spite of her intentionally vague words. And what did she mean by things were about to get interesting? He didn't ask because he wasn't sure he wanted to know and figured he'd find out soon enough.

Like it or not, Ava was involved in this case somehow, and

with their limited leads, he had to chase the ones that popped up. Dead ends were a part of the job—more often than not—but occasionally, there were those leads that panned out.

He could only pray Ava could convince her friend to reveal her father's real name—or at least the name he used with Jesse Fields. The more they could find out about her father, the more they would find out about those he associated with—which might lead them to the killer. And if it took a trip to DC to do that, then he was okay with it. "Do you think this friend of yours could give us a list of aliases? See if any are missing from our list?"

"I think she probably could, but I doubt she would. I'm actually skeptical that she'll tell me my father's birth name." She paused. "What if I'm wrong and this is just a wasted trip? Will your SAC be super mad at you for following the whims of a childhood friend?"

"No way. It's not a whim. It's a legitimate lead. Right now, those are few and far between. And if it turns out to be a dead end for the case, at the very least you have a nice visit with a lady you love."

Her expression softened. "Yes, that's true. Thank you, Caden."

"Of course."

Fifteen minutes later, he pulled to the curb of a home located in McLean, Virginia. A very nice home.

Ava blew out a low breath. "Well, I guess this is it."

"Ava?"

"Yeah?"

"What exactly does your friend do at the CIA?"

She cut him a look from the corner of her eye. "Hmm?"

"Spill it."

"He's the director. John Sparks."

Oh boy. Caden shut his eyes for a brief moment. Ava sat still. Quiet. He opened one eye and looked at her. She worried her bottom lip with her teeth and kept her gaze on the house. He should have known. He knew her father was CIA, and she'd said the person she'd tried to get information from knew everything there was to know about her father, so . . . in hindsight, it made sense. "All right, then, let's do this."

She turned her eyes to him. "Are you sure? I really don't mind if you want to sit this one out."

"I'm sure."

"Okay, but you're not here as a fed, you're here as a friend. Just follow my lead, will you?"

That would be an unfamiliar role. "I'll try."

"Cade . . ."

"All right, all right. You can introduce me as your boyfriend. That's probably more believable than just a friend, right?" Her jaw swung open and he tapped it. She snapped it shut and let out a husky chuckle that washed over him in a way that set his nerves singing. He cleared his throat. "Ready?"

"No."

"Oh. Why not?"

"Because we need to clarify something. She'll never believe that you're my boyfriend, because I don't do the whole dating-slash-boyfriend thing—and she knows that."

He blinked. "You don't? But I remember you going out on dates." And he hadn't liked it at all, but since she'd never shown even a hint that she was interested in him—as an adult, not a flirty teen—he hadn't pursued her. Much.

"First dates mostly. It's a little embarrassing to admit, but I've rarely had a second date." She paused. "Definitely never a third. If I had a third date with someone, I would probably wind up marrying him because that would be huge."

Disbelief rendered him speechless. This time it was she who tapped his swinging jaw. Finally, he found his voice. "Now, wait a minute. I have a hard time believing that."

"Well, it's true."

"But . . . why?"

She sighed and rubbed her eyes. "Various reasons. Mostly because I wasn't willing to give what most of them wanted. Other reasons include unwilling to be—" She swallowed and looked away.

He narrowed his eyes. "Be . . . ?"

"Vulnerable. Open. Honest. You know, all of those things that are kind of important when you want to build a relationship? I try, but I'm not very good at it because I've lived a lie—that included multiple *sub-lies*, if there is such a thing—since I was fifteen years old."

Tears sparked in her eyes, surprising Caden. "Hey, it's okay." He could count on one hand the number of times he remembered seeing her cry.

She swiped a hand under her lashes. "It's fine. Sorry. I must be more tired than I thought."

"We don't have to do this."

"Yes," she said, her voice low, "we do. I do. I want to help you figure out who's killing these people, but if I'm honest, this is for me just as much. I want to know who my father is. *Was*. And who might be coming after me."

"Right. I'm ready when you are."

She climbed out of the car and waited for him to join her. Then linked her fingers with his. "Come on, boyfriend, maybe it's time to let Julie think I've turned over a new leaf."

Caden's heart was the object that turned over, but he kept his surprise—and happiness—to himself and let her lead the way. With a mental note to learn more about why those first dates never morphed into seconds. Because he definitely wanted a second date—no, a *third* date.

Assuming he ever got a first one.

He smiled. He'd get a first date—and a third one.

Someway, somehow.

ELEVEN

Ava's heart thundered in her chest as they approached the front door. Caden's large hand tucked around hers boosted her courage like nothing else could have. And calling him "boyfriend" had sparked a gentle hope in her heart that she couldn't ignore. What would it be like to let herself fall in love with Caden? If she was honest with herself, she'd concede that it wouldn't be a lengthy fall. But even more intriguing was the question, What would it be like to let herself be loved by him?

Heat fired in her cheeks and she ducked her head to get her emotions under control. *You don't date for a reason. Think about something else.*

But the fact was, her reason for not dating was gone. A fact that pierced her heart with sadness but allowed hope to filter through the cracks.

She took a deep breath.

While she and Julie talked on a regular basis, Ava had rarely dropped in on the woman unannounced. Only the fact that she'd been received with open arms the few times she'd done it allowed her to put one foot in front of the other.

She pressed the doorbell, then tapped her foot while she waited. She'd pace if Caden didn't have a firm grip on her hand.

"You're nervous," he said.

"A little."

"Should we abort?"

"No way."

The door opened and Julie Sparks stood there. Her eyes lit up when she saw Ava. With a very proper squeal, she pulled Ava into a hug. "What are you doing here? I'm so glad to see you." She released Ava from the embrace and slid her hands down to Ava's, which forced Caden to release the one he'd been holding. "This is such a welcome surprise." Her gaze landed on Caden. "And please, tell me who you've brought with you."

Ava made the introductions. "Sorry for dropping in unannounced."

"Are you kidding? I'm thrilled. Come in, come in." Julie backed toward the sitting area just off the foyer. When they were settled in the cozy den with Ava and Caden on the couch and Julie in the wingback chair near the fireplace, the woman leaned forward. "I noticed you two holding hands." She batted her eyes. "Is there anything you need to tell me?"

Ava cleared her throat. "Nothing other than we're friends . . . um . . . good friends." The point had been made. Holding hands with Caden had done the job of avoiding an explanation for his presence.

"Uh-huh. Well, that's wonderful, my dear."

"I hope we're not interrupting your bridge game."

"No, not today. Loretta had back surgery last week and Sonya has a new grandbaby she's visiting. So I'm free this afternoon." Her smile faded. "I can't tell you how sorry I am about your father. I know it's been eight months, but it seems like a lifetime."

"Thank you. And again, thank you for the flowers. They were beautiful." Exactly what she'd stated in her thank-you note.

"How's your mother doing? John gives me a report every so often, but I haven't had an update lately."

"She's about the same. The doctors have given her three to four more months—or she could go at any point."

"Oh dear, I'm terribly sorry."

"I am too."

Julie tilted her head. "So, what brings you here?"

"Well, of course, I wanted to see you, but I also had some questions about my father I was hoping you could answer."

A microexpression of wariness flickered across her face before she clasped her hands between her knees and flashed a brilliant smile. "Of course. What would you like to know?"

"Well, I know you, John, and my father went to the same high school. I was just wondering if you could tell me some stories about him. Like the time he played the practical joke on you at the homecoming dance."

The woman's face went blank and her jaw dropped a fraction. "How did you know about that? Did Paul or John tell you?"

"No. I actually heard the three of you joking about it when I was around eighteen or nineteen years old. I asked my father about it, but he never gave me a straight answer. I was really disappointed too. It sounded like a great story and I've wondered about it ever since."

"I see. Well . . ." She shrugged. "It was a silly thing. I've always hated surprises. Truly." She paused. "Not your visit, of course, but at the dance, they had a miniature float as a decoration. Your father hid confetti inside it, and when I was crowned homecoming queen, he had it rigged to explode when he pressed some kind of button. It scared me to pieces. Everyone had a good laugh, and eventually, I forgave him."

And there was her confirmation that they'd been in high school together. It had been an educated guess based on the conversation, but . . . Ava forced a laugh. "That definitely sounds like my dad." She sighed. "Julie, I came here for another reason too."

"What's that?"

"I've discovered some things that point to the fact that Paul Jackson wasn't my father's real name. I need to know—what name did he go by in high school?"

Julie's expression tightened and she had that deer-in-the-headlights look. "I . . . uh . . . I don't really remember. You're right, he went by another name, but I've just called him Paul Jackson for so many years that . . . I can't think of what he called himself in high school." A nervous titter escaped her, and she threaded her fingers together. Then her features smoothed, her eyes blanking.

"I see," Ava said. "Of course. Maybe I shouldn't have asked. I suppose if he'd wanted me to know, he would have told me. On that note—" Ava stood. "It was a long trip and I need the ladies' room."

"Of course," Julie said, her countenance lightening, relief tingeing her words. "You know where it is."

"Thanks."

As Ava left the room, she heard Julie ask Caden how long he'd known Ava. She hurried down the hallway and found John's study, slipped inside, and went to the wall-sized bookcase. "I know they're here," she muttered. "I've seen them a dozen times." She ran her fingers over the books, looking for a specific one.

There. John's high school yearbook. McLinder High School. Her father had lied about that too, obviously. Quickly, she flipped to the senior year section and found the page that should have her father's picture there. No Paul Jackson. "Surprise, surprise." She went back to the beginning of the senior pictures and studied each one. She found John Sparks easily enough.

And Julie Tate. She flipped the page and scanned. Flip, scan, flip, scan. Until she gasped. "Seriously?"

Someone had cut out the picture of one of the seniors and blackened the name with a sharpie. *Unbelievable.* But she knew the last name would start with a W. It could be her father, or it could be someone John simply hated, so he'd removed the person from the book. But she didn't think so.

Ava finished looking at the rest of the pictures before she let her hand hover over the page that had the small square a third of the way down.

Footsteps in the hallway sent darts of fear through her. If Julie caught her in the study with the book . . .

With no time to snap a picture of the page, she ripped it out and shoved the paper into her pocket. Once she had the album back in its spot on the shelf, she hurried toward the door.

The footfalls came closer.

"Ava?"

Ava grabbed one of the pictures from the mantel next to her head, trying her best to get her heart rate under control.

"Ava? Are you all right?" Julie's voice came from just outside the door.

She forced a smile and peered out. "In here, Julie."

Her friend stepped inside, a frown creasing her brow. "What are you doing in John's office?"

Ava waved the picture at her. "I'm sorry. I got sidetracked. I remember being in here as a kid and wanted to see if it was the same." She smiled, hoping it was normal and not fake. "It is. I was just walking down memory lane, looking at all of the photos in here of your family." She pointed. "I don't remember these, though. You've added a few new ones."

"Oh." Julie dropped her gaze.

Ava bit her lip. "I'm sorry. I shouldn't have come in here, I guess. I just couldn't help thinking that you and he have all these pictures of your loved ones and I have . . . very few. Of Dad, anyway. I guess I was feeling a bit jealous. I'm sorry."

Julie's expression turned tender, and being the compassionate woman she was, she pulled Ava into a hug. Needles of regret stabbed at Ava's conscience, but . . . her words weren't a total lie.

When Julie released her, she sighed. "Oh, my dear, no need to feel jealous. Take a close look around. Do you see John or me in any of those pictures?"

Now that she mentioned it . . . "No."

"That's because they're fake. I don't know any of the people in those pictures, but I couldn't stand not having photos. So . . . I've created a little fantasy world. I've put together the family I'll never have." She stroked Ava's cheek with such love that Ava's throat closed. "I suppose that's another reason I've cherished having you in my life. You're the daughter I never had."

"But—"

"I know. It's pathetic. And truly, I almost don't even see the photos anymore. However, if I took them down or threw them out, I'd miss them." She chuckled. "Definitely weird and sad, but there you have it. I don't even have a picture of you because if it landed in the wrong person's hands . . ." She shrugged.

Unsure what to say, Ava studied the pictures once more. There weren't a ton of them, but enough to make the room— and the mantel in the den—feel cozy. Homey. "It's not weird or pathetic," she said, her voice soft. "It's actually a really good idea. I think we have to find comfort where we can. My father was so meticulous to never be in a photograph. No family pictures, nothing. His wedding pictures are in a safe-deposit box along with the negatives."

"He had his reasons for that. The same with John."

"I know. And if Mom tried to sneak pictures of Dad and me when I was little, the photos always managed to get lost." She paused. "What were the reasons? I know there are other CIA officers who live fairly normal lives and have pictures in their homes. Why was my father—and John—so different?"

Julie sighed. "Even I don't know the complete answer to that, but I can tell you this. You know John and your father were good friends and grew closer than brothers while working with the CIA. Has your father ever mentioned Lucas Moreno?"

"No."

"That's probably not his real name anyway, but the three of them were tight friends. Lucas got married and had a son. About a year later, something went wrong with a case—they trusted the wrong person, or someone was paid off, I really don't know the details. All I know is that Lucas's wife and baby were killed in retaliation—a car bomb. Lucas committed suicide shortly after that, and that's when John and your father made a pact to do nothing that could come back to their families." She cleared her throat. "It's one reason John and I never had children. Your father wasn't quite willing to give all of that up, apparently."

"My mother was pregnant with me when they got married," Ava said. "My dad may have decided the same thing, only got caught when Mom told him she was pregnant. But I didn't know about Lucas. Thank you for telling me."

"Come on, honey, let's go back in the den and I'll get us something to drink and a snack. Then we'll talk about lighter things. Your friend has to be wondering what's taking us so long."

"Sure. Okay."

When they returned to the den, Caden's worried gaze caught hers and she offered him a tight smile. But once Julie disappeared into the kitchen, Ava settled next to him on the couch and patted her pocket. "I think we need to visit the local high school."

○ ○ ○

Caden stepped outside, conflicted, but relieved as well. He'd nearly had a conniption fit when she'd disappeared, knowing full well she was going snooping. When Julie had excused herself to go check on Ava, it had been all he could do not to give everything away with an attempt to stop her.

So, he scrambled for a plan while he watched her walk down the hall and finally followed on silent feet. And overheard the exchange just inside the director's office. It hadn't surprised him. Fake families, secrets, and subterfuge. Lies. It was all part of the life Ava's father—and others—had chosen. Great personal sacrifice for the good of the country.

When their conversation wrapped up, Caden slipped back into the den and they enjoyed the next hour of Julie telling them lighthearted stories of Ava's father. Mostly his penchant for practical jokes, his fascination with puzzles and foreign languages, and his amazing ability to crack a code.

But now, they were back in the rental car heading for the high school her father had attended.

It was late, but a call to the principal had garnered them an after-hours appointment. Ava rode beside him, her features smooth. Serene. She was one of the few people he couldn't always read, and quite honestly, he found it a bit unnerving. "What are you thinking?"

"That I'm not sure she bought my reasons for being in John's office."

"Hmm. Maybe not, but if she didn't, she put on a good show."

"And I feel bad betraying her trust like that." She paused. "In spite of the fact that she's been lying to me my entire life."

"About your father."

"Yes, but who knows about what else?"

He shot her a sideways glance. "But you've basically lied to everyone in your life as well. Like your mother and Nathan? Us?"

"Us?"

"Heather, Sarah, Brooke, me?"

She bit her lip and sighed. "I've tried not to. I've done my best to simply avoid any conversation about my father, but"—she shrugged—"yes. If someone asked me outright what he did for a living, I lied."

"Why?"

"To protect him, of course."

"Exactly. And you know that's why she and John haven't told you everything there is to know about your father. They're protecting him—and possibly you as well."

"But he's dead. What's the point in keeping it from me? It's not like I'm asking them to take an ad out in the paper or post it on social media. Mom and Nathan don't know and I wouldn't tell them, but since I know as much as I do, I think I deserve to know who my father was. All of it." She leaned her head back. "If I didn't know what I know and was living in blissful ignorance, that would be one thing, but I haven't had that claim since I was fifteen. I have questions I think I deserve answers to." She fell silent. "Or if I don't deserve them, then . . . I need to know that too."

He turned onto the high school property, wound his way to the front office, and pulled into the nearest parking spot. A silver Ford Taurus was already in the principal's reserved space. Ava unbuckled and climbed out with determination stamped on her features. "Let's do this."

He followed her to the door, and she pressed the button that would alert anyone inside to their presence. Caden held his badge to the camera.

The door buzzed and Caden reached around to open the glass door. A young man about their age walked toward them, hand outstretched. "Hi. I'm Dr. Ronald Pearson, principal here."

"Thank you for seeing us, Dr. Pearson," Ava said.

"Of course. Please call me Ron." After the handshakes, he motioned for them to follow him. "Come on back to my office and you can tell me what this is all about."

"Actually," Ava said, "this won't take too long. I just need to see a couple of your yearbooks. If you still have them." She gave him the years they were looking for.

"They'll be in the library. I'll show you." He led them into the library to a wall dedicated to past volumes of yearbooks. He went to the year Ava had given him and used a forefinger to tilt the book from its space and into his hand. "Here."

He handed her the book. She opened it to the page she'd torn out from the other book and gasped.

Caden looked over her shoulder. "Unbelievable," he muttered. The page was gone, the ragged edge against the binding a pointed message.

The principal met his gaze. "Who would do this?"

"Someone with a lot to hide," Ava said. She pushed the book back into its spot. "What about his freshman through junior years?"

"Probably the same," Caden said.

They checked anyway. He was right.

Caden rubbed a hand across her tense shoulders. "All right, I have another idea."

"So do I."

He raised a brow. "Contact one of the classmates and ask to see their book?"

She shot him a tight smile. "Great minds." She pulled the yearbook page out of her pocket. "There are several possibilities here. All we have to do is find one of them, call them up, and ask them for the fifth name on page seventy-four."

"Should be easy enough. I'll get Daria to see what she can find while we work our way back home." He sent the text along with the high school information and a picture of the page from the yearbook. When he finished the text, he looked at the principal, whose gaze was ping-ponging between him and Ava. "Thank you so much for your time."

"Of course. I'm happy to say this was the most excitement I've had today. I hope you find who you're looking for."

"Me too," Ava said. "Thank you again." She nodded to Caden. "I guess that's all we can do for now."

The man glanced at his watch. "I have a conference call in exactly three minutes. I'm going to head to my office. You can let yourselves out?"

"Of course," Ava said.

The man hurried back toward the office when Caden's phone pinged. "Daria said she's on it and should have something for us soon. She's getting ready to send me a long text explaining what's on those old disks." He took Ava's hand. "Ready?"

"I'm right behind you." When she didn't pull from his grasp but allowed him to hold on all the way out to the car, he decided he might be making some progress. The thought tightened his chest for a moment. Asking Ava out was one thing. Letting her see he was serious about a relationship with her was another. She was so skittish about the idea of dating, he didn't dare voice his interest. Besides, she knew.

He had a feeling the only reason she hadn't run from him was because he didn't push the issue. He let go of her hand to open the door and she climbed in.

"Thanks," she said.

When they were on the road, she turned to him. "Thank you for coming with me. I honestly wasn't sure what we'd find. Truthfully, I was halfway afraid it would be a wild-goose chase, but this trip only cemented that someone doesn't want to make it easy for me—or anyone who decided to look—to find out who my father actually is. Paul Jackson was just an alias."

"Yeah, that picture was cut out of the yearbook long before you—we—started this quest. Which means someone was afraid another someone would go looking at some point."

"Yes."

She sighed and fell silent, and Caden drove, glancing over at her every so often. "What was it like?" he finally asked. "Finding out your dad was in the CIA. I mean, that's every kid's dream come true, right?"

She gave a light snort. "In the beginning maybe, sure, it was kind of fascinating. But that awe faded fast. In the end, it was awful. Truly awful. It just taught me how to be a world-class liar."

TWELVE

Her words hung in the air between them, but it was too late for her to recall them. All the emotions that simply holding his hand had sent swirling through her had obviously rattled her brain.

"Ouch," he said.

"I know. I'm sorry. I shouldn't have said that with such bitterness. I've had a good life. A different beginning than I would have picked, but I'm at a point now where I like what I've done, what I've accomplished, and who I am."

"And that's one of the things I like most about you."

She raised a brow. "What?"

"You're just . . . you. At least the you I thought I knew. The more I'm around you lately, the less I think I know—but I still like you."

A small burst of laughter slipped from her. "Do I say thanks or act insulted?"

"It was a compliment." He shot her a sideways smile. "Seriously, you don't seem to worry about what other people think. You do what needs to be done and you don't whine about it if it's unpleasant."

"Ha. That's what being in the Navy will teach you." She paused. "And trust me, I've done my share of whining."

He laughed just as his phone rang. "It's Zane. Put it on speaker, will you?"

She tapped the screen.

"Hi," Caden said, "you're on speaker with Ava and me as I'm driving back to the airport. What you got?"

"Other than a bad cold?" The voice didn't even sound like Caden's partner. Before Caden could get a word in, Zane started coughing.

Caden raised a brow. "Dude, you need to get in bed. That sounds worse than a cold."

"Ah, probably bronchitis. I'll get Patty to call in an antibiotic or some cough meds or whatever after I hang up with you." Ava thought she remembered Caden mentioning Zane's sister was a doctor at the hospital. "Putting my health issues aside," his partner continued, "Daria called and said she found something interesting."

"What's that?"

"The family that was killed in San Diego, the Holdens? They were going by an alias."

"Witness protection?"

"No. That's the weird thing. The Marshals claim no knowledge of them."

Ava frowned at Caden, who shrugged. "So, what was their real name?" he asked.

"Sidorov."

"That's Russian," Ava said, her voice low.

"Yes, ma'am, it is." Zane coughed again, a deep cough that made Ava's chest hurt just listening to it.

"How did she find that out?" Caden asked.

"She asked for all of the information found thus far on the cases. She also used remote access on the kid's computer and found he'd been doing a search on a genealogy website. Kid even did one of those DNA test things and found out he had cousins in Moscow."

"Wow," Ava said.

"Once he had that information, he ran with it. Found some old record albums of his father's. The old man was in a band back in the early 1990s." Zane paused for another coughing fit and Ava winced. "Sorry. Anyway, Daria took what he had and went further, tracking the dad down to his old workplace."

"Why do you say that like it's important?" Caden pulled into the airport parking lot and found a spot near the rental office.

"Because that's how she found Vitaly Sidorov. From there, she found pictures, birth records, marriage licenses, et cetera. And the fact that after the year 1995, they disappeared. From Russia anyway."

"And they ended up in the United States," Ava said.

"Exactly."

"Okay. Thanks."

"Oh, one other thing. Daria said she was sending us a video and that we should be sitting down when we watch it. She said it was pure evil and very hard to watch."

Caden frowned. "All right. She mentioned something in a text about having something from those floppy disks."

"Yeah, that's what it is. Said it was some Russian dude torturing prisoners. She thinks. She's trying to identify the victims—and the perpetrator."

Ava shuddered at the mental images.

Zane hacked up another lung and sniffled. "Okay, I'm going to see what Patty can do and then get some sleep. Sorry to bow out on this, Cade."

"Not to worry. You're still staying in the loop. Take care of yourself—or let your doctor sister do it. Ava and I'll be back in about three hours."

"Sounds good. Bye." He hung up on another round of coughing, and Ava sighed.

"He sounds like he's going to be down for the count for a few days."

"Yeah." Caden frowned. "He rarely gets sick. But when he does, it's around this time of year." He nodded to the tarmac. "Chopper's here."

"Let's go."

Once they were buckled in on the helicopter, they both took the opportunity to get some rest and soon found themselves back on the ground and headed toward Ava's home. She shot a group text to Heather, Sarah, and Brooke.

> How's the puzzle going?

Sarah's reply came instantly.

> We made a little progress. Heather and I are still working on it. Brooke said she couldn't keep her eyes open so she crashed on your couch. LOL.

Ava passed the information on to Caden, who nodded. She texted back.

> We'll finish it up when we get back. Have you been keeping an eye on the security monitor?

> Sarah
> Of course. We're fine. There's been nothing to indicate anyone's watching or any attempts to get in your place.

> Good, good. Thank you so much for your help.

> Sure thing. We'll catch up later.

This time it was his phone that buzzed. He glanced at it. "That's Daria."

Ava put it on speaker before he could ask and he shot her a quick smile. "Hi, Daria, what do you have?"

"First, I sent you some footage from the floppy disks found at the Fields home. Just . . . be aware, it's seriously mind-numbing to think someone's that evil. And you know that's saying a lot, considering who my father was."

"Okay, thanks for the heads-up, Daria."

He heard her take a deep breath, then blow it out slowly. "Also, I managed to get in touch with two of the people from the yearbook page that you sent me. They both verified the man in the missing picture went by the name David Winters in high school. However, they both said he was dead. When I did a search on Winters, it appears that he was killed in a car wreck when he was a sophomore in college."

"And I'm assuming you cross-referenced the name David Winters with our current case?"

"I did. And there's nothing. Probably because he's dead—or at least his name is."

"Do you have a picture of this guy?" Caden asked.

"I do. It should be on your phone now."

The notification flashed and Ava glanced at Caden, asking for permission to look at it. He nodded and she swiped to open the text. And her heart crashed. "That's not him."

□ □ □

Caden raised a brow. "What? Are you sure?" Into the phone, he said, "Daria, I'll talk to you in a bit. Thank you for everything."

"Of course. It's my job. And I'm good at it, in case you haven't noticed."

He couldn't help but smile at the little dig, but his heart was hurting for Ava, who'd fully expected this man to be her father. He pulled onto the shoulder of the road and turned on the hazards, but left the vehicle running. "Let me see."

"Wait a minute," she whispered, her voice so soft he barely heard it. Her gaze stayed glued to the screen of his phone. "I take that back. I think this actually *is* him. Granted, I've never seen a picture of him this young, but now that I take a closer look . . . see the scar on his lip?"

"Yeah. It's the same as your dad's."

"He used to rub that scar whenever he was thinking. And his eyes . . . Caden, this *is* him." She sighed. "Well, obviously, he didn't die in the car wreck, but it looks like he had some extensive plastic surgery."

"And he changed his name."

"The perfect cover for a CIA officer. If someone got a clear enough picture to run through facial recognition, he'd come back as not even in the system—or depending on how much change was done to his bone structure, as a possible match to a dead man?" Ava shook her head. "Which is probably why he was so obsessed with never having his picture taken." She shuddered and Caden reached over to wrap his hand around her cold fingers. "If he came back as a dead person," she continued, "that would open a whole 'nother can of worms, wouldn't it?"

"It would. We need to get that puzzle finished and get into your dad's computer."

She nodded and frowned. "I don't want the girls at my place anymore. I want them to leave before someone decides to go after me again." She palmed her phone. "I'm going to text them to go home." She sent the message and looked at him. "I understand why Heather was so adamant about everyone staying away from her when someone was after her a few months ago. She finally accepted that she needed to let others help her, and then Asher got shot and she was devastated. Still is. She can't talk about it without tearing up. I get it now. Just the thought of someone breaking into my apartment while my friends are there is terrifying."

A few months ago, Heather had run into trouble that had required help from her friends. Help that had ended up in a shootout, with Asher taking a bullet. He fully recovered, but it had been touch and go for a bit in the beginning.

"Sarah just told you that they're fine, right?"

"Yes. For now. I plan to keep it that way."

"Asher doesn't worry about what happened," Caden said. "Heather shouldn't either."

"Easy to say. If I was in Heather's position, it would still bother me."

"Okay, I'll concede that I'd probably feel the same way."

She shot him a half smile. "Thank you."

"Now, while we're sitting here, I'm going to call Daria back with one more request." He dialed and Daria answered halfway through the first ring.

"What's up?"

"One more thing," he said. "Can you see if there's any connection between the Sidorovs and Ava's father? Use the names Paul Jackson, David Winters, and Dimitri Golubev."

"Got it. I'll let you know if something comes up."

"Thank you."

He hung up and found the video footage Daria had sent. And warned him about. With a quick tap, he started the video. A man tied to a chair came into view. The quality wasn't great, but it was in color and probably the best that technology had to offer back then. Caden could tell the room had cement blocks, a single overhead lightbulb, and a table off to the right. The anonymous cameraperson zoomed in on the table, and Caden's heart thudded when he realized what he was seeing.

Torture instruments. The camera panned to the walls, capturing the display of hooks and chains. In the middle of the room stood a long, bloodstained table. A man lay on it, his face contorted with pain. His torturer acted as he released a hideous laugh, and the man screamed. His cry echoed through the vehicle and Ava gasped. Bile crawled up the back of Caden's throat and he shut off the video. "You don't want to watch this."

"You shouldn't either."

"Yeah, probably not, but unfortunately, I don't always have the option of not seeing stuff I'd rather not see." He tucked the phone back in the cupholder. "But I can watch it elsewhere."

He shut off the hazards and put the truck in drive to head back down the road. Five minutes later, he took the exit that led to her apartment, dreading the viewing of what he knew was on the rest of that footage. But that could wait for the time being. Right now, he needed to focus on the present situation. "You know, you've got a really nice route through here. It has a driving-through-the-mountains kind of feel." The two-lane road wound below a canopy of dense trees.

"I think the developers did that on purpose. Being close to Mom was the priority in choosing my apartment, but I'll admit that this drive is a lovely perk."

Behind the trees, unseen from the road, were evenly spaced homes, three to four acres each, many with horses and other animals that needed the room to roam and graze.

A buzzing sound caught his attention. "You hear that?"

She frowned. "Yes. Sounds like a hum or—watch out!"

From his left, a . . . drone? . . . came at him hard and fast. He jerked the wheel to the right and the machine zipped past. "What the heck was that?" Caden spun the wheel, skidded onto the shoulder, regained control of the truck, and sped back into the lane.

Ava turned in her seat. "It's coming back. Flying just below the trees."

"I see it." Definitely a drone, but not one of those fun kind of machines kids like to play with. In the rearview mirror, he spotted the large quadrotor drone flying back toward them and gaining ground.

"There's a car in front of you getting ready to turn." She kept her voice low and calm, but the tightness in it betrayed her tension.

He was going to have to slow down or wind up in the turning car's trunk. He slammed on the brakes as the drone dipped down in front of them, turned, and headed toward him once more. He yanked the wheel to the right, onto the shoulder, and then surged around the vehicle. He wasn't sure how he didn't clip the bumper, but he made it. The drone followed, lowering, rising, then plunging once more to zip past him . . .

. . . and turn.

The machine hovered, then came straight toward them, mimicking its earlier move. "Oh, you're kidding me." His heart thundered as he noted the mounted weapon. "Get down!"

Ava ducked. Caden did the same as a spate of bullets peppered the glass. The windshield cracked and splintered but held. When Caden looked back up, a car was pulling out of a side road, and he had no choice but to slam on the brakes and swerve down the embankment to his right.

His truck bounced and rocked. His ears told him the drone was following.

Tree limbs scraped the passenger side, wind rushed through the holes in the windshield, and Caden spun the wheel to miss crashing headfirst into a looming tree. He aimed for the space between two of the towering trunks.

The truck crashed through the middle and jerked to a halt, triggering the air bags, throwing Caden back against his seat and forcing the air from his lungs.

Stunned motionless for a brief second, he sucked in a deep breath, praying he hadn't broken a rib. The breath hurt, but not like the lightning pain of a punctured lung. "Ava, you okay?"

"Yes." She groaned, released the seat belt, and pushed her own air bag to the side. The residue from the air bags filled the cab and she coughed. "I think. Where's the drone?"

"Don't know."

Ava rubbed her head with a wince. When she pulled her hand away, blood coated her fingertips.

The back window shattered and Ava dove to the floorboard while Caden shoved on his door. The drone zipped overhead, hovered, and turned once more. The operator must've had some serious training in order to control the thing that well. He pushed on the door once more with no success.

"My door's jammed! Can you get yours open?" He glanced back to see the drone coming back for another pass. "Ava? We've got to get out of here." He grabbed his weapon from his arm holster. He aimed it and pulled the trigger just as the machine returned for another round.

Caden missed and the drone soared away.

Ava slid back into the seat and fought with the door while he looked for his phone. It was gone from the cupholder. Great. Heart thundering in his ears, he started to crawl over the console to help with the door, only to look up and see the drone hovering, taking aim. "Down!"

She went to the floorboard once more while he dove over the console and onto the back seat floor. Bullets riddled the truck once more.

"How many bullets does that thing have?" Ava yelled. "I've already counted forty-five."

She'd counted? "No idea. We've got to go." He peered over the back seat and out the missing back window.

"This door's jammed too," she said. Fear and anger mingled in her voice, sending a desperation through him to get her to safety.

Caden lifted his head and saw nothing. The drone had disappeared as fast as it had shown up. But that didn't mean it wouldn't be back. It was now or never.

He kicked out the rest of the glass, then rolled back toward Ava. "Come this way."

She climbed from the floorboard onto the seat, then grasped his outstretched hand and let him pull her next to him.

"I'll go out first and help you through."

"Be careful, Caden, he could just be waiting for one of us to pop our head out that window."

"I know. Which is why we've got to move fast. I'm going to roll out and into the truck bed. You follow my lead and then we're going to run into the shelter of the trees. Got it?"

"Got it."

The now familiar low hum reached him. "Hurry!" He rolled out and didn't bother to ask Ava if she was ready, he just pulled her out beside him. She landed with a grunt but kept moving. "Into the woods," he said.

"I'm right behind you."

He vaulted over the side of the truck bed and hit the ground hard, turned to help Ava to find her mid-jump. She landed beside him and he grasped her hand. Together, they bolted for the trees, the drone closing in fast.

THIRTEEN

Ava stayed with Caden, waiting for more bullets to come their way. A tree limb scraped along her cheek and she gasped but kept going. The drone followed, weaving in and out of the trees, like it had a mind of its own.

"This way," Caden said. He leapt over a log and she followed, lost her footing, and only Caden's grip on her hand kept her from going down.

The drone fired once more, a *rat-a-tat-tat* of bullets. She whirled and shoved Caden to the ground, throwing herself down beside him. A sharp sting zipped across her arm and she cried out.

Caden turned and fired at the machine. Missed again, hitting the trunk of the tree next to it. He yanked her to her feet and propelled her beneath a huge horizontal tree trunk, then swooped in beside her. The bullets stopped and the buzz from the drone faded. Seconds ticked past. Did she dare hope it was gone for good? For now, they were safe, tucked into a nature-made dugout. A little cave that, hopefully, to the drone operator, looked like they'd simply disappeared. She shuddered, not wanting to think about the creepy-crawlies she might be sharing space with.

And, man, her arm hurt.

"Can't you shoot it down?" she asked.

"If I could get behind it. Whoever's operating it isn't letting that happen. Right now, he can't see us, so let's just sit here for a second."

"Sure." She breathed out a low groan.

"Ava?"

The sheer terror in his voice jerked her head up and her mind off the grossness of insects and reptiles. "What?"

"You're hit."

She was? "I guess that's why my arm feels like it's on fire?"

"Probably." He pulled her sleeve away from the bloodied area. She looked and grimaced. "Hold on," he said. He reached under the long-sleeved T-shirt he was wearing, grabbed the hem of his undershirt, and brought it up to his mouth. With his teeth, he got a hole started, then ripped off enough to fold into a makeshift bandage.

"I don't hear the drone," she said, her eyes searching the trees.

He stopped for a second to listen. "Then we need to get this taken care of." He pressed the material to her wound and she hissed. "Sorry. Can you hold that?"

She used her other hand to do so. "I think it's just a graze."

"Yeah, it is. Doesn't mean it's not painful, though." He pulled another strip from his shirt and tied the bandage in place. "Do you think you can run if we have to?"

"If it means staying alive, I'll manage."

Admiration glinted in his eyes for a brief second. "Okay, now for the really important question. Do you have your cell phone on you?"

"No, I didn't have time to grab it."

He grimaced. "Same here."

"Fabulous."

He paused for a moment, thinking, listening. Ava listened too.

"Should we go," she asked, "while it's not here?"

"Let's wait it out for a few minutes." His eyes scanned the woods and she could almost see his ears twitching. He glanced back at her. "You okay?"

"Sure."

"So, why don't you date?"

She blinked. "You want to know why I don't date while there's a psycho drone trying to kill us?"

"If you talk, it'll keep your mind off the pain."

"Oh." Would it? Well, in that case . . . "Because I've given up on it. After a series of lousy dates, I decided it's not for me."

"Like?" He eased his head out of the opening and she waited for him to pull back before answering.

"Like, an example of a lousy date?"

"Yeah."

"Um . . . one guy had his mom meet us at the restaurant."

He jerked. "What?"

"For real."

"Wow."

"He said she always paid for the first meal to show how generous she was. Really, it was obvious she wanted to check out who her baby boy was seeing."

"Creepy," he muttered.

"Then there was the guy who seemed all right at first, but at the restaurant, he ordered for me without asking what I wanted, told me how I should style my hair, and said he would allow me to keep working—at least until the kids came." She shifted and winced. But he was right. The talking had helped in more ways than one.

"Unbelievable. Any more?"

"Too many."

"Keep talking."

"Then there was Chris. I met him in the Navy. He just wanted a babysitter for his four kids. Our first date, he invited me over for dinner and then said he had to run out for a few minutes to pick up a prescription for the oldest. He asked if I minded. Of course, I said no. He was a single dad, right? Six hours later—after no answers to my calls or texts, he came back drunk and asked me if I was free the next night."

Caden had no words.

"I called child protection on him and that was the last I heard from him. There's more, but you get the idea."

"Boy, do I." After another minute, he said, "We'll pick up there later. For now, let's head back to the truck. I'm hoping our attacker will think we've kept going through these woods instead of doubling back."

"Works for me." Her arm throbbed and she ground her teeth against the pain. She'd whine about it later. Right now, she wanted to get someplace that didn't include bullets.

He held her hand and peered around the edge of their hiding place. "I don't see it."

"Or hear it." The words had barely left her lips when the familiar buzz sounded to her left. They drew back, and it flew past them, paused, spun, and came back to sweep over them. "Caden?"

"Yeah?"

"I think we waited too long. It's looking for us."

"It sure is. He was probably scanning the woods where we should have been running, and when he didn't see us, came back."

On the next pass, Caden rolled and launched himself to his feet, his hands gripping a three-foot tree limb. As the drone came even with their hiding place, Caden swung. The wood connected with the machine and sent it spinning, then smashing to the ground. "I was always better with a baseball bat than a gun," he said.

Breathing hard, Ava scrambled up and hurried to join Caden in his approach to the drone. "Be careful," she said. "He could be waiting for us to get closer before setting that thing off again."

"I don't think so, but we'll act like that's the case."

Sirens in the distance reached Ava. "Someone called the cops."

"Good."

The machine sputtered, then hissed.

Then went silent.

"Where do you think he is?" Ava asked. "The guy holding the remote?"

"Could be anywhere, unfortunately. Some of these things have a pretty impressive range." He glanced at her. "How's your face?"

She lifted her good hand, only now noting the sting. "A branch got me."

"And the arm?"

"Burning like crazy."

The sirens grew louder. "Hold tight, help's coming."

"I'm fine." Truthfully, while she was technically fine—as in still alive—nausea clutched at her and weakness hit her knees. She slumped to the ground and Caden whirled to rush to her. "Ava?"

"I'm okay. Just . . . feeling a little woozy. Probably the adrenaline crash." And maybe the wound in her arm?

He gripped her good arm and helped her to her feet. "I don't want to leave you here alone, but I don't want to leave the drone either."

"You think there are prints on it? He didn't leave any on the mace-slash-chloroform container."

"I know. I doubt the guy would be dumb enough to leave

some, but you never know." He paused. "I need to take it with us. You think you can walk back the way we came?"

"As long as I'm not dodging bullets, I think I can handle it." Her words sounded more sure than she actually felt.

"Okay. Stay put for a minute."

He approached the drone, his posture wary, his movements slow. Ava watched, her stomach in a knot, praying it wasn't a trap. Caden pulled off his T-shirt, tossed it over the machine, and waited. Ava almost expected the thing to jerk to life and start shooting again, but nothing happened.

Some of Caden's tension must have eased, because his shoulders relaxed a fraction. Ava could tell he wasn't making any assumptions, though. He pulled the shirt away and moved closer, staying to the side, out of the path of any bullets that might still be in the weapon.

With care, he placed the shirt over the machine again, then stepped around behind it and unplugged the battery. Ava released a low breath she didn't realize she'd been holding. He picked up the drone with a grunt.

The sirens had quieted, and Ava figured they'd found Caden's truck. "You lead the way," she said. "I'll keep up."

Caden nodded, his worried gaze slipping over her in a quick assessment, pausing briefly on her bloodied left arm.

"Go," she said, her voice soft.

He nodded and headed back down the trail he'd blazed on their run from the drone. Ava bit her lip on the throbbing that pulsed through her arm, her head, and her cheek. She could complain later. For now, she'd concentrate on putting one foot in front of the other.

o o o

Caden couldn't help casting glances over his shoulder at Ava. He was worried. While she stayed with him, she kept her head down and her breathing seemed too shallow for his peace of mind. "You okay?"

"Yeah."

"Would you tell me if you weren't?"

"Probably not."

About what he figured.

After another minute of walking, when he glanced back, she stumbled and latched on to a tree. He set the drone down and reached for her. Snagging her good upper arm, he pulled her against him. "We're almost there. I'll send someone back for the drone. Let me help you."

"No. Just give me a minute. The world is kinda spinning."

"Put your arm around my waist."

"I—"

"Unless you want me to carry you."

Her right arm went around his waist. From the road, he could hear the commotion—people talking, engines running, radios crackling. She gripped a handful of his shirt and wobbled once more. Caden swept her up into his arms.

"Caden!"

"Give it up, Ava. Kind of like you did dating."

She groaned—a sound that was half laugh, half protest—and leaned her head against his shoulder. "Fine."

Caden carried her the rest of the way. As he broke the tree line, the first person he saw was Zane. He wasn't surprised one bit. If the roles had been reversed, he'd have gotten off his deathbed to help too.

Zane, red-nosed but looking slightly improved, hurried toward them. "Way to scare a partner, man."

"Yeah."

"Ambulance is one minute out."

"And the drone is about a two-minute hike north through those trees. Just follow the trail I left."

"Drone?"

"It's a quadrotor outfitted with a machine gun. I unplugged the battery, but be careful."

Zane's eyes widened. "She catch a bullet from the drone?"

"I'm still awake, guys," Ava said, sounding slightly annoyed. "Yes, Zane, the bullet from the drone *grazed* me, but I'm fine."

"That's a relief."

"No kidding."

She shut her eyes and Caden could feel the tension running through her. She was in pain. A head wound from the truck crash, a bullet to the arm. Even the scratch from the branch on her cheek. All of it had to add up to severely uncomfortable. And she simply lay in his arms with her eyes closed.

"They found Mickey Fields," Zane said.

"What? Where?" The ambulance pulled up and Caden headed straight for it.

Zane followed. "He's in the hospital. He's been shot."

"Shot?" Ava's head lifted. "Seems to be a lot of that going around. Is he okay?"

"He's alive."

"Which hospital?" Caden asked.

"Mercy One."

Ava turned her head and groaned when he stepped up to the ambulance.

Caden shot her a frown. "Don't even say you don't need to have that arm—and head and cheek—looked at."

"I'm not."

"Good." He looked at the paramedic who'd run around to open the back. "Don't bother pulling anything out. Head to Mercy."

"But—"

"You can check her on the way." He climbed in with Ava

still in his arms. With the paramedic's help, he got all the way in with only a small grunt.

"You did *not* just imply that I'm too heavy, did you?" Ava's words were slurred, her eyes bleary. Caden knew her well enough to understand where the snarkiness was coming from. Whenever she was scared or in pain, she got snippy.

He set her on the stretcher. "Never."

"I should hope not." She turned her head to the paramedic, who had already begun to remove the bandage on her left arm. "No painkillers, understand?"

"An addict?"

She laughed, a breathy, sarcastic sound. "No. A target. I need to be aware of my surroundings."

Caden gripped her hand. "I'm here, Ava. Let him give you something—" Her gaze never wavered from his. He glanced up at the paramedic. "No narcotics."

He nodded.

Just as the ambulance started to move, a fist pounded on the passenger door. The paramedic lowered his window, and Caden heard a cough, then "Here, take this." The man handed the items back to Caden. Ava's purse and Caden's cell phone. He smiled.

Ava gave a relieved sigh. "I can't tell you how grateful I am someone thought to grab that."

"It was Zane. I could tell by the cough."

Fifteen minutes later, they were rolling her out of the ambulance and into the hospital. They bypassed the waiting area and were led straight back to a room.

Zane appeared shortly after, coughing into his elbow and looking miserable once more.

"You might want to get checked out while you're here," Caden told him.

Zane shot him a look that should have sent him six feet

under. "It's a cold. A miserable cold. Patty insisted on examining me and said I'm just a wimp, but she gave me cough meds and a steroid shot to keep it from turning into bronchitis."

Caden shook his head. "Go home. We're fine. And I don't want to be breathing your air."

"You need a bodyguard or something. Every time I turn around you two are in trouble."

"Funny." He sobered. "I don't know what's going on, Zane. Has Daria found anything else with the Russian connection? She hasn't texted me—or if she has, I missed it."

"She did and you missed it. I guess you were running from a bullet-spitting drone when she passed on the information. She's making progress. She's pretty sure that all three families—the Sidorovs, aka Holdens, the Baileys, and the Fields—came over from Russia sometime in the early nineties. They all changed their names to American ones, and they've taken great measures to hide their Russian heritage. Whoever helped them was very skilled and had a lot of resources to make their Russian past disappear."

"My father could do that," Ava said. "Maybe that's the connection. He helped them get out of Russia? The nineties? That was about the time of the fall of the KGB, but not everyone was happy about that."

"And the KGB never really disappeared. They just renamed it the FSB. Maybe these people were agents for your father?"

She shrugged and winced. "It makes sense. And if they were in danger, he'd relocate them."

"But right in your backyard?"

"Not all of them. Just the one family. The others that were killed were in San Diego, Texas, and Oregon, right? And the one in Oregon, Bridgette O'Reilly, was the sister of the guy whose family was killed in Houston—Carl Bailey."

"Yes."

She rubbed her forehead. "Trying to keep it all straight is giving me a migraine."

"I can relate. But yes, you're right on the families and how two of them, at least, are connected."

"So, maybe my father had a reason for—"

The doctor's arrival cut her off and sent Caden and Zane from the room. For the next hour and a half Caden paced the hallway while Ava's wounds were tended to, including a quick trip to radiology for X-rays.

"You've been hanging around Ava too much," Zane said.

"Why's that?"

"She does the same thing. Paces when she needs to think."

He was right. She did. Caden stopped and raked a hand through his hair. "It works."

Zane narrowed his eyes. "I know that look. You've thought of something."

"No, not really. But while we're here, I want to check on Mickey."

Zane frowned. "He's not awake yet or someone would have called."

"I know," Caden said, "but I don't care. I want to go see him." He paused. "Has someone notified his grandparents?"

"Not sure."

"Let's go find out as soon as Ava can leave."

"Ava's leaving." Caden turned at her voice. She stood in the door, a butterfly bandage on her cheek, another on her forehead, and her arm in a sling. "Where are we going?"

"You're sure you're up to going anywhere?"

"I'm sure. The bullet was just a graze. I'm losing the sling as soon as you break me out of here. I have some painkillers in my pocket that I'll probably flush, and everything else is minor—even the knock on the head."

"No concussion?"

"Not even close."

"All right, then." He looked at Zane. "Sounds like she's in better shape than you are."

Zane rolled his eyes and Ava covered a smile with her good hand.

"Let's go." Zane coughed into his elbow and led the way to the elevator. "He's out of ICU, but they're keeping him in a secure room with a guard on the door."

"Excellent."

"The officer who called it in said Mickey was terrified. His last words were, 'Don't let him kill me.'"

"He saw his family's killer."

"That's what it sounds like, and now the killer has to make sure Mickey can't identify him."

Two floors up and a walk down a long hall took them to a corner of the square tower. The officer on duty looked up from his phone when they reached the glassed area that led into the room used for quarantine—or in Mickey's case, protective custody.

Caden and Zane flashed their badges. "We're here to see Mickey Fields."

"You'll have to run that by the medical staff." He nodded to someone behind them. "Like her."

A nurse stepped into the area and sized them up. "Can I help you?"

"Would it be possible to see Mickey Fields?" Caden asked.

"He's still mostly unconscious."

"Mostly?" Ava asked.

"He's in and out."

Ava took a step forward. "Have his grandparents been notified?"

"I'm not sure. He hasn't had any visitors, so . . ."

"Maybe we could wait with him until his grandparents get here?" Zane asked.

"Just one of you."

"I'll go," Caden said. "No need to give the poor kid the cold on top of all of his other issues."

Zane scowled.

Ava's phone buzzed. "I guess that's my cue."

FOURTEEN

Ava recognized John's number. She grimaced, surprised it had taken him this long to call. Knowing she was about to be raked over the coals, she excused herself and stepped into the hallway. Zane motioned he was going to get a drink from the cafeteria. She waved him on, then swiped the screen. "Hi, John."

"What do you think you're doing?"

The low, lethal tone to his voice stopped her. Then anger bypassed her filters. "I have a right to know who he is." She paused. "Who he was."

"No, you don't. You don't have any rights when it comes to him. He set things up the way he did on purpose. If you want to honor him, you should respect that!"

His words hit home. And yet—

"You don't know what you're doing," he continued. "The fine line you're walking. The people you may be putting in danger. You need to—"

"I'm trying to protect people! You wouldn't help me, so I had to take things into my own hands."

"And you lied to Julie. You used your friendship with her, her love and trust in you, to get something that you know you shouldn't have. What do you think that yearbook page is going to tell you?"

The guilt she'd been fighting ever since her visit washed over her like a tsunami. He wasn't wrong. She'd justified betraying Julie's trust in order to save lives. But how often had he done the same? Didn't necessarily make it right, but something pushed her to see this through to the end. "Does she know?"

"No. I wouldn't break her heart like that. She thinks of you as a daughter, you know that. Do you remember the times you called her, crying because your own mother was passed out, and what did Julie do? She talked to you, encouraged you, told you what to do and how to help Nathan, remember?"

"Of course I remember." And she did. The memories were more than vivid, tumbling one over the other.

"And you go and pull this stunt. I thought more of you."

Ava hesitated, hearing something more in his voice. Something . . . she could almost put her finger on. And then it hit her and she gave a short, humorless laugh. "Lay on the guilt trip all you want, John, but you admire me. You're impressed at what I did, aren't you? It's what any good officer would have done— including betraying someone they love to get to the truth." The last part of the sentence was hard to choke out, but it was true.

"A good officer wouldn't have left evidence behind."

"You only knew what to look for because you know me."

He went silent. Then cleared his throat. More silence.

She sighed. "All that aside, have you talked to the people at the FBI? Did you get the pictures? If so, then you know why I can't just let this go."

"Ava! Listen to me! Your ingenuity may have impressed me, your actions show you've got what it takes to join the organization, but right now, you don't understand the ramifications of what you are doing."

"Then tell me!" Her shout echoed in the hallway. She glanced up to see several people looking at her. With a silent groan, she turned her back. "Then tell me," she said again. This time low and in control.

"Ava?" She turned. Caden stood just outside Mickey's room, frowning. "You okay?"

She nodded and he slipped back inside, but not before shooting her another concerned glance.

"I can't tell you, Ava, but if you don't stop what you're doing, you're going to put people at risk. People you love."

"Who? Mom? Nathan? Are they in danger?"

"I'm telling you to stop. That's all." He hung up.

Ava lowered the phone and drew in a deep breath. She wanted to release it in a scream. Instead, she blew out slowly. Took another breath and did it again. She dialed Sarah's number.

"Hello?"

"Hey, I need a favor."

"Sure. What's wrong?" Sarah's instant understanding that she was serious sent waves of gratitude through her.

"I don't have time to go into it right now, but my mother may be in danger because of what I'm working on. Do you think Gavin could check on her and make sure she has some kind of security?"

"Oh, Ava . . ." Sarah's compassion reached through the line. "Yes, of course. I'll get him to do it right now."

"I'll explain later, okay?"

"Okay. Anything else you need?"

"Uh . . . no. Thanks."

"You hesitated. You need the puzzle finished, don't you?"

"Yes, but I'll get to that soon."

"Or I can just go do it."

Ava groaned. "No, Sarah. I'm a target. If you go to my place, you might be a target too."

"Look, I'm a journalist. I go into crazy situations often. I think going to your place to do a puzzle is kind of low on the danger scale. But if it'll make you feel better, I'll get Gavin or a police buddy to go with me. It'll be fine, I promise."

Ava hesitated. Sarah made a good argument, but . . . she hated to let someone else do it. It was something she'd wanted to do herself, but this was too important to let sentiment get in the way. "Fine. If you're sure."

"I'm sure. I'll let you know when it's finished."

"Okay. Thanks, Sarah." She almost hung up, but hesitated. "Does Gavin know anyone in Durham?"

"I don't know. Probably. Why? Oh. You need someone on Nathan too."

"Yes."

"I'll get right on it and tell Gavin to text you when it's all arranged."

"Thank you."

"Be careful, Ava."

"Always. We'll talk soon."

She hung up and pressed the phone to her forehead. Her arm throbbed in time with the beat of her heart, and she realized how close she'd come to being seriously injured. Or worse. Whoever was after her wasn't playing around.

Wait a minute . . . *including betraying someone they love.*

She'd said those words because she'd heard them before. Her father had said them when training her. John had said them in some fashion more than once.

Had John been the one operating the drone? Or had it been someone he'd sent to take care of her?

But why?

Because she wouldn't stop looking for the truth?

Her jaw hardened and resolve centered itself like a ball in her stomach.

Well, whoever it was, for whatever reason, had just ensured

she'd see this through to the end. Until she found the truth—or she was dead.

○ ○ ○

Nicolai stepped out of the stairwell, adjusted the ball cap, and made his way down the hall. His eyes scanned the rooms, not seeing what he was looking for, but knowing it was only a matter of time before he found it. After all, how many patients were likely to have a guard outside their door?

When this floor yielded him nothing, he took the stairs to the next. In the ER, there might be a patient from the local prison, but the officers on guard always wore the prison uniform. Nicolai wouldn't bother to stop for those.

Most likely, the room he was searching for would be set apart. At the end of a hallway.

Two floors later, he found it.

Nicolai stepped to the side and leaned against the wall like he was simply taking a break from visiting the patient in the room just ahead of him. He pulled his phone from his pocket and lowered his head. Thus far he'd managed to avoid the cameras by taking the stairs and keeping his head down in the hallways.

Once he managed to kill Mickey Fields and the dead teen was discovered, there would be a full-on search for him on security footage, but they'd find nothing. Nothing they could work with to identify him, at least.

Now, to get in and get the job done. He stuffed his right hand into his pocket and curled his fingers around the plastic bag. For a moment, his vision dimmed and all he could see was the woman being tortured, her screams echoing in his mind even after all these years. He shuddered and focused his attention on the business of the floor. Nurses, doctors, physical therapists, visitors. It was a beehive of activity.

And was that Ava Jackson? His heart rate picked up and his

breathing quickened. Yes, that was her, pacing outside the room at the corner. With her arm in a sling? Had she caught one of the bullets from the drone? He frowned. He hadn't thought any of them had found a mark, but maybe so.

It had been a risky move to use the drone, but it was the best he'd been able to come up with at the time. His intention had been to take out the truck and the agent who seemed to have no other purpose in life except to protect Ava Jackson. Then he'd planned to chloroform Ava and take her with him. Yet, once more his plan had failed miserably.

His fingers tightened over the plastic bag in his pocket.

One man stepped out of Mickey's room and joined Ava and the other agent. Nicolai recognized them from the Fields's neighborhood home as leaders in the investigation. Special Agents Caden Denning and Zane Pierce. He'd wanted to know who he needed to watch out for. Some intel about the agents determined to stop him from completing his mission might come in helpful. Especially since it looked like Agent Denning had more than a professional relationship with Ava.

The three of them headed for the elevator, leaving the lone guard to settle into his chair next to the door. Nicolai had to give the officer credit. He didn't slouch and he didn't pull out his phone. His gaze was alert and intent.

A worthy adversary.

But Nicolai was smart—and more determined than ever to make sure the teen died. He had a list of people to kill and this loose end was delaying his timeline.

But he'd be patient. Watchful. And it wouldn't take him long to figure out how to make the busy floor work in his favor.

▢ ▢ ▢

In the hospital cafeteria, Caden pulled out a chair for Ava and waited for her to drop into it before sitting next to her.

Zane's medication was wearing off and he'd decided to head home to catch a few hours of rest.

Ava sipped on the Coke she'd ordered while she waited for the burger and fries to come up.

"You okay?" Caden asked.

She met his gaze with a sigh. "Yes and no."

"Wanna explain?"

"Physically, I'm all right and I'm grateful to be alive. Everything could have turned out much different."

"I know." He could honestly say that had been one of the more terrifying moments in his life. He'd had a few harrowing ones with his sister, but running from a drone spitting bullets, fighting his desperate fear that he wouldn't be able to keep Ava safe, had just claimed top spot. He tried to conceal the shudder that rippled through him, but the effort wasn't necessary. Ava's eyes were open, but he didn't think she was seeing anything but her thoughts.

She blinked. "How long are we going to wait to see if Mickey wakes up?"

"I figure maybe an hour or so. The nurse seemed to think it could be sooner." Their number was called and Caden went to get the food. When he returned, he set the bag with her burger and fries in front of her. He'd chosen a hot dog with a side of chips and a bowl of fruit.

She took another sip from the Coke, then rubbed her forehead before pulling the food from the bag. "I need to check on my mom and Nathan." She stabbed one of his strawberries with her fork and popped the piece of fruit in her mouth.

"I thought that's who you were on the phone with earlier."

She looked up at him. "No, that was John."

"He let you have it, huh?"

"And then some. He figured out I'd ripped that page from the yearbook." She went for the mandarin orange next.

"Wow. That was fast."

"That's John. He's predictable in some ways, but smart. Very, very smart." When she stole the piece of apple, he pushed the bowl in front of her. She ate two blueberries and looked up. "Especially when it comes to people he knows. And he knows me pretty well." She frowned. "Did I just steal your fruit?"

"No, I gave it to you."

"Oh. Thanks." She snagged two more strawberries.

He laughed, then turned serious again. "He's mad you got past him."

"Hmm," she said. "Mad and impressed all at the same time." She told him about the conversation, and Caden's shoulders knotted with each word. When she fell silent, he did too.

"Caden?" she finally said.

"Yes?"

"I've known John since I was fifteen. He's always been there for me and my family. He and Julie both. What kind of person does it make me that I think he's capable of trying to kill me to keep me from finding out all I can about my father?"

Caden leaned back. He could tell she was truly conflicted and wished he could ease her mind. "He's CIA, Ava. You never know what's going on beneath the surface."

"Meaning I don't know if I can trust him or not."

Caden nodded. "Unfortunately."

"I hate that my mind goes there, but he's adamant that I leave things alone. That I'm endangering those I love." She shrugged. "Then again, I don't have all of the information that I might need to see that. So, what do I do? Drop everything and take a chance on letting a killer go free because he says that's what I need to do? Do I ignore that little voice in my head that says all is not as it seems?"

For a moment Caden didn't speak. Then he cleared his throat. "Can you do that?"

It was her turn to fall silent. Then she raised her head and shook it. "I don't think so. I don't want to put anyone at risk, especially not my family, but I also can't let a killer go free—free to kill again—if I have an ounce of power to help stop him."

Caden reached across the table and squeezed her hand. "Finish your burger, Ava, then we'll check on Mickey again."

She took three bites, then wrapped the food and slid it back into the bag. "I can't eat right now."

Caden hadn't had that problem. He'd been starving and the food was hot and fresh and he'd wolfed it down. She'd eaten all the fruit, though. "We can go back up there," he said, "if you're ready."

"Sure." Ava stood, and stuffed her leftovers into her purse, then patted it. "I owe Zane a thank-you for grabbing this."

Caden pulled out his phone and waved it. "Me too." He placed a hand on the small of her back and followed her to the elevator.

Her shoulders lifted, then lowered with a big sigh, and he slid an arm around her to tuck her against him. When she didn't pull away, hope sprouted that he might get that first date. Maybe even the second. If he managed a third, he might be able to relax a fraction. While they rode the elevator in silence to Mickey's floor, Caden wracked his brain trying to remember what Ava did for fun, besides puzzles. He came up with movies. She liked to binge-watch classics.

"When you binge-watch the classics," he said, "what kind of food do you like to go with them?"

She jerked her head to stare at him. "What?"

"I was just thinking. There's no way I'm leaving you alone with this maniac on the loose, so until he's caught, we might as well make the most of it."

"Oh. Okay. Right."

"So . . . food?" The elevator chimed and the doors slid open. Ava stepped out and Caden kept his hand on her back.

"I'm not a big cook. I might pop a frozen dinner in the microwave and cut up some fruit or something."

He stopped in the hallway and turned her toward him. "I'm sorry, did you say *frozen dinner*?" This time, he didn't even attempt to hide the shudder that swept over him.

She smiled. "Well, it's better than starving."

"No. It's not. Okay, tonight, we're going to cook at your place and I'm going to make you a decent meal. You like steak, right?"

"Love it."

"Asparagus and baked potatoes?"

"Yum."

"Then it's a . . ." *Don't say the word* date. "Deal. I'll cook, but you have to clean up."

The laughter spurted from her and she nodded. "Perfect." Her smile faded. "But I really need to stop in and check on my mother."

"We can do that before dinner." Which was turning into something close to a midnight snack.

She hesitated. "You don't think I'm putting her in danger by visiting, do you?"

"I don't know," he said, his words slow, his eyes narrowed. "Although, now that you bring it up, I think maybe it might be best to stay away from the facility for now."

Ava bit her lip on the immediate protest he could see forming and nodded. "You're probably right."

His phone buzzed, distracting him. He glanced at the screen. "It's Daria."

"You take that," Ava said, "and I'll head on down to Mickey's room."

Caden frowned at the thought of her going on her own, but he wouldn't be long. "All right. Hopefully this won't take long." She walked away and Caden pressed the phone to his ear. "Hi, Daria, what's up?"

FIFTEEN

Ava was so glad he hadn't said the word "date." She would have had to decline. But if he was "making" her clean up, then he wasn't thinking date, so that was good. Right? They were just two friends hanging out, watching classics and eating food not cooked by her. It was a win all the way around. Wasn't it? Of course it was. So why did she feel . . . deflated?

From the corner of her eye, she studied Caden and admitted if she was going to date anyone, it would be him. Assuming he was interested. Which she was pretty sure he was.

So why hadn't he said, "It's a *date*" instead of "It's a *deal*"?

Well, duh. She'd told him she didn't date, so being the gentleman he was, he wouldn't push the issue. "Just take it one day at a time," she muttered. "It's not like you have time for dating right now anyway." Not with a killer after her.

However, while the thought of not visiting her mother saddened her, the thought of Caden fixing dinner for her tonight softened the blow. She'd admit it made her happy to have something to look forward to besides dodging bullets and running from bad guys.

When Ava reached Mickey's room at the end of the hall, she

frowned. The guard was gone. She glanced back over her shoulder and didn't see anyone. Maybe Mickey had been taken for a test or something and the guard had gone with him. Ava eyed the chair, the fatigue swamping her. She was so tired. Physically and emotionally tired. Her head throbbed, her arm ached, and her cheek stung. Surely no one would begrudge her the guard's chair until he needed it.

She sat, knowing it could be a while before they returned. She could still see Caden where she'd left him, phone pressed to his ear, pacing back in the small area near the elevators.

A noise came from inside the room and she stood. Were Mickey's grandparents waiting inside? Surely they were here by now. She knocked and pushed open the door. A man dressed as a surgeon, complete with head covering and mask, stood next to Mickey's bed.

With a plastic bag held over the teen's head.

"Caden!"

Ava launched herself at the man and tackled him to the floor. Her injured shoulder slammed onto the tile. Pain swamped her and the breath left her, but she was desperate to keep the momentum of her surprise attack and forced herself to her feet.

He was doing the same and she pushed herself forward once more to land an elbow in his throat. Only she missed when he stepped to the side. Pain radiated through her head as his hand, wrapped in her hair, snapped her back. She let out a scream when the door slammed open.

"Ava!"

Caden. The man swung a hand up and aimed a weapon at Caden. Then brought it against her temple. "Back up or she dies."

Caden stopped, his eyes locked on hers. They flicked to her attacker. "Let her go."

"She's my ticket out of here. Back through the door."

"Check on Mickey," Ava cried. "He was suffocating him!"

Caden glanced at the boy in the bed, pulling at the bag and gasping for air. He started toward him.

The weapon pressed harder against her head. "No, no. Do not move."

Ava's heart pounded while Caden's gaze darted between her and Mickey. "Security is on the way up here," he said.

"Then I'd better be leaving now." Her attacker continued toward the door and stepped out, the weapon still on her head. He swung her around to face the security Caden was talking about. Ava didn't think he'd shoot her until he was out of the hospital. At least not unless he was provoked and had no way out. Or unless he had a way out and thought he could shoot her and run. Hospital security had their own weapons drawn and aimed at the two of them.

"Let her go! Put the weapon down!"

Their mingled shouts echoed in her ears and the man simply ignored them, pulling her along until he got to the stairs.

"Open the door." His order was low, his voice steady.

"Mickey saw your face, didn't he?"

"I'm not here to talk."

He backed through the door, pulling Ava with him, and a plan formed in her mind as he spun her toward the stairs. As soon as she placed her foot onto the first step, she gripped the rail with her left hand and bent her knees to drop to the step in a sudden move. The gun slid from her head as she'd hoped. At his surprised grunt, she released the rail, shifted to her right, and shot up, her hands latching onto his wrist before he could aim the weapon at her once again.

She had to use her wounded arm and her shoulder burned, fire shooting along her nerves.

"You stupid—!" He jerked hard, almost unbalancing her from the narrow step. Before she fell, she yanked on his arm and banged it against the rail. He gave a shout and the weapon tumbled from his fingers. His left hand grabbed her hair and yanked her head back.

Ava cried out but swept a leg against his knee. He lost his grip on her and gravity worked in her favor. He tumbled toward her, and she grabbed the rail with her left hand once more, using her right to lash out, hitting the back of his head. She gave it an extra push, her fingers tangled in the mask strings, snapping his head back. She yanked the mask from his face. He gave another scream as he fell, his arms pinwheeling, scrambling to grab something to stop his fall. He bounced and crashed down the steps to the bottom.

When he landed, he lay still, his leg twisted at an awkward angle. The door behind Ava slammed open. Her attacker rolled, keeping his face from her.

"FBI! Stay there!"

"Police! Don't move!"

The officers' shouts behind her seemed to spur him to shake off the effects of the fall. He lurched to his feet, favoring his right leg, and pushed out of the exit.

"Get him!" Caden's shout resulted in hospital security pounding past her. She dropped to the step, head reeling. "Ava!" Caden's grip on her upper arm almost made her smile. Even in the midst of the chaos, he made sure he didn't grab her wounded one.

She turned to him. "I'm all right." A sigh slipped from her. "Do you have an evidence bag?" She held up the mask by the strings. "Maybe this has some DNA on it."

□ □ □

Caden gaped. Then snapped his mouth shut. Would she ever stop surprising him? "Yeah, I'll get one." As soon as he stopped shaking. When she'd screamed his name, it had echoed through the floor of the hospital, sending his adrenaline into overdrive. He'd darted into the room to see the man dressed as a surgeon with a gun to her head. Caden had been unable to do anything but watch him pull her into the stairwell, then race after them. He'd opened the door just in time to see the man take his tumble down the steps.

Caden waved to one of the hospital security officers. "I need an evidence bag. You have one?"

"Be right back."

Caden sat beside Ava while she held the mask as she'd grabbed it. "You think they got him?" she asked.

"I don't know. If not, at least now we should have a face to circulate."

"There aren't any cameras in this stairwell, but maybe they got him as he exited?"

"Exactly. I'm going to request that footage now."

She nodded and he sent the request.

The door opened once more, and the officer handed Caden the evidence bag. "All right," Caden said to Ava, "just slide it in there, nice and easy."

She did so. He sealed the bag and labeled it. Then met her eyes. "Are you okay, Ava?"

"I'm . . ." Her throat closed and she fought the wave of pure exhaustion that wanted to overtake her. "I'm alive, but honestly, I just want to know Mickey's okay, then go home and finish that puzzle and find my dad's password to his computer and find out what's on there that he might or might not want me to see and I still want to know what Daria found out about that code and what it means and—"

He wrapped his fingers around hers, stopping the flow of words. "How about I take you home and you try to get some sleep?"

"Sure. Why not?"

The fact that she didn't argue with him said a whole lot

about the state of her mind. He passed the evidence bag off to one of the task force members. "We need DNA off this ASAP. See if he's in the system."

"On it."

He disappeared, and Caden helped Ava to her feet, through the crowd, and out of the hospital. He'd take her statement in the comfort of her home. Then he'd call Daria and ask her about the code she'd discovered in the newspaper clippings. She'd said she—and the others—were still working on it, but he agreed with Ava. They needed that information.

"Wait a minute," she said. "We still need to find out if Mickey's okay and talk to him, don't we?"

He glanced at his phone. "Mickey's okay. You got there in time. I'll get one of the others to talk to him and I'll take you home."

"No, it's fine. Let's go see if he's awake and if we can get anything from him."

"All right. If you're sure you're up to it."

"Just catch me if I keel over."

"Always."

"And what happened to my steak dinner?" She scowled. "I'm not passing on that. We had a deal."

He gave a low chuckle. "Let's see how you feel after we check on Mickey. Deal?"

"No deal. I'm expecting steak and I want to get that puzzle finished. I think that's going to be the key to a lot of this."

"That works for me."

Caden shook his head and led the way back to the room. The staff eyed her with expressions of disbelief, relief, and awe. A nurse approached her. "Are you all right? Do you want someone to take a look at you?"

"No, thanks," Ava said. "He didn't hurt me. I'm fine."

The man nodded, but looked unsure. However, he said, "I know you were wanting to speak to Mickey. He's awake."

"Where was the officer on his room?" Caden asked.

"We found him in the bathroom, unconscious. He's currently recuperating in a room down the hall."

Caden frowned. "But he'll be all right?"

"Yes. He'll have a headache, but other than that he was unharmed."

"That's a relief," Ava murmured.

Caden nodded. "Is he awake? Can we talk to him?"

"Yes, I think so. Follow me." He led them down to the third room on the right. "We had this one open and put him here to treat him quickly."

He knocked and pushed the door open. The officer sat propped up in the bed, his eyes closed, face pale from the trauma. A white bandage covered part of his head. Caden thanked the nurse and turned to the patient, who blinked his eyes open.

"I'm Agent Caden Denning," he said, showing his badge. "This is Ava Jackson. Do you mind if I ask you what happened?"

"Sure, you can ask, but I can't give you a description."

"Tell me what you can."

"The guy was dressed in surgical scrubs. Had a hospital ID badge and said he was the surgeon who'd patched up the kid's shoulder." He pressed a thumb and forefinger to his eyes. "And I let him in."

"What made you check on him?"

"I don't know. Just had a weird feeling about the whole thing. I stepped in, and he was getting ready to put a plastic bag over the boy's head. I yelled at him and he turned and sucker punched me. Then he used the phone by the bed to clock me in the head. That's the last I remember."

Caden handed him a card. "Sorry about that. Hope you heal up quick."

"Thanks."

"If you remember anything else, give me a call, will you?"

"Of course."

They stepped out of the room and made their way back to Mickey's. Another officer had been stationed there, and Caden hoped Mickey would be able to give them more information than the officer had.

"What are you two doing here?" The voice was familiar, angry and low.

Caden turned. "Hello, Mr. and Mrs. Fields."

Jesse Fields approached, the tension radiating from him. He held a steaming cup of coffee and had just stepped out of the small break room across the hall. "I asked what you were doing here."

"I'm here to talk to Mickey," Caden said.

"He's still unconscious."

"The nurse said he was awake," Ava said. "Why are you fighting so hard on this? Your family was *killed. Murdered.* And there's a connection with my father, whether you want to admit it or not. You know something, so why don't you help them find the person who did this?"

Caden placed a hand on her arm. "Easy, Ava."

Jesse's nostrils flared and his wife sucked in a sharp breath. She sniffled and dabbed her eyes with a tissue. "Jesse," she said, her voice soft, "maybe—"

"Shut up," he fired at her.

Fresh tears filled her eyes and slipped over her lashes.

He groaned, walked over to her, and took her in his arms. "I'm sorry, honey, I'm sorry."

Without a word, she pushed past him into Mickey's room.

Jesse locked eyes on Caden. "Leave us out of this."

Ava raked a hand over her head. "Mr. Fields, there's no leaving you out of this. You're in this whether you like it or not." Her voice was low. Subdued.

Mr. Fields looked like he might explode at any moment. Ava would be right behind him.

"I need to speak to Mickey ASAP," Caden said.

"He can't tell you anything."

Caden's phone buzzed. He glanced at the screen. Daria. "I'm sorry, I need to take this. Ava, come with me?"

She sighed and nodded.

He pressed the phone to his ear. "Yes, Daria?"

"I think I might have some information you're going to find interesting."

"Lay it on me."

Daria cleared her throat. "All right. I'm just going to go over everything, so stay with me. The first family, the Holdens, were murdered in San Diego, California, last month. Second one, the Baileys, was two weeks ago in Houston, Texas. The third, the Fields family, was in South Carolina, and the fourth was in Portland, Oregon. All of these families have living parents who have a connection that I think I've figured out."

"What is it?"

"They were all high-ranking—and I mean, high—Russian KGB."

He blinked. "What? How did you find that out?"

"I have friends in high places. Namely the CIA."

"You're FBI. Why would you have CIA friends?"

"Ha ha. Cute. And it's only one friend, but just be glad I do and that she's willing to share—albeit off the record. Anyway, that's the connection to all of the families, I think."

"They weren't officers, they were assets," he murmured.

"Exactly. High-ranking Russian officials selling their country's secrets to the United States."

And Ava's father had no doubt recruited them. But . . . "How did they all come to be in the United States?"

Ava's phone rang and she leaned against the wall to take the call.

"From what I can gather," Daria said, "the CIA officer who

recruited them—and whose name was not divulged even by my friend but could very possibly be Ava's father—managed to get them out one by one starting in the late eighties and into the early nineties."

"So that would have been a bit before the KGB was disbanded—officially—and shortly after. Why, after all these years, would someone be unhappy about that and come looking for them? Why kill their families, but not them?"

"I'm not sure. I'll let you work on that angle, but I have one more bit of news for you. ViCAP sent me a notification of a murder that might not be related, but there were enough markers that it caught my attention."

"What is it?"

"A couple living in New Mexico were found dead six weeks ago. The wife was shot point-blank in the foyer of the home, but evidence shows she was moved postmortem to the sofa. The husband committed suicide as evidenced by the spatter on the window behind him."

Caden frowned. "Why would that have anything to do with our case?" Although the fact that the woman was moved to the sofa was interesting.

"I'm getting there. Even though he shot himself in his office, he, too, was moved to the sofa next to his wife."

"Well, that's definitely a flag."

"Indeed. Anyway, the couple, Max and Yvonne Kirkland, were supposed to have been on a plane to the Turks and Caicos to meet some friends at an all-inclusive resort. When they didn't show and weren't answering their phones, the friends asked someone to go by and check on them."

"And found them."

"Right. Turns out they don't have any children together, but Yvonne had a son from a teenage relationship. In the office where Max killed himself, this son, named Gregory, found a box that he remembered his mother telling him contained pictures from her husband's 'former life.'"

"Former life, huh?"

"Yeah. I don't have all the details there, either, but it looks like Max and Yvonne are really Maksim and Yelena Kuznetsov."

Caden froze. "Let me guess. From Russia."

"Yes. Well, he was Russian. She was American. Her birth name was Yvonne. When they lived in Russia, she went by Yelena. And here's another piece of interesting trivia for you."

"He was high-ranking KGB?"

"You win the prize—and it looks like he was the first one in this particular group to defect."

"The first of many?"

"Definitely quite a few.'"

"So how did he wind up with an American woman?" Caden shot a glance at Ava, who was still on her phone, her forehead creased.

"Yvonne came from a wealthy family," Daria said. "Old money on her mother's side. Her father was an FBI agent working with defectors—questioning them, guarding them, et cetera. When she finished college, she was offered a job at a prestigious girls' school in Moscow teaching English as a second language. At some point, she met Maksim and they hit it off. Reading between the lines, it looks like this was all set up by her father to get Maksim to defect. It worked. Long story short, he followed her to the US in 1990 and changed his name to Max Kirkland— and gave Yvonne's father names of other high-ranking KGB officials who could be turned. For the right price."

"I see."

"All of that information is on file here, of course. I didn't have to dig too deep to find it."

"So why did ViCAP flag it? The positioning on the sofa?"

"That and the missing pictures. Other flags were home invasion and gunshot to the head, a single intruder who knew the family's routine, and a couple of others. But mostly the missing pictures and bodies on the sofa."

"Okay, thanks, Daria. This is a huge help." But a bigger help would be questioning Jesse Fields yet again and presenting him with the information he now had. If questioning Mickey had to wait, he could grab Mr. Fields and see what he had to say about the information Daria had just shared. His phone dinged and his lips turned upward. Finally.

Two attachments—a still shot and a video from hospital security. He stared at the picture grabbed from the footage, then played the video to see how the picture had come about. The man slipped out of the stairwell, keeping his head turned from the camera, but he stumbled and fell, then wrapped his hand around his knee.

A worker dressed in scrubs rushed over to place a hand on his shoulder—probably to ask if he was okay—and the man looked up for a split second to shove the hand away.

That split second was all that was necessary to get a clear shot of his face.

"Perfect," he breathed. "Now to run you through the facial software system and nail your hide to the wall." Then throw it in prison. He sent the picture to Daria with the text.

I need to know who this is ASAP.

On it.

Oh, I need a vehicle. Mine is full of bullet holes.

Insurance would probably total it. He grimaced. He'd really liked that truck.

◻ ◻ ◻

The multimillion-dollar luxury yacht had been Nicolai's home for the past four months when he wasn't at the house with his aunt. It boasted three levels of indoor and outdoor living, with a swimming pool and bar area on the top deck. The five staterooms were spread out over the second level. And the bottom deck . . . well, that was his special place.

Nicolai maneuvered the speedboat into the garage of the yacht. The hydraulic-operated bay served his purposes and he hadn't minded spending the money for it. He'd moored the floating mansion to the dock of a private island he'd . . . procured.

Once he was finished with his mission, he planned to have the yacht towed from the lake to the ocean so he could sail away and never look back. For now, though, while he hated to use this slice of paradise as his hideaway, it was the only place he felt confident in keeping his prisoner secured. It was a place where his aunt wouldn't hear things she was better off not hearing.

Like his prisoner screaming for mercy.

It had taken him this long to find the man. Having him escape now would mean the end of everything.

And while his mission was nearly finished—and getting nearer with each family he killed—it would not end because something went wrong, like that unexpected change in routine in Oregon, or the Fields boy escaping, but because his plan succeeded. He'd worked around the routine issue and he'd take care of the kid soon. Mickey was running scared and would make a mistake before too long.

Once he had the speedboat parked, he climbed out onto the decking and made his way up to the room he'd had specially designed for this mission. He peered through the small window. His prisoner sat on the bed, his head in his hands, wrists shackled to the steel loop on the far wall. He wore a pair of jean shorts and his upper torso was bare, revealing the evidence

177

of the beatings he'd endured over the last three months. But he was still in excellent shape. Nicolai noted the rippling muscles that had only strengthened with the man's time in the room. Good. Nicolai wanted him healthy. At least for now. He tapped the button on the wall next to the keypad. The low hum started, reeling in the chains attached to his prisoner. The man could still sit on the bed, but there would be no slack in the chains, keeping Nicolai safe from a possible attack. Once the chains were taut, he keyed in the code and pushed the door open.

The man on the bed looked up but didn't move. He'd learned the hard way that resistance was futile. However, while he was calm, he wasn't broken. His eyes glittered and his nostrils flared. Nicolai squelched the slight flicker of admiration for his adversary. He hadn't thought it would take this long to break him, but his enemy was stronger than he'd given him credit for.

"Did you see me kill them?" He smirked. "I know you watched." The small camera he'd attached to his glasses had captured each moment and relayed the scene to the television hanging on the wall opposite the bed.

"I watched. I watched them all. I also watched a kid take you down and get away. Nice going."

Nicolai's fingers curled into fists and his breathing quickened while his rage boiled. He drew in several deep breaths. He wouldn't be goaded into acting outside of the plan. If he killed the man on the bed, everything else would be for naught.

He picked up the remote, aimed it at the television, and pulled up the photograph that had started everything.

With gleeful anticipation, he watched his opponent. The man stared at the screen, still and silent. Then turned his gaze to him. "Is that supposed to mean something to me?"

To say his reaction was woefully disappointing was an understatement. For a moment, the killer wondered if he'd gotten it wrong. His fist shot out and caught his prisoner in the ear. The man fell back onto the bed and stayed there, eyes still open, brow furrowed in pain.

Nicolai stepped forward, intending to get in a series of punches, but when his captive just lay there, the killer stopped, drew back, and stared. Always before, his prisoner had fought back.

Nicolai's gaze went from the television screen back to the man on the bed. A slow smile curved his lips. "I won't hit you with my fists anymore," he said, his tone soft. "I won't take a chance that I might accidentally kill you. Oh no, my friend, you won't escape through death until I'm ready for you to die. Soon, you'll have company and you'll know what it's like to sit helpless while someone kills the one you love."

He walked out of the room, heading to prepare a meal for his prisoner. He needed to make sure the man kept up his strength. Nicolai's mind went to the picture. He'd gotten it right. He'd gotten it very right.

CHAPTER

SIXTEEN

Caden drove the rental Daria had arranged for him to the apartment complex, turned into the parking lot, and found the spot outside Ava's unit.

Sarah had texted and let them know she'd finished the puzzle about an hour ago—in spite of Ava's worry about her being at the apartment. She'd left to go to work but asked to be kept up-to-date on whatever they could tell her.

Ava had fallen asleep about halfway there and he'd let her snooze. He didn't blame her. She'd been through a lot, and while she appeared to be holding up well, it had to be mentally as well as physically exhausting. Even a few minutes of rest would do her good.

When he shut the engine off, she rolled her head toward him and blinked. "I fell asleep."

"Guess you needed it."

"Apparently."

"You still in the mood for some steak?"

"Hmm. Yes. Always. I seem to have gotten a second wind and am not the least bit tired at the moment. What about you?"

"The same. I'm actually starving."

"Then a steak sounds great." She frowned. "But I don't have any food here."

"I know. While you were sleeping, I pulled over and ordered groceries from the app on my phone. They should be here in the next"—he checked his phone—"few seconds or so."

Her brows rose. "Wow. That's truly impressive."

"I aim to please." He got out of the rental and walked around to open the door for her. When she placed her hand in his, he was struck once more by her fragile surface appearance. Yet, beneath that surface was a strength born of necessity—and training.

While she unlocked the door, he glanced around the area, his gaze probing the trees, the cars in the parking lot, looking for anything that was out of place or rang his inner alarm bells. Fortunately, for the moment, all seemed still. Peaceful and silent.

Once inside, he locked the door behind them, and Ava pulled her phone from her pocket. "Make yourself at home. I'm going to call and check on Mom real quick, then I'll take a look at the puzzle and the laptop."

"Sounds good. I'll grab the groceries when they get here and get started."

"Thanks, Caden."

He smiled and she studied him a moment. Caden stood still, wondering what she was seeing. Thinking.

A knock on the door sent his hand reaching for his weapon and Ava raised a brow. "I doubt the bad guys knock," she said.

He dropped his hand with a rueful shrug. "It's become a reflex."

Ava raised the phone to her ear. "Hi, Tammy, this is Ava. I just wanted to check on my mother." She walked to the laptop and shook her head. She mouthed, *Still running*, to Caden.

He nodded and went to the door, peered out the window, and saw the groceries left on the welcome mat. With one last glance around, he opened the door and snagged the three bags. Once he was back inside with the door locked, he couldn't help but wonder if someone was out there watching. If so, he hoped that person saw him and realized Ava wasn't alone. She needed a good night's rest, and he planned to see that she felt safe enough to get it.

He walked toward the kitchen, but the puzzle on the table caught his attention. Like Sarah had said, it was finished. All but one piece. He stared at the picture—which was actually a lot of pictures, numbers, letters, a blueprint. He couldn't make any sense of it but hoped Ava would know what it meant.

With the groceries spread out on the counter, he quickly threw together the salad, covered it, and slid it onto the shelf in the refrigerator. Then he prepped the potatoes and the steak.

Her grill was outside on the little patio at the back of the apartment and he got it going. The area was more open than he'd like, but he took comfort in the trees along the fence line and the fact there were no tall buildings in sight for a sniper to take aim from.

Although, he supposed one of the trees would be good enough for that. He scanned them, and while nothing alarmed him, he made a mental note to warn her about the possibility of someone hiding in one.

While the grill heated, he returned to the kitchen to find Ava bent over the puzzle. She held the last piece in her hand. A tear dripped from her lashes to splash on the puzzle. She wiped it away and sniffed. "Sarah left this one for me to finish it."

"Seems fitting."

With a nod and deep sigh, she placed the piece in its home, then rested both hands on top of the finally completed puzzle.

"Well?" He walked over to stand beside her. "Does it mean anything to you?"

"Yes, so many things. I'm not sure if there's supposed to be a message in here or if it's just a collage of different places where we've been and he thought it would be fun for me to walk down memory lane." Her finger traced the foreign symbols. "But after learning all we've learned over the past few days, the Russian makes me wonder . . ."

Him too. "Okay. While you're studying, I'm going to be making the steaks. If I remember correctly, you like yours medium rare?"

"Uh-huh. Thanks."

He smiled. Her absent-minded response said she was in full concentration mode, and he wished he could see inside her brain just to get a glimpse of the way it worked. "I'll put these steaks on the grill."

"Hmm."

He shook his head, amused she could fall that deeply into thought so fast.

For the next twenty minutes, he cooked and she never moved. When he set the plate in front of her, she looked up and blinked. Then gasped. "Oh, Caden, I'm so sorry. I got so immersed in thinking about the pictures on this thing that I . . ." She shrugged.

"Zoned out?"

"Something like that." Ava looked at the food and an audible rumble came from her stomach. She flushed and he laughed.

"I'll take that as a compliment."

"You should."

He blessed it and she cut a bite out of her steak. After chewing and swallowing, she closed her eyes and nodded. "Yep. You're hired."

"What?"

"As my personal chef."

He laughed. "I'd be happy to cook for you anytime, Ava."

Her eyes widened a fraction and then she smiled. "Well,

thanks. I may take you up on that." Then she sobered and her eyes went back to the puzzle. "As crazy as it sounds, I think I may know the password."

o o o

He stilled. "Okay."

Ava noted his reaction and picked up her fork. "I'll try it after we finish eating. I want to enjoy your efforts."

Twenty minutes later, she pushed her plate to the side. "I don't think I can wait any longer."

He huffed a short laugh. "I thought you'd never finish. Go, please."

While Caden watched, she went to the laptop and typed in the password. Her heart thudded and expectation hummed.

Caden's statement that he'd be happy to cook for her anytime resonated with her. She was almost tempted to analyze it and see if she could find a hidden message in his words. Then decided she was being silly. Not everything had a hidden message. Some messages were loud and clear. He was interested but wouldn't push her. And he'd cook for her if she'd let him. She would.

The password screen opened to the desktop and she let out a low laugh of disbelief. "Seriously, Dad?"

"You're in?"

"I'm in."

"How'd you know?"

"Every place on the puzzle is a location where we actually *did* a puzzle."

Caden frowned. She picked up the laptop and carried it to the table, sitting next to him so he could see. "Okay."

"And every time he presented me with a new puzzle, he had a phrase."

"Ah, and the password was the phrase."

184

"It was. I'vegotapuzzleforyou,Ava-girl. In Russian. Complete with punctuation." She shook her head. "It got so that when he walked in the door with a puzzle in hand, I'd try to beat him to the saying. We'd wind up saying it together and have a good laugh. Right up until about a month before he was . . . before he . . . died." Dead, but no body to bury. She frowned and shook her head. He was gone.

Wasn't he?

"So," Caden said, "what about the other things on the puzzle? Even I can recognize that the letters are part of the Russian alphabet, but no clue what they mean. And what about the blueprint?"

"I think the letters were to let me know if I figured out the password, I had to enter it using the Russian keyboard. The blueprint is familiar, but I can't place it."

"It's a house," he said, "but not the one you grew up in."

"No. It's definitely a different floor plan. And it's not the one he had in Virginia either."

He sat back. "All right, you ready to see what's on the laptop? Maybe that will answer some of the questions."

She drew in a deep breath and nodded. "Sure."

She ran her finger over the trackpad to wake up the screen and pulled up the password box once more, entered the phrase, and stared at the desktop. "Okay, Dad," she whispered, "what am I looking for?"

"He's got folders all labeled in Russian," Caden said. "My skills are rusty, can you interpret?"

"Rusty?"

"Okay, nonexistent. Can you help me out?"

She moved the cursor over the first little blue file icon in the right-hand corner of the screen. "Why don't we just start clicking through them?"

"Perfect."

For the next twenty minutes, she continued to click while her mind raced. "Okay, this is getting us nowhere," she muttered. "Let's try something else."

"Is it just me or is there not a lot on there."

She checked the hard drive space. "Good observation. While it doesn't look like there's a lot from this vantage point, the storage meter says there's quite a bit. I just have to find it." She yawned and took a sip of her Coke. "Sorry."

"Should we try again after you get some rest?"

"No way. We've come this far, I'm not stopping now."

"I'm going to check in with Daria and see if we've got anything on the mask or the face."

Ava nodded and kept her attention on the screen. When she moved on to the search history, she straightened. Her father knew to clear the history and how to do a good job of it so no one would be able to find it. But Ava found quite a few websites that sparked her interest.

Scuba diving equipment?

A wet suit?

Air tank?

She sucked in a sharp breath and scooted back. "He's not dead," she said. "Caden, he's not dead."

"Hold on, Daria." Caden looked over at Ava. "What?"

"My father. He's alive and I think he wanted me to figure that out."

SEVENTEEN

The complete lack of color in Ava's face worried him. "Hang on a sec, Daria." He walked over to Ava and sat beside her to place a hand on her shoulder. "Ava? You okay?"

She swallowed, her eyes wide, still on the laptop screen. "He's not dead. He's really alive." A tear slid down her cheek and she swiped it away.

"Who's not dead?" Daria asked.

Caden muted his phone. "Ava? Look at me."

She blinked and stood. Raked a hand over her sloppy ponytail. She spun and gripped the back of the chair and met his eyes. "I have to find him."

He held up a finger. "Hold on just a second. Let me finish talking to Daria and then you can show me what you found. Okay?"

"Yes. Yes, of course. I'm sorry. Finish your call." Color had crept back into her cheeks and now her eyes sparked with renewed life. She settled back into her chair and swiped a finger over the trackpad to bring up the screen once more. "I'm going to keep searching and see if I can learn anything else."

"Okay. Good." He unmuted Daria. "I'm back. What were you saying?"

"Everything okay?"

"For the moment."

"All right, well, anyway, I sent this to Zane, but he may be passed out somewhere, thanks to his cold medication. Facial recognition got a hit, but we might need Ava to verify. There were several to choose from. I had our forensic artist take a look, and she said she had no doubt it was the first one the system found."

Caden straightened. "Who?"

"A guy by the name of Nicolai Kuznetsov."

"Wait a minute. Isn't that the last name of the—"

"Couple found dead in New Mexico? Yeah."

"Whoa." Okay, he had to admit that one had come out of left field for him.

"I know, right? Here's the big one, though. Brace yourself."

"I'm braced."

"The mask had some DNA on it, but the person isn't in the system."

Shocking. They couldn't expect to be that lucky twice, could they?

"However," she said, "it does match DNA found at a particular crime scene."

"Which one?"

"The couple who was found dead in New Mexico."

"What!"

Ava's eyes went wide at his shout.

"The couple who was—"

"I heard you."

Daria fell silent and so did he. Then he realized Ava was still watching him. "So, the mask that Ava pulled off the guy in the hospital has DNA that matches the crime scene in New Mexico."

"Yes."

"Wow." Now they were getting somewhere. "How is Nicolai related to the dead couple?"

"Looks like a son. Not the one they called to the crime scene. That was Yvonne's kid. Nicolai is a son from another woman." Daria paused. "I just don't know who yet, but I will. Talk to you when I know more."

She hung up and Caden did the same with a frown, then filled Ava in. "So, this Nicolai went to his father's home and killed them. Then set out on a killing spree that spans all over the US." He paused. "What in the world did that father do to send his kid over the edge and incite him to murder?"

"Not just murder," Ava said. "Suicide. He killed himself. Why? What could your son do or say that would be so awful that you would rather kill yourself than face it?" Ava shook her head. "I can't imagine."

Caden narrowed his eyes. "Okay, your turn. Why do you think your father's alive?"

o o o

"Because of all of the scuba stuff that he bought about a week before he supposedly died." Ava drew in a deep breath and scrubbed a hand down her cheek. She might have been tired earlier, but her adrenaline was now surging like nobody's business. She was wide awake and ready for action. "Where did they get Nicolai's picture for the facial recognition database?"

"Looks like they flagged him at the airport about eight months ago. He flew in from Japan, I believe."

"Japan!"

"Yes, why?"

Ava pushed the laptop to the side and leaned forward. "Caden, my father was on the Donghae–Vladivostok ferry. He was headed to Donghae when he went over the side. And you're telling me this Nicolai Kuznetsov flew to the United States from the same place my father was headed?" She scoffed. "I'm having a hard time believing that was a coincidence."

"I would have to agree that it seems a bit of a stretch."

"A major stretch." She paused. "Can you get the security footage from the airport? I want to watch it and see if my father arrived around that time."

Caden hesitated, then nodded. "That would prove without a doubt that he's still alive, wouldn't it?"

"Yes."

"All right. Let me make some calls."

While he got on his phone, Ava went back to the laptop. Folder after subfolder, file after hidden file, she worked her way through the conglomeration of information. Her father had tons of documents and intelligence that she sifted through, scanning for something that would capture her attention. Finally, with the next click, she straightened. "Caden?"

He was at her side in an instant. "You found something?"

"Maybe."

He sat next to her and she pulled up the black-and-white photo. "Wonder if that's the picture that disappeared from the Fields home."

He pointed. "And that looks suspiciously like a young Jesse Fields."

"Maybe we need to make another trip to ask him a few more questions?"

Caden sighed. "I'm not sure that's going to accomplish much." He paused. "But what if we get his wife alone? She seemed like she might have something to say before Jesse shut her down."

Ava raised a brow. "That's a possibility, but how do you plan to do that? Jesse seems to hover pretty close."

He rubbed his chin. "Yes, he does. Maybe there's a reason for that other than offering comfort." He studied the picture. "There are five men. The one on the left is the one whose family was killed in San Diego. The one beside him was Houston. The next one was Jesse."

"He's killing them in order of the picture," she whispered.

"What?" He blinked. "I don't think so. The fourth family killed was the sister of the San Diego family. Wouldn't she have been second?"

"Maybe." She shrugged. "What if she wasn't home and he had to move on?"

He frowned. "But he's obviously been watching and studying these families. He'd know if she was going to be home or not." He paused. "Unless she broke routine and he had to adjust the plan."

"It happens all the time."

"Yes," he said, "it does. I'll get Daria to check." He tapped the request, then turned back to the picture. "This is getting awfully convoluted. Who are the fourth and fifth guys in this photo, I wonder?"

"I don't know, but we need to find out quickly and warn them to protect their families."

"Assuming it's not too late," he muttered. "Can you send me the picture? I'll have Daria run them through facial recognition and see if she can track them down."

"Of course." She logged into her own email account and sent him the photo.

While he busied himself once more with his phone and contacting Daria, Ava went back on the hunt. Two hours later, Caden was in her recliner napping while he waited for a response from Daria, and Ava finally stood up from the computer to stretch and rub her eyes.

Despair hit her hard. She was no closer to finding an answer to where her father could be hiding out or what the blueprint picture on the puzzle could mean.

Caden lowered his feet with a thud, and she jumped. "You okay?" she asked.

"Yeah. Got that footage from the airport from Daria."

"I have an adapter. Can you plug it in to my television so we can watch it on a larger screen?"

"Sure."

She got it for him and within seconds was watching the footage from the airport about eight months ago—two weeks after her father was reported missing and presumed dead.

"Daria managed to find the place where they got a good shot of Nicolai's face for the software," Caden said. "I told her we'd scan backward from there."

"He used his real name and passport, didn't he?"

"He did. Guess he didn't think it mattered." The video played and for the next hour, they watched the twenty-four-hour period prior to Nicolai's arrival at JFK airport until Caden pressed pause. "There."

"What? Where? Did I actually miss him?"

"It was a brief flash, but I think so." He rewound and played it while Ava leaned forward as though that would help her see better.

But she finally caught a glimpse of the man he was talking about. "I don't know, Caden. That's awfully iffy. It's mostly the back of his head." But it *could* be. She desperately wanted it to be. "Can you keep going backward? See if we can get him coming off the jetway?"

Caden pressed the rewind button and the video jerked backward.

"How about that one?" he asked.

Ava stared, her jaw dropping. Her father's face appeared on the screen. Larger than life and definitely alive.

o o o

"I knew it," she whispered. "I knew it." A sob slipped from her and she pressed her fingers to her lips. "I was too scared to believe it, but deep down, I knew."

Caden swiped a thumb over her cheek before the tear had a chance to drip from her chin. "If your father has gone to these lengths to fake his death, then Nicolai must be after him."

"But how did he survive? I saw the video. John showed it to me," she said, her voice low. "And I bought it."

"Not completely, you didn't." He paused. "You think he doctored it?"

"I don't know what to think." She picked up her phone and tapped her chin. "How do I approach this?" He raised a brow and she shrugged. "I could come right out and ask him, but he'd just deny it."

"Ava, can I ask you a question?"

"Of course."

"Who do you trust?"

She blinked. Once, twice, then looked away. Then back. "You. I trust you."

Her words slammed into him with the punch of a tsunami, scattering every sensible thought and emotion and leaving him reeling in the aftermath. "What about Sarah? Heather? Brooke?"

"Yes. Up to a point. But the problem is, I've never been able to *fully* trust them. I know they care about me. I know they love me. I know they trust *me*. The problem is, I've had to be so careful with what I said that I could never let myself be vulnerable with them."

"Because of your father."

She nodded.

He shook his head, unable to fathom not being able to trust

those you loved. "And the main reason you never go on a second date?"

"No, it's the main reason I've never gone on a *third* date. I've had the occasional second one."

"Oh, right. You're going to marry the guy who gets the third date."

She narrowed her eyes, then huffed a short laugh. "Quit messing with me."

He nudged her. "Come on, it's making you feel better, isn't it?"

"A bit." Her smile faded. "But John's going to give me some answers. Maybe by calling him this early, I'll catch him off guard." She tapped the number and waited. "Come on, come on." Just when Caden figured she'd have to leave a voice mail, she said, "Hi, John, it's me." She put it on speaker and set the phone on the table.

"Ava."

The man sounded aloof, chilly. Not like she'd just pulled him out of a deep slumber. She must have thought so, too, as she grimaced and shot him a glance. "I . . . want to ask you something."

"All right."

"When you came to my house and showed me the video of my dad falling off the ferry, I was . . . in shock."

"I'm sure." His voice warmed a few degrees. "Maybe I shouldn't have shown you the footage, but I didn't figure you'd believe it if you didn't see it."

"I know. You were right. I wouldn't have. I know you want me to leave things alone. And maybe I should." Caden could see where she was going and was impressed that she never actually lied. "But I think I need to see that video again. I think it will help me come to terms with . . . things. Can you send it to me?"

A long pause followed her words.

Then a heavy sigh. "Yeah. Sure. If you think that will help."

"I really think it will."

Another pause. "I can't decide if you're playing me or not."

A short laugh escaped her. "Playing you? Because I want to see a video of my father falling to his death? Right. Thanks, John. Have a good rest of your day." She hung up and Caden gaped.

"Okay," he said, "I didn't expect that. What now?"

"We wait for him to send the video." Caden snapped his lips shut about the time her phone pinged. She waved it at him. "And there it is."

"Once again, I'm not sure whether to be impressed by you or scared of you."

She bit her lip and her eyes clouded. "And there you have it."

"What?" He frowned.

"Why I don't do relationships. I'm too much a product of my upbringing."

Caden wanted to slap himself. "Ava, that's not what I meant, by any stretch of the imagination. I think you're absolutely amazing. I mean I thought you were incredible and wonderful before all of this. Now, I just admire you even more."

She gave him a sad smile and reached out to cup his cheek. "You're a good man, Caden. A wonderful man, really. Any girl would be blessed to call you hers."

"But not you?"

Her eyes widened and she cleared her throat. "Of course I would be. But you don't deserve to wonder if I'm playing you every time I ask you for something."

Anger flashed. Mostly at Ava's father for not shutting her down the minute he learned of her hacking and snooping. "Wow. You really think I would go there? Glad to know you think so much of me."

He might as well have reached out and slapped her. The stricken look in her eyes said his barb had found its target.

He sighed. "Ava, I'm sorry, that's—"

She looked away. "Let's just watch the video, then you can go."

His phone buzzed and he let out a harsh sigh, swiped the screen, and barked, "What?"

"Dad's had a heart attack," Sarah said. "He's on his way to the hospital."

Caden bolted to his feet and Ava's eyes went wide. "I'm on the way," he told his sister. To Ava, he said, "I've got to get to the hospital. Dad's had a heart attack." His own heart threatened to jackhammer out of his chest.

"I've got to go," Sarah said.

Ava grabbed her purse and darted for the door. "Let's go."

EIGHTEEN

Caden used his hazards and horn and flashed his lights as he sped through town, parting traffic much like she envisioned God must have divided the Red Sea. Ava clutched the handle attached to the roof of the car to keep from slamming against the door.

"I knew he wasn't feeling well," he said, "but in no way did I think it was this serious."

"That's the general for you."

"No kidding." His jaw flexed. "He's never been one to let on when he was feeling bad. I should have known when he let Sarah take him to the doctor that something was wrong."

His phone rang while he took a turn a little faster than Ava would have liked, but she understood his rush. She tapped the screen for him and he shot her a look of thanks.

"Caden here."

"It's Daria." Her voice filled the car's space.

"I know. I've got you programmed in my phone."

"I'm honored. Okay, so do you have a minute?"

"I have about seven minutes and then I'm going to be offline for a while." He told her about his dad.

"Oh no. I'm so sorry. All right, I'll talk fast. According to a neighbor I managed to track down, Bridgette O'Reilly and her three children of Portland, Oregon, took an emergency trip to Houston when she heard her brother and his family had been murdered. After everything was over, she and her children returned home, and she confided in the same neighbor that she couldn't go back to work yet. She was having a very hard time coming to terms with their deaths and had decided to take an impromptu trip to her parents' second home in New York. She chartered a plane and there they stayed for a few weeks. The day she and the kids returned, they were killed."

"He was waiting on them," he said. "He knew their itinerary. How?"

"She had it on her refrigerator for the neighbor who was coming over to take care of the cat, so if he was in their house beforehand . . ."

"Right. Were their deaths before or after the Fields family was killed?" he asked. His eyes scanned the road, and while he drove with skill and precision, Ava knew he was using the call to keep from worrying about his father. She wasn't sure it was working.

"Before," Daria said. "However, they were *found* after the deaths of the Fields family. But you know that."

He raked a hand through his hair, then down his cheek. "All right, thanks, Daria."

"I'm still working on gathering information about your guy Nicolai. I hope to have something soon."

"I'm heading into the hospital. I have a feeling this might wind up being a 'hurry up and wait' kind of thing. If I don't answer a call, definitely text."

"Will do." She paused. "I'm saying a prayer for your father."

"Thanks, Daria," he said, his voice suddenly slightly husky. "I appreciate it."

He hung up and nodded to Ava. "Wait for me to come around and get you, okay?"

She raised a brow. "Okay."

He opened her door and leaned in a fraction. "I'm sorry, Ava. I didn't mean to be harsh."

"You weren't harsh. No apologies necessary."

He offered her a strained smile and held out a hand. She placed hers into his and he helped her out of the seat. Then he shut the door and slid an arm around her shoulders, tucking her close. No doubt thinking he was protecting her in case there was a sniper trying to get a bead on her.

While Ava considered herself self-sufficient and able to take care of herself, she wasn't opposed to his help. Or being this close to him. In fact, she liked it just fine. What she didn't like was him putting himself in danger with his protection.

He held the glass door open for her and she slipped into the air-conditioned chill of the hospital. Together, they made their way to the emergency room waiting area, where they found Sarah and Gavin sitting next to each other, holding hands. Sarah looked up and her eyes connected with her brother's. "You came."

"Of course I did." He frowned and Ava's heart hurt for him. He was batting a thousand today for getting his feelings knocked around. She squeezed his hand.

Sarah blinked and sniffed. "Sorry. I didn't mean . . ." She waved a hand. "Of course, I knew you'd come. I don't know why I said that."

"So what's the verdict?"

She shrugged. "I don't know anything yet. They're still back there working on him."

Gavin rose. "I'm going to go grab coffee for all of us." He looked at Caden. "Two creams, no sugar." Then turned to Ava. "Black and loaded with sugar?"

She gave him a small smile. "Yeah. Thanks."

He leaned over and kissed Sarah's forehead. "Hang in there, hon, the general's one of the most stubborn men I know."

Sarah nodded and bit her lip. "Yeah."

She stood as Gavin headed down the hall toward the cafeteria, and Caden stepped forward to hug his sister. She leaned her head against his chest and Ava looked away. She and Nate were so far apart in age, she felt more like his mother than his sister. She'd had to adopt that role at an early age, thanks to their mother's alcoholism battle. She pulled her phone from her purse and sent him a simple text.

I'm thinking of you and I love you.

There, that was more sisterly than motherly, wasn't it? Or maybe it was a bit of both, but hopefully, he'd take it as it was intended.

"Hey, guys."

Ava turned to see Brooke with her very round tummy coming toward them. She embraced them all, then took a seat with a sigh and put her feet up on the chair opposite her.

Caden shook his head. "You didn't have to come down here, Brooke."

"Oh, please. I wanted to. Asher would have come too, but he and Travis are working security for someone." She eyed them. "How's the general?"

"We're still waiting to hear," Ava said, taking a nearby chair.

Sarah settled next to Ava and took her hand. "How are you doing?"

Ava shrugged. "I'm hanging in there. Glad Caden has allowed me to help him on this case some." And very anxious to watch the video burning a hole in her phone.

"Yeah, he's told me a little about that, but not much. He's

been very tight-lipped about it." She stuck her tongue out at her brother and he rolled his eyes.

The levity was a coping mechanism. They meant no disrespect to their father. Ava knew that and offered the siblings a smile.

Caden's phone rang and he snagged it. "Hi, Daria. Hold on a second."

"She found something else?" Ava asked.

"I'm going to find out. Come get me if the doctor comes out about Dad, will you?"

"Of course," Sarah said.

He walked to the corner of the waiting room and leaned a tense shoulder against the wall. Ava's phone buzzed and she glanced at the screen.

> Nate
>
> Love you too, big sis. I really do. I also appreciate you. And no, NOTHING IS WRONG, I promise. Just had a bit more sleep yesterday and I'm feeling generous.

Ava bit her lip on a laugh, relief flooding her. He was a good kid. He'd be okay. She shot a glance at Caden. His broad shoulders had slumped, as though he simply had too much weight on them, and while he was strong, Ava sighed, wishing she could do something to help. Anything to take some of the stress from him. But for now, she'd simply be here and support him. Exactly what he'd do for her.

o o o

Nicolai stood in his special room and inhaled. It had taken him months to put this together. He strolled to the instrument wall and stroked the collection of knives he'd hung from largest to smallest.

Next, he envisioned what he could do with the saw. But he would only use that as a last resort. Maybe to help hide the body when he was done. He doubted he'd need it, but it was good to be prepared. Then there was the assortment of whips. He even had a cat-o'-nine-tails he'd crafted himself.

Everything was in order. He thought about using it on his current prisoner, but Nicolai would have to move the man to this room, and he simply didn't want to take a chance on him escaping. Because as soon as he was out of the room next door, he would attempt it.

When he'd started on his quest for justice for his family, he'd never envisioned this type of thing. But slowly, his vision had changed after learning about his enemy's daughter.

Nicolai turned and walked to the table at the center of the room. His masterpiece. He checked the straps by pulling as hard as he could. They held strong. He had a stack of candles that he would place around the table and light them to give the room an eerie atmosphere. Not only was he going to physically torture his intended target until he became bored, but toying with her mentally might actually be more fun.

He stilled and rolled that word over in his head. *Fun?*

Since when had the killing become something he enjoyed?

Interesting. He'd have to examine that emotion later.

Nicolai made sure the television on the wall was on and that the camera was positioned just right, then walked to the door and turned once more to survey his handiwork. Yes, it had all come together nicely.

Now to find Ava Jackson and put it to use.

□ □ □

Caden pressed the phone to his ear once more. "Okay, Daria, what's going on?"

"I'm sorry to bother you while you're dealing with your dad, but I can't get ahold of Zane. I think he's still down for the count with that cold."

"That's okay. I'm in wait mode anyway. Fill me in." He glanced over his shoulder and saw the ladies huddled together. Good, they would keep Sarah occupied. He noted Gavin's stance, his attention focused on the door.

He could focus on Daria's words because no one was going to get to Ava right now.

". . . looks like we've got a possible location on Nicolai."

"Where?"

She gave him the address. "It's a rental, but it's not in his name. Once I knew who he was, I was able to go in and find out all kinds of stuff about him. His family died when he was ten years old, and he was shipped off to live with an aunt in Kostroma. She's a descendant of the Romanovs, never married, and had no children. But she had tons of old family money—like 'many, many millions' tons. Reports are that she doted on Nicolai. He excelled in school in spite of the tragic loss of his family, went on to university, and graduated with honors about two years ago."

"Graduated in what field?"

"Computer science."

"So, he's definitely smart."

"Very."

"How did his family die? That's waving a huge red flag for me. He has a dead family and he's killing families. There's got to be some connection."

She sighed. "That's where it gets kind of muddy. Some reports say it was an intruder. Others say it was a car accident. One report even says it was a murder-suicide by his mother."

"She killed the kids and then herself."

"Maybe. But the house burned down, too, with all of them in it. So, who knows? It's like they threw out the causes and said, 'Pick one.'"

"Well, regardless of how they died, they're still dead and that would mess with anyone's head."

Daria let out a humorless laugh. "Yes, well, not everyone with a tragic childhood or past turns out to be a serial killer."

Caden flinched. "Daria, I didn't mean to—"

"Forget it. I don't think about it most days."

Daria's father had been as evil as anyone Caden had ever encountered. And she'd helped bring him to justice, earning herself hero status in his eyes—and a place at the Bureau. He didn't quite buy that she was past thinking about it most days.

"You've learned from your experiences and are a better person because of them," he said. "Don't let anyone tell you any different."

"Thanks, Caden, I'm fine. So, anyway, back to the aunt. Her name is Vanya Tunicova. Nicolai's mother was her sister. In the last six months, she's rented short term. Some are extended-stay hotels, others are corporate apartments, and one was an Airbnb she stayed in for about a month. All of her moves correspond to the killings."

Finally. "He's moving her with him, letting her rent the places and keeping his name out of it. Is the address you gave me an Airbnb?"

"It is."

"Is Nicolai staying with her?"

Another sigh. "I've been unable to confirm that. Right now, there are two agents watching the house, as well as local police."

"All right, tell them not to spook her. I want to talk to her."

"Well, good luck. I put on my acting hat and my Southern accent and called the Airbnb landline. She answered, and I asked her about speaking to the man of the house about a food service with home delivery. She spat a flurry of Russian at me, and while I understood every word she said, I pretended like I didn't just in case it would tip her off."

"What'd she say?"

"Nothing earth shattering. Basically, that she didn't need a man to tell her if she could order food, that she was the one who cooked and put the food on the table, and that if she wanted to sign up, she would. She also mentioned that I needed to join the current century and realize that women were allowed to use their brains and make decisions for themselves. On and on about that until she finally hung up. So, sorry, I didn't get a good feel for whether Nicolai was there or not. However, local officers are on the way to assess the situation and see if they can find out for sure."

"Good." He thought about it with one eye on the ladies and one on the woman at the desk in the waiting area. All information went through her. If the doctor wanted them to know something, she'd get the call. "Listen, I can't leave until I know whether my father is going to live or die. Zane is on sick leave. Frank Green is familiar with this case. Can he go out and question the woman?"

"Not without an interpreter."

Caden rubbed his eyes. "Okay, what about a contract linguist?"

He could hear the clicking on the keyboard. "Yeah, but not one close by." More clicking. "It will take someone a while to get there. Even pushing the paperwork through and all that, it'll be several hours."

He sighed. "Fine. You get it arranged and we'll have to pray he's not out there killing again while we're waiting."

"Or . . ." She drew out the word.

"Or what?"

"You could use Ava. I'm sure we could add linguist to her consultant contract pretty easily."

"Um, no. We're not using Ava."

"Use me for what?"

Caden's head snapped up to see Ava holding two cups of coffee. "Oh, hey."

"She heard you, didn't she?" Daria asked.

"Yes."

Ava raised a brow at him and handed him his coffee. He sighed. "If I tell you what we don't want to use you for, you're probably going to insist we do it, aren't you?"

Amusement flickered in her eyes. "It's kind of scary how well you've gotten to know me."

"He'd recognize you."

She shrugged. "I'll wear a disguise. A wig, a hat, and some sunglasses should do the trick. Who will recognize me and what do I need a disguise for?"

"Ava—"

She simply stared at him and he groaned. His stress level was going to kill him if nothing else did. Into the phone, he said, "Daria, I guess you'd better run that contract linguist thing by Gary."

She snickered, then cleared her throat. "I'm on it."

He hung up and turned to Ava, who had her arms crossed and that brow still as far north as it could go. "What are you not wanting to use me for?"

He rubbed his forehead, wishing he had a few ibuprofen he could pop, but told her what Daria had found out and what he was thinking. "I would go with you," he said, "but I don't feel like I can leave just yet. Frank is a top-notch agent. He'll watch out for you and you'll have backup close by if anything—" He scowled. "But nothing is going to happen, so it's fine. Right?"

"Of course. So, if Nicolai's not there, you think the aunt might know where he is and you want to do a kind of recon?"

"Something like that. We've got agents and local officers watching, but I don't want to scare him off by approaching or using direct force if we don't have to. I don't want to run the risk of the aunt being an innocent pawn in all of this."

She shrugged. "I'm happy to help."

"I'm shocked."

She wrinkled her nose at him. "So, when do we do this?"

"I'll let you know." He spotted the doctor at the door, his gaze roaming the waiting room. When the lady at the desk pointed at Sarah, Caden took Ava's hand and led her to join the group.

Sarah stood, coffee cup in one hand, Gavin's fingers gripped tight with the other. "Well?"

The doctor sighed. "It's hard to say what's going to happen at this point. He's definitely had a heart attack. It was touch and go for a while there, but we've got him stable for now and are transferring him to surgery. He's got a ninety-five percent blockage in two arteries."

Sarah gasped. "Can we see him?"

"He's unconscious. I'd rather you wait until we get him through surgery. He'll be in ICU for a while after that."

Sarah bit her lip and nodded. "Who's the cardiologist?"

"Dr. Dale Haywood. He's the best."

Caden felt Ava's hand slip from his. "I'll want to double-check that with Heather." He glanced at Ava and noticed her texting.

She looked up, caught him watching, and waved her phone at him. She'd texted Heather almost before he'd finished forming the sentence.

The woman continued to stupefy him. How had she known? It didn't matter. Hopefully, Heather would answer within the next few minutes, or his father was going into surgery with someone whose track record they didn't know.

And while his father was fighting for his life, Caden would be fighting to catch a killer before he struck again.

NINETEEN

Four hours later, Ava sat with Sarah and Brooke, itching to pull her phone out and watch the video John had sent but didn't feel like she should, while Caden paced and Gavin examined something on his phone. Every once in a while Caden would walk over and sit next to her and take her hand in his. Then he'd give her fingers a squeeze, rise, and resume his trek from one side of the waiting room to the other.

She didn't mind waiting with Caden. On the contrary, she was more than happy she could be here for him.

But the thought of her father being alive wouldn't leave her alone. Where was he? Why hadn't he tried to get in touch with her? Was he okay? In danger? What was her next step in locating him?

"Ava?"

She jerked from her thoughts and lifted her eyes to find Sarah next to her. Brooke had disappeared, but a small smile curved Sarah's lips. "She's in the bathroom."

Again. "Bless her."

The smile flipped. "What's going on with you, Ava?"

"What do you mean?"

"We haven't had a chance to have a good discussion." Sarah glanced at her watch. "The doctor said it could be another hour and I've been thinking."

Uh-oh. "About?"

"You've never said why someone's been attacking you. Why your mom and Nathan might be in danger. Even Gavin said Caden's been vague and noncommittal."

And yet, her friends continued to help without knowing all the details. She shook her head, more grateful than she could express. But now that her father might still be alive, she had to revert back to her secrets. Her lies.

Didn't she? What could she say?

As much of the truth as she could. She cleared her throat. "I'll explain as much as I can if you promise not to ask questions about anything you don't understand."

"Oookay. I'll do my best."

Ava nodded and rubbed her eyes. "My father used to work for the government years ago." Sarah's brows rose, but she stayed silent. "His travel writing was a cover to explain away his many absences—although," Ava continued, "he did do the travel writing, too, simply because he enjoyed it." Which was true, because he'd often read them to her before sending them off to his editor—or whoever. "Anyway, before he died, he must have gotten involved with some sketchy people, because they've now started coming after me. And the case that Caden's working on is somehow connected to whatever my father was involved in."

Sarah's eyes widened. "Sketchy people who do what?" She clapped a hand over her mouth. "Can I ask that?"

"Sure. Unfortunately, I don't know. That's the problem. But Caden thought I could help them, so that's why we've been spending so much time together."

Sarah snorted. "That's not the only reason."

209

Heat climbed into Ava's neck and cheeks. "Hmm. Well, regardless, it *is* the main reason."

Sarah fell silent, then sat up and took Ava's hand in hers. Ava raised a brow and met Sarah's gaze.

"Ava," Sarah said. "You know I love you. You're the sister I never had and always wanted."

"I feel the same."

"But if you break my brother's heart, I'll have to hurt you."

Ava's jaw dropped and Sarah's lips twitched, but her eyes glinted with worry. Ava squeezed her friend's hand. "I love Caden, Sarah, I always have. You know that."

"You've loved him as a brother."

"No, that's not true. I had a vicious crush on him as a teenager."

"Oh yeah, I remember that. I used to be jealous that you liked him so much."

"What?" Ava laughed. "You never let on."

Sarah shrugged. "I didn't want to lose your friendship. I knew you liked Caden, but I knew you genuinely liked me, too, and weren't trying to use me to get to him."

"Like a lot of girls did," Ava said, her voice soft. "I remember."

"It's just that you don't date, and I'm worried he's going to fall for you." She paused. "If he hasn't already."

"He knows how I feel about dating. We've discussed it."

Sarah blinked. "Oh."

"Please don't worry. We'll be all right." She hoped.

"Sorry if I was sticking my nose in where it didn't belong."

Ava almost laughed. "You're a journalist. I don't think it's something you can help."

"Hey, now . . ." Sarah sighed and looked away, her gaze turning anxious once more.

Ava scanned the waiting room to find Caden talking to a man in his midforties. The newcomer had on khakis and a black shirt advertising a food delivery service. Wow, that was fast. Special Agent Frank Green?

Caden caught her eye and waved her over.

She patted Sarah's hand. "Hang in there, my friend. I'm going to see what Caden wants." She walked over to the men and Caden made the introductions.

Frank nodded. "Glad to meet you."

"And you."

Caden looked at her. "Are you sure you're up for this?"

"I can do it." If it would bring her one step closer to finding her father, she could do just about anything.

"All you have to do," Frank said, "is just tell me what she's saying."

Caden shifted and shoved his hands in the front pockets of his jeans. "I don't like this." He looked at the agent. "Can't you wear an earpiece and a mic so she can hear and just tell you what the woman is saying?"

Ava laughed. "Caden, come on. How's he supposed to answer her? Of course I have to be there."

"She'll have on a wire too," Frank said. "Backup will be seconds away."

"A lot can happen in a few seconds," Caden said, his voice hard.

Ava laid a hand on his arm and squeezed. "I'll be fine. Like Frank said, there will be cops and feds all over the place."

"I still don't like it. Things could go sideways and you're not a trained agent."

"No, I'm not, but I *am* a world-class liar, so I think I'll do just fine."

◦ ◦ ◦

Ava's frosty words stopped him and he sighed. "That's how you describe yourself. No one else would. Ava, I'm sorry, I'm just not comfortable with this."

"You don't have to be. All you have to do is remember that I'm very capable of taking care of myself and trust me—and the agent that you requested for this, not to mention all of the backup—to do it."

He'd thought he'd be all right leaving her in the hands of an extremely capable agent. He wasn't. But she was right. He thought about going with them, but while Sarah had Gavin there for support, Caden had to stay.

The general was still his father, regardless of their rocky relationship. If Caden left and the man died, he'd never forgive himself. Then again, if something happened to Ava . . . "Fine. You're right. Just text often." He paused. "Or better yet, call and leave your phone on so I can listen in."

"If I can do it, I will," Ava said.

That helped. Sort of.

With his heart in his throat, he watched them leave, heads bent, already working on their plan.

"You can go with them," Sarah said from behind him.

He turned, her pale face and worried eyes searing him. "No, I can't. What if he—"

"Then I'll call you."

"But—" They shared power of attorney and if worse came to worst . . .

"Frank's an excellent agent," he said. "I've worked with him numerous times. It will be fine."

She raised a brow, but whatever she was going to say was interrupted when a nurse in scrubs walked up to them.

"We're moving him to recovery in a few minutes," she said.

Caden put an arm around Sarah as they both took deep breaths. "How did he do?" Caden asked.

"The doctor will be out to see you soon and—"

Bells and alarms went off in the hallway. The nurse whirled

and ran, and medical personnel swarmed to the area, calling out orders, shouting for meds and a crash cart.

All Caden could do was hold his sister and pray.

o o o

Ava glanced at the man beside her in the silver SUV. He was good-looking in a rough sort of way. He sported a crooked nose, and a faint scar ran from his temple to his chin.

He caught her looking and smiled. "Knife fight with a mean dude who thought he could win."

"Looks like he almost did."

"Not even close."

"Hmm."

He laughed. "All right, it was close." He took a left at the next light, then glanced at her again. "So, tell me how you know Caden and why he's so twitchy about trusting me with your safety."

Ava gave a mental scoff and chose her words carefully, giving him the bare bones of the story, then asked, "What made you want to join the FBI?" By the time he finished telling her, he was pulling up next to a large van.

"This is the command center," he said. "Everyone here will be listening in. Agents will be standing by ready to storm the place if necessary."

"Let's hope it won't be."

"Exactly. The home sits on three acres and has a barn in the back. It's a lakefront property with a dock. From what I've been told, there's no security system per se, but it looks like he's got some homemade alerts rigged."

"Lovely. Any drones in sight?"

He gave her a tight smile. "I heard about that little adventure, but you'll be happy to know we've not seen any drones."

"Then I should be fine."

"Okay, so we're going to drive right up and knock on the

front door. I'll start talking, and when she responds in Russian, you take over. When she asks you how you know Russian, you can tell her—"

"My family was from Moscow."

"And if she starts talking about all the cool places there?"

"I can handle it, I promise." Her father had made certain she knew the city as well as he did. Because he actually loved everything about it. The history, the culture, and the innocent people who weren't involved in the whole game-of-spies thing. And he'd passed that on to her.

In the command vehicle, Ava met the other agents, and they went through the plan several more times before she was out-fitted with a wire. "Now," one of the agents said, "I'll be able to hear you and you'll be able to hear me. And you and Frank will be able to hear each other. If you hear my voice, I might be communicating with Frank or someone else on the team. If that happens, just be sure not to give away the fact that someone's talking in your ear."

"Got it."

In spite of her brave words, her heart pounded in her throat. It had been so long since she'd had a good night's sleep, and she was pulling on all the reserves to battle the exhaustion yanking at her. What if she messed up and said the wrong thing? What if the aunt refused to speak to her? What if Nicolai was in the house and they just didn't know it? She touched the wig and the glasses and prayed it was good enough to hide her true identity.

Before she knew it, she found herself decked out in a GOOD-N-FAST uniform and headed up the drive with Frank beside her in the driver's seat.

She pressed her palms to her thighs and drew in a deep breath.

"You okay?" he asked.

"Yes. I'm ready to find this killer and see him in prison." Although, to be honest, she'd love a few moments alone with him—as long as he was tied up and harmless—so she could question him. There was the very real possibility he would know where her father was. Or at the least, if he was still alive.

She prepared herself for the fact that even if she got the chance to ask him, he might not tell her. Assuming he knew. And she was okay with assuming that.

At the top of the horseshoe-shaped drive, Frank parked, and she climbed out of the passenger seat. She shut the door and waited for him to walk around to join her. "Nice place," she said.

"Very."

The house was a two-story Victorian that looked like it had been renovated recently. In the distance, to her left, she could see a red barn and land that stretched to the edge of a wooden fence. Beyond that, to the right was Lake Savannah. The lake was huge, covering over two hundred miles of shoreland, numerous private islands, and several marinas.

"Do you see any booby traps?" she asked.

"Not yet."

Frank rang the bell and stepped back, clipboard in hand, pleasant expression on his face.

"Stay focused, you two. Here we go." The voice sounded way too close and Ava nearly jumped out of her skin. Then remembered the nearly invisible earpiece in her canal.

Ava pasted a smile on her lips and waited. Seconds later, she heard the footsteps on the hardwood. The curtain to her right moved and she gave the woman a small wave.

The door opened. A woman in her sixties—older than Ava had expected—dressed in jeans and a long-sleeved pink T-shirt, towered over Ava and would have met Frank eye to eye had she not been leaning on a cane. She also had a phone pressed to her ear. "Da," she said, "da. I know. It's fine. Of course. I will take care of everything. Please do not worry." She spoke in clipped Russian and Ava listened intently. "See you later." She hung up and raised a brow. "Da?" she asked. "I . . . speak no . . . English. Please. You go." The words were clear in spite of her heavy accent and Ava could tell she'd practiced them diligently.

Getting into her role, Ava smiled. "You're Russian?" she said perfectly in the foreign tongue.

"Da." The woman narrowed her eyes. "You speak it?"

"I do," Ava gushed. "It's so exciting to meet someone who does too. My name is Melissa. I studied it in high school and took a trip to Moscow when I was in college."

"Oh, Moscow. How I miss my great city." She placed a hand on her chest and closed her eyes as though remembering days gone by. Then she blinked and shook her head. "I am Vanya Tunicova. Very nice to meet you, Melissa. So, you are selling me something?"

"Not me, I'm in training, but this is Steve and he'd love to tell you about our product." Ava looked at Frank, repeating everything in English.

"It's a home food delivery service," he said. "I would very much appreciate the opportunity to tell you more about it if you're willing to listen." He held up his briefcase, indicating he had material he'd like to show her.

The woman hesitated.

"Get Frank inside if you can, Ava," the voice said in her ear. "She seems to like you."

Ava wasn't so sure about that. She translated Frank's words, then said, "You have a very lovely home."

"Bah." She waved a hand. "It's a rental until my nephew decides where he would like to settle down. We've moved and moved and moved. I'm very tired of it. I'm ready to go home to Moscow. He has promised it will be soon."

"I'm sorry."

Still she hesitated. "How do I know you're not here to rob an old lady?"

"Ah, I assure you, Ms. Tunicova, we're not here to rob you," Ava said, "but I certainly understand your hesitation. You have a lovely porch. We could sit out here instead?"

She translated everything for Frank—and the people listening in.

A harsh groan from someone in the van echoed in her ear, but it wouldn't do any good to insist they enter the home if the woman didn't want them there. At least if they were sitting on the porch, they could keep her occupied and talking. Or it could make them targets for a sniper named Nicolai. Ava wanted to slap her head and keep her mouth shut.

The woman stepped closer, her cane thumping on the wood floor. Her gaze held Ava's before she gave a low grunt. "You have nice eyes. You can come in to do your presentation."

"Well . . . thank you."

"Good job," the voice said. "You're a natural."

Ava did her best to keep her face neutral. She didn't want to be a natural. She wanted to find out where Nicolai was.

"Come in, come in." She waved them in, and Ava stepped into a foyer with an oversized chandelier hanging from the high ceiling. Ms. Tunicova led them into the formal sitting area to the left. She patted Ava's arm. "You sit there on the sofa." She motioned to the one under the window. Ava took some comfort in the fact that the blinds were closed. With her cane, Ms. Tunicova pointed and said to Frank, "You take that chair by the fireplace." Ava translated and Frank raised a brow but lowered himself into the assigned seat.

Using her cane as leverage, Ms. Tunicova settled herself beside Ava with a grunt and pulled an album from the coffee table in front of them. She handed the book to Ava. "Pleasure first, then business, da? Your food presentation can wait just a few minutes, okay?" She patted the album. "Open it, if you will?"

Ava shot a glance at Frank, and although he was frowning, he nodded. Ava flipped the cover open and recognized Red Square in Moscow. "It's beautiful."

The woman nodded and coughed, then touched her throat. "I left my water in the kitchen." She pulled the album from Ava's lap. "Would you be so kind as to get it for me?"

"Um . . . sure."

"Get it and see what you can see," the voice said.

Ava shot Frank a tight smile, rose, and walked into the mammoth kitchen. It was truly a gourmet space. But she wasn't here to admire the scenery. She spotted the cup on the counter and paused. The room off the kitchen stood open. She hurried to it.

"I need more time, Frank," she whispered.

"Ah, Ms. Tunicova," Frank said, "I have my translate app. Maybe we could talk a bit with that?"

"What a silly man," the woman muttered. "Melissa? Did you find it?"

"I did." Ava pushed the cup over, and the water splashed across the granite, ran down the cabinet, and onto the floor. "I'm so sorry, I spilled it! Let me clean this up and get you another glass. I'll be just a minute."

"There are paper towels where you can see them, I believe."

"Yes, ma'am," she called. "Okay, guys," she said in a soft voice, "there's a room off the kitchen. It doesn't look like hers."

"Good job, Ava. You're a natural. See what you can find."

Why did everyone keep saying she was a natural? "Frank," she whispered, "keep her occupied with the photo album, please. Use Google Translate or something. It's better than nothing."

He cleared his throat. "Hey, what is this?"

Ava heard the mechanical voice translating—not exactly accurate, but it got the point across.

"Oh, let me show you these pictures. They're from when I was a child."

While the woman droned on and Frank acknowledged her

monologue with a grunt every so often, Ava cleaned up the worst of the spill, dropped some paper towels over the water on the floor, then darted into the bedroom.

"Definitely a guy's room," she said, her voice soft. "He's a serious cologne lover. Whew. There are scrubs on the bed. I'm sure those are what he wore when he snuck into Mickey's room to kill him. And there's a desk." Heart in her throat, she made her way to it and pulled out her cell phone. She snapped a picture of the surface, then opened the top drawer. Nothing. She worked her way down and found . . . nothing.

She moved to the nightstand with one ear turned toward the door. "I'm almost done," she called. "Don't want to miss any and risk you slipping."

"That's fine, dear, thank you for your consideration," the woman answered. "I'll wait. Just enjoying my memories of Moscow with your friend."

Ava sprinted back to the room and went to the nightstand once more. She opened the drawer and stopped. A small calendar lay on top of everything. With no time to study it, she opened it to the current month and snapped a picture, then the next page, then the next. She closed it and shut the drawer.

She heard Frank gasp. "Frank?" Then the thud of the cane on the floor. What had she heard? "Frank," she whisper-hissed. "Answer me."

"Melissa? Do you need help?"

Ava's hands shook from the adrenaline coursing through her. She hurried from the room and stepped into the kitchen just in time to drop to the floor and grab the sopping paper towels. "No, ma'am, I've got it."

She wiped the rest of the water up and stood as the woman's cane rapped hard on the floor. "My dear, are you quite all right?"

"Ava," the voice said into her ear, "we haven't heard from Frank in too long. Check on him."

Ava tossed the paper towels into the trash and motioned to the woman. "Why don't we finish looking at that album, then my friend can do his presentation?"

When the knife appeared in the woman's hand, drawn from the top of the cane, all Ava could do was blink. "She has a knife!" she hissed in English.

"Your friend is out of commission for now," Ms. Tunicova said.

Ava could hear the agents scrambling in the background, the earpiece picking up their shouts and orders.

"Ava?" the voice said. "We're coming. Just hold on, help is on the way."

Spotting the bloodstain on the knife, Ava stumbled backward. "What did you do to him?"

"Nothing he didn't deserve for lying to me." She shook the cane at her. "I should blow you all up."

"Put the knife down, please," Ava said, her voice low, doing her best to keep her cool. "You don't need that." And Frank? What had she done to him?

"On the contrary, my dear Ava Jackson, I very much need this knife. Nicolai has promised me my pound of flesh and I intend to get it."

She'd seen through her disguise and knew her name. The woman had been playing them from the time she opened the door. "But why?" she whispered. "What did I do to you?"

"Not you. Your father."

"Where is he?"

"He's dead, you know that."

"Is he?"

The woman's strange smile sent goose bumps pebbling her skin. "And soon you will be too." She shook the fist with the cane piece once more. "One way or another."

"There are federal agents all over this property," Ava said, proud of herself for keeping her voice calm. "They've been listening in on everything and know you're here and they know you have a knife. So, why don't you put it down and save us all a lot of trouble?"

The woman screamed and charged at Ava, the knife aimed at her face.

Ava ducked, swung her arm around to land on the woman's wrist—just as her father taught her. Ms. Tunicova released another scream as the knife flew from her fingers and skidded under the table. She dove after it and Ava scrambled from the kitchen and into the sitting area. "Frank!"

The agent still sat in his chair, but blood dribbled from the corner of his mouth. He blinked and tried to say something. Ava ran to him, heard agents at the front door.

She turned to see Ms. Tunicova coming at her once more, eyes wild, mouth twisted in a soundless snarl, the knife held firmly and once again aimed at Ava.

TWENTY

The gunshot echoed through the room and the bullet whizzed past Caden's cheek and struck the woman. He swung his weapon up to the scene in front of him.

Nicolai's aunt had stumbled backward, but still held the knife above her head.

"Put the knife down!"

She gasped and spun, her arm lowering.

"Drop it! Now!"

He noticed the bright red stain spreading across her shoulder and down her arm. The knife tumbled from her fingers and hit the carpet with a dull thud. Caden darted forward, his weapon on her. Other agents rushed inside. "Take care of her," he said. He kicked the knife away while she leaned heavily on the cane with her good arm. Her other arm bled, but the bullet was a through and through, as it was now buried in the doorframe. She'd live.

She said something, but he didn't understand her words. Probably condemning them all to Hades. He hurried to the wounded agent while the others dealt with Ms. Tunicova. She didn't fight, just clutched that cane like it was her lifeline, refusing to let it go. "I need for walk," she said in English. "I need for walk." He wondered absently how many other English words she understood and spoke.

Her voice faded to the background as Frank's eyes locked on his, then closed. His gun slipped from his slack fingers and Caden grabbed it before it hit the floor.

He shoved it into his waistband, then holstered his own weapon. "Ava? You okay?"

She met his gaze for a brief second, then nodded and focused back on Frank. "Help me get him on the floor and raise his legs. Quickly!"

He hurried to follow her lead, and together they maneuvered Frank to the floor and Ava grabbed the pillows from the sofa to shove under his legs. "Where are the paramedics?"

"On the way."

"He's got a stab wound in his neck," she whispered. "And one in his chest. The one in his neck seems to be the worst. Put pressure there."

Caden pulled off his shirt and pressed it to the neck wound. "Hold on, buddy." He looked over his shoulder. "Get the paramedics in here now!"

Frank's eyelids fluttered and she stroked his cheek. "Shh. Be still, Frank. You're going to be okay." She looked up, tears swimming in her eyes. "He saved my life, Caden. She would have stabbed me, too, if he hadn't shot her."

He nodded, his heart racing at the mental picture.

"What are you doing here?" she asked.

"Sarah sent me. I'll explain later." Two paramedics pushed through, rolling a stretcher between them. When the lead paramedic dropped to the floor beside Frank, Caden moved and pulled Ava with him. "Let them do their job."

Ava pointed to Ms. Tunicova. "She knows something about my father." She pushed away from him to get to the woman's side. Two agents flanked Ms. Tunicova while she stooped over her cane. The knife had been sheathed in the top, but the rest of it did its job and kept her from falling to the floor.

Seeing Ava, she curled her lip. "He'll get you for this." She coughed and let out a wheezing sigh. She muttered something else and Ava narrowed her eyes.

"What did you say?"

She muttered the words again and coughed. Then cackled.

"Ten seconds?" Ava asked. "Ten seconds to what?"

"What does she mean?" Caden asked.

"No idea." Ava reached out to grip the woman's arm. "Tell me what you know about my father."

The agent held up a hand. "Ma'am, back up. We need to get her to the hospital to treat that arm, then she'll be available for questioning."

Ava glared. "You don't understand—"

Caden rested a hand on her shoulder. "Come on, Ava. Let them take her. We'll regroup and go question her after she's seen and in custody."

With a low, frustrated sound, Ava stepped back. The agents led the woman toward the front door. Her cane thumped the hard floor with each slow step, and Caden noticed Ava shudder with every thud.

"She knows what Nicolai is doing," Ava said. "She's aware and she's protecting him."

"We know that now. Nothing of that sort showed up when Daria did her investigation of the woman. I never would have agreed for you to walk into this kind of situation."

"You didn't know. No one did. I agreed to this, so don't dwell on it." She rubbed her eyes, then dropped her hand. "I'm grateful Frank intervened when he did." The cane pounded on the porch and Ava's frown deepened.

"What is it?" he asked.

"Something she said."

"What?"

"'I should blow you all up.'" Her eyes widened. "The cane, Caden."

"What about it?"

"Get it from her." She raced toward the door, with Caden behind her. "Get the cane from her!"

The old woman made a sudden spry movement and pulled away from the officers who held her, darting down the porch steps and onto the drive. Taking advantage of their surprise, she raced toward the dock and the boat.

"Stop her!" Caden called.

She turned. "I'll blow you up!" The English words echoed around them. "I'll blow you all up!" Her thumb moved as an agent from the left tackled her. She screeched and lay still.

Ava whirled. "Get out of the house now! She detonated it!"

"Ten seconds," Caden whispered to himself. He raced for the house. "It's a bomb! Get out of the house!"

That's what she'd muttered. In English. Ten seconds.

Ten.

"Get out! Get out!"

Agents scrambled out the door.

Eight.

The paramedics hit the front porch steps with Frank between them.

Seven.

Six.

"Go! Go! Five seconds!"

Four.

Three.

Two.

One.

A pause. Nothing.

Had he miscounted?

An explosion from the back of the house rocked the ground. The paramedic in the rear fell to his knees, then scrambled up, grabbed the stretcher, and raced for the ambulance.

"Run!" Caden grabbed Ava's hand and yanked her after him. Another explosion took the roof off, sending debris their way. Caden shoved her into the driver's side of the SUV and climbed in even as she scrambled across the console and into the passenger's seat. He threw the vehicle in reverse and raced backward.

Officers continued to hold the screeching woman down on the ground while pieces of the house rained down. Fortunately, they were far enough away that it didn't reach them.

"She just blew up the evidence," Caden said.

Ava nodded. "But I got some pictures, so maybe they'll help."

He turned to her, eyes wide. "You got pictures?"

"I got pictures."

"Well, then. Once again, you've impressed me."

She gave a half laugh, half groan, then dropped her head into her hands.

"How'd you know it was the cane?" he asked.

"I'm not sure." She looked up. "I just connected it. The 'ten seconds' thing, her insistence that she needed the cane, saying she was going to blow everyone up . . ." She shrugged. "It just made sense. And if I was wrong, well . . . then so be it."

"You saved everyone's lives. Frank's and the paramedics, for sure."

"I'm just glad the first bomb was at the back of the house, not the front."

Caden nodded. "He did that on purpose."

"In case he needed time to get out?"

"Yeah. That and the ten-second delay."

Ava's jaw tightened. "Well, no more escape plans for him. We need to catch him, Caden."

"I know." He spun the wheel toward the hospital. "Let's go find Mickey and his grandparents. This time, we're not taking no for an answer."

"I want to watch the video John sent me."

He nodded. "As soon as we pull in the hospital parking lot, we'll watch it. In the meantime, can you send those pictures to me and we'll see if there's anything that can tell us where your dad is."

o o o

Nicolai lowered the binoculars as the last ambulance pulled away. His anger smoldered just like the house he'd come to call home. Anger at the feds, yes, but mostly himself.

He'd been too arrogant, assumed no one would have a clue as to who his targets were or why he'd chosen them. But he hadn't counted on Ava Jackson being a part of the plan. How could he? He hadn't known she existed when he started putting everything together five years ago. He'd been so careful. Meticulous in his research and planning. How had Paul Jackson managed to keep his daughter a secret for so long?

It didn't matter. What mattered now was that he knew about her, and the new plan would have to suffice. As long as she wound up dead—and suffered greatly while dying—in the end, that's all he was interested in.

However, he would like to know if his aunt would survive. He'd seen the blood on her before they tackled her. At least she'd managed to do as he'd instructed and gotten rid of the evidence.

But that blood . . . it was a lot. Then they'd cuffed her before placing her on a stretcher and sliding her into the ambulance.

He hoped she would recover. She was the only one left in this world that he cared about. She was loyal and loved him without reservation.

Just like his mother and sisters had.

Grief choked him. Even now he could picture their absolute terror just before the bullets took their lives. And his mother . . . his gentle, kind, loving mother. How she'd tried to protect him—to protect them all.

While he'd watched from his hiding place. Unable to move, to breathe, to save them. He'd started to leave his hiding place, and only the sheer panic in her eyes when she realized what he'd planned had kept him still. And he'd watched them die.

He'd been unable to save them, but he could finally get them justice.

Soon.

He raised the binoculars once more, then headed to the vehicle he'd stolen that morning. He'd watched everything play out on his phone, thanks to the hidden cameras in the house. He'd known it was a trap the minute he saw the car heading up the drive. And then Ava had climbed out and walked up his front porch steps. After all he'd done to get to her, she'd come to him.

And he'd been powerless to do anything about it.

Unable to get his aunt out in time, he'd only been able to call her and warn her to play along.

And it might have gotten her killed.

Time to find out.

And he still had the kid to deal with.

What was the saying? Two birds with one stone?

Yes. Two birds. Or three or four.

o o o

Once again, Ava found herself in the hospital parking lot. She pulled her phone out. "Are you sure we have time to watch it?"

"It'll take them a few minutes to get Frank stable," he said. "They won't let us see him before then. And we've waited this

228

long to talk to Mickey, we can wait a little longer. You pull up the video while I send a text to Sarah." He paused. "Speaking of texts, you never once texted me while you were in the house. And you didn't call me and leave your phone on so I could listen in."

She gaped. "You were serious?"

He scoffed. "Are you kidding me? Of course I was serious."

"Oh. Sorry."

"I was terrified for you, Ava."

"Is that how you came to be there?"

He grimaced. Then shrugged. "Sarah kicked me out. She said I was driving her crazy with my pacing and muttering and constant phone checking. When Dad was finally stable, she practically shoved me out the door and told me to go find you."

"So you did."

"I did."

She reached up to stroke his cheek, noting he needed a shave. "I'm glad you did."

His eyes darkened, and she dropped her hand, then looked away, not ready to admit her growing feelings for the man. But she'd admit her teenage crush was nothing like her adult one. Ava could feel his gaze on her for a long moment before he turned his attention back to his phone.

After he finished his text, he looked at her. "All right, I'm ready when you are."

Ava held the phone so he could see it and tapped play.

John had sent her the part where her father was at the rail— just before he went over. The whole video was three minutes total.

He was standing there, looking out to sea.

"It's hard to tell if he has any scuba equipment on him," Ava said. "And an air tank would be too bulky."

"But a small one would fit right in that backpack he's got on his shoulder. Maybe even two or three of them. The backpack is a hiking bag. It's big. And waterproof, if I had to guess."

"That might give him enough air to get to shore. With flippers, he could go pretty fast."

"And a wetsuit underneath that coat would help keep him warm."

"They found his coat," she said. "The water was around sixty-eight degrees. Cold—and uncomfortable—but not cold enough to kill him."

People walked past him on the deck. It wasn't terribly crowded, but enough so that someone occasionally blocked her view of him.

And then he was falling overboard. People screamed, pointing, some pulling out their phones and racing to the railing to shoot video or snap pictures.

"Go back," Caden said.

She glanced up, saw his brow furrowed, and slid her finger across the screen to rewind the footage. "What did you see?"

"I'm not sure. We may have to throw it up on a bigger screen, but let it play again."

She did as he asked.

"Stop. There."

She tapped the screen. "What?"

"Rewind once more."

Hanging on to her patience, she did so and hit play. What was he seeing?

Caden tapped the screen this time. "There. The guy that walked behind him and kind of bumped his backpack. I think I saw his hand slip something into one of the pockets on the side."

"What? Really?" She watched again, this time in slow motion. When it got to the part Caden was talking about, she gasped. "He did. What do you think it was?"

He met her gaze. "I think it was a tracker and that's how he followed your father from Japan."

Ava processed that idea. "You think it could have survived being in the water that long?"

"Sure. There are waterproof trackers."

"Right." She knew that, it was just . . . "Okay, that makes sense." She shook her head. "Unbelievable." A lump formed in her throat and she closed her eyes. "But Nicolai wouldn't have known my dad was going over. Unless he pushed him."

"No, watch again. He's kind of bumped from behind by another guy walking past, but he went over the rail under his own steam." He pointed. "There. His hands were on the rail and he kind of just hauled himself over."

"He's alive," she whispered. "I don't really care how he wound up in the water. What matters is, he faked his death and I bought it."

"I thought we cleared that up. You didn't buy it," Caden said.

"Yes. And no. But mostly yes. I didn't want to believe he was truly gone, of course, but I think I was starting to accept that he was. Until the whole weird password thing. I couldn't figure out why he'd change it when he was so adamant that I memorize the sequence of when he'd change it and how."

"Now you know."

"Now I know. But how do we find him?"

"We find Nicolai."

Her heart clamped. "What if my father's in trouble? What if Nicolai did something to him?" She remembered the words of his aunt. "I asked Ms. Tunicova what I had done to cause her to hate me so much, and she said it wasn't me, it was my father."

"So, all of this is some kind of revenge against him?"

"I think so."

"And if they get you, they get their ultimate revenge."

She swallowed. "Yeah. Sounds like it. But she didn't say anything about Nathan." Ava narrowed her eyes. "I don't think they know about him."

He nodded. "He's got someone watching him, and I know the guy reported to Gavin that he hadn't seen anything that alarmed him."

"Good. That's good."

He squeezed her hand. "Let's go see if Mickey or his grandparents have anything to offer."

A few minutes later, he led her into the hospital, and she followed him to the elevator, up to Mickey's floor, then down another hallway to the door of Mickey's room. He still had the guard. And the grandparent bodyguards who stood near the nurses' station.

Caden approached Jesse. "Mr. Fields."

The man straightened and adjusted the hem of his shirt. "What do you want?"

"I'd like to show you a picture."

Mr. Fields blinked. "All right."

Caden pulled his phone from his pocket, scrolled to the picture of the five men, and turned the screen so he could see it.

The man gasped and turned gray. His wife placed a hand on his arm.

"Jesse!" She turned to one of the nurses. "I think he's going to have a stroke."

Two of the nurses moved toward him, one reaching for her stethoscope, the other a wheelchair. She pushed it behind him. "Sir, sit down. Your color isn't good."

He held up a hand. "No, I'm all right." His gaze lifted to meet Ava's. Then Caden's. "I think it's time to tell our story."

TWENTY-ONE

Ava stilled. "Yes," she said, "I think it's time. Please tell us."

Jesse looked up at the nurse. "Could I borrow your conference room?"

She glanced at the other woman, who frowned, and Caden flashed his badge. "Please."

Her eyes widened slightly, but she nodded. "All right, but I want to check his vitals first."

"Of course."

When she finished, she looked at Mr. Fields. "Your heart rate is too fast and your blood pressure is borderline high."

"I'm not surprised," the man said, "but I think once I get this off my chest, I'll feel better."

At first the nurse hesitated, then sighed. "All right. Follow me."

Five minutes later, they were seated in the conference room one floor above Mickey's. The nurse paused at the door and turned. "Please get someone if he looks like he needs it."

"We will," Ava assured her.

Caden nodded and the nurse left.

"Okay," Caden said. "I'm not going to drag this out. Please, start talking."

The man locked fingers with his wife and drew in a deep breath. He let it out slowly. "I believe you've already figured out much of it, but I'll start with the fact that you have a very good ear, young lady. I've never had anyone call me out on that accent before." His gaze held Ava's and she gave him a tight smile.

"There's a reason behind that," she said, "but go on, please."

"I grew up in Moscow. My father worked for the government and I quickly followed in his footsteps. By the time I was in my late twenties, the KGB was in full force, and I joined their ranks to work alongside my father." He cleared his throat, and Ava rose to snag a water bottle from the tray near the door. She handed it to him. "Thank you." He took a swig.

"And you knew my father, didn't you?" she asked.

"Yes. Later, but yes, I knew him very well."

She nodded.

"I still don't know his real name, but he went by Dimitri Golubev when I knew him."

"We figured that part out."

"Ah. I guess I didn't hide my surprise very well at hearing that name, did I?" He waved a hand. "Anyway, your father somehow figured out that a friend of mine wasn't happy with the way things were being done in our country and offered him a way out. That friend then came to me and offered me the same deal."

"Explain that," Caden said. "Who recruited you?"

"Maksim Kuznetsov," Ava said, her voice soft. "Am I right?"

Jesse blinked and his wife gasped—the first sound Caden had heard her make since they'd walked into the room. "Yes," Jesse said. "How did you know?"

"It was a guess," Ava said.

"A very good one. Max and I were good friends. He came to me and told me he'd made a deal with the US and did I want in."

Caden leaned forward. "Just like that?"

"Yes."

"He wasn't afraid you'd turn him in?"

"I wouldn't. He knew that. We were closer than brothers. He told me he was leaving, explained everything, and promised if I worked for six months, gathering intel and found one person to take my place when I was gone, that this man—your father— would help me and my family defect to the US."

"There are five of you," Caden said. "Where are the other two? We've tried to locate them, to warn them that someone is killing your families, but we've not been able to find them."

"I don't know. We've not kept in touch."

"It doesn't matter," Ava said, looking up from her phone. "The pictures I took before Nicolai blew up the house have their names and addresses. They'll be warned and protected, right?"

"Yes," Caden said. He squeezed her shoulder on her good arm. "You did phenomenal." He turned back to Jesse. "Back to you and the Baileys. I know you kept in touch with them—or at least Michael did. We found a photo of their family on the mantel in his home."

Jesse paled again. "Yes." He rubbed a hand over his head. "He shouldn't have put that out. We weren't supposed to com- municate."

"Let me guess . . . another son?"

"No. Nephew."

Caden held the picture out once more. "Which one's your brother?"

With a shaky hand, the man pointed to the last one in the row. "Gordon Bailey. Carl was his son. I knew something was wrong as soon as I heard Carl and his family had been killed. And then Carl's sister and her three children in Oregon."

A sob broke from him, and his wife bowed her head into his shoulder. Together, they wept. Caden looked up to see tears dripping down Ava's cheeks. She took a deep breath and grabbed a box of tissues from the table near the door. "Here."

"Jesse?" Caden asked. "Why is Nicolai Kuznetsov killing families?"

The man shuddered and swiped a hand over his wet cheeks. "I don't know." He shook his head. "I truly don't know. Unless—"

"Yes?"

"Unless it has to do with the fact that when his father left Russia, he left his family."

"Left them for Yvonne?" Ava asked.

"Yes. Irena, Max's first wife, came to me one day shortly after he defected and asked me if I'd known what he'd planned. I denied everything, of course. I had to."

"How would Nicolai know the connection to my father?" Ava asked.

Jesse frowned. "I don't know that either."

"It has to be the picture," Caden said to Ava. "Somehow, someone connected your father to the picture."

"Of course he was connected to it," Jesse said. "He's the one who took it."

Ava gasped. "Why would he take a picture of men he was helping defect?"

"Simple. So we wouldn't back out. We were a package deal. If one of us backed out, then we would all pay the price for it."

"He was blackmailing you?" Ava paled and swallowed hard.

"No, no," Jesse said. "We all agreed to do what he asked us to do, but he wanted to make sure we understood that changing our mind wasn't an option."

"Who else had this picture?"

"We each had one."

"Including Max?" Ava asked.

"Of course."

"Well," Caden said, "I guess we know where Nicolai got his information."

o o o

Ava's head pounded. Her cheek had started to itch as it healed from their dash through the woods, and her arm ached every time she moved it. She was tired. Tired of being attacked every time she turned around. Tired of running. Tired of being unable to see her mother or brother. Tired of a lot of things. But pity parties would have to wait. She could fall apart later.

While Jesse and Caden continued to talk, she stepped out of the conference room and looked up to see John at the nurses' station, his forehead creased, lips turned down. Watching her.

She walked over to him. "Hi."

"Hi."

"What are you doing here?"

"Looking for you. I heard about the attempt to grab Nicolai going sideways, the explosion. And your part in all of it." He shoved his hands into his pockets. "Can we talk?"

Of course he'd heard about it. "About?"

He huffed a short, humorless laugh. "Life."

"My father's?"

His jaw tightened, but he jerked a nod. "I guess it's time I gave you some answers."

She studied him. John had been her father's friend for years. *Her* friend. Julie's husband. How could she have thought he'd had anything to do with the attempts on her life? The guilt nearly suffocated her. "Okay, that would be great." Then again, would he believe her if she told him her dad was alive?

Or did he already know?

Her heart hammered at the thought. If he'd known all this time—

"Can we grab some coffee from the cafeteria," he said, "then find a quiet spot away from any listening ears?"

"Fine. I just need to let Caden know where I'm going."

He nodded. "You sure you want to interrupt that?"

Ava shot a glance at the conference room's window. Caden and Jesse were still deep in conversation. She noted the intense look on the men's faces and hesitated. "No, I guess not." She pulled her phone from her pocket and sent Caden a text.

> Heading to the cafeteria with John. He said he wanted to talk about my father. I'll keep you updated.

She followed John to the elevator and stepped inside. Neither spoke as they descended to the first level. John led the way to the cafeteria and ordered two coffees. She loaded hers with sugar, then faced John. "Where do you want to go?"

He looked around. "It's kind of crowded in here. How about my car? At least that way, I know no one's listening in."

Ava frowned. "I really don't want to leave the hospital."

"Why not? You have your phone. I'm parked in a law enforcement spot right outside the door. You can be back inside in seconds if you need to."

She sighed and rubbed her eyes. So tired. "No, let's find an empty room or something."

A muscle jumped in his cheek, but he shrugged. "Fine."

He led the way out of the cafeteria, checking his phone as he walked.

Her phone buzzed and she stopped to check it. John hovered nearby. It was Caden's return text, asking her to please not leave the hospital and to let him know where she was at all times. She smiled—and enabled her location services for him. He could now track her. She should have done that ages ago.

Her phone rang, flashing her mother's facility number. "John?"

He looked up. "Yeah?"

"Hold on. I need to take this."

"Of course."

Ava slid the bar at the bottom of the screen and pressed the phone to her ear. "Hello?"

"Is this Ava Jackson?"

"Yes."

"I need to let you know that your mother's taken a turn for the worse, and if you want to tell her goodbye, you need to get here pretty quickly."

Ava closed her eyes and drew in a deep breath. "I see. All right. I'm on my way." She looked at John. "I need a ride to the nursing home. We can talk on the way."

"Your mom?"

"Yes."

He pulled his keys from his pocket. "Then let's go."

□ □ □

Nicolai stood at the information desk outside the cafeteria, watching Ava. Would he never find her alone? Or with someone who didn't look like they could defend her? He had to bide his time, wait this out. He couldn't afford another mistake.

He'd checked on his aunt and learned she'd been released to police custody. They'd question her, but she wouldn't tell them anything. In fact, she'd do her best to buy him the time he needed to complete the mission. Once he was finished, he'd find a way to get to her and then they could disappear.

And if he couldn't, then, as much as it pained him, he'd leave her behind for a short while.

You can do this, Nicolai, she'd said only days after his mother and sisters had been killed. Tears streaked her cheeks, but her eyes burned with a strange light. One he'd finally identified as pure rage. *It's your duty to avenge our family. For too many years, our enemies have gotten away with their traitorous acts. And now your mother died because your father betrayed his country. But worse, he betrayed his family. So, what are we going to do to make sure they pay?*

I will kill them, I will kill them all. I promise.

That's a good boy.

He blinked back into the present as he climbed into his vehicle. He had two more families to finish off, but not until Ava and her father were wiped from this earth. If he didn't act now, he could lose his chance. And that wasn't an option. His breathing had quickened and sweat dripped into his eyes. He swiped it away, swept the police parking placard from the dash, and fell in behind them.

TWENTY-TWO

Ava shot a text to Caden explaining her sudden departure from the hospital.

> But don't worry, I'm with John. Everyone's on the lookout for Nicolai. I'll be fine. You can meet me there whenever you're able.

He wouldn't like it. Knowing she was with John wouldn't offer him any comfort at all, but she'd been deployed when her father supposedly died. The grief of not being able to say goodbye was still with her. She wasn't going to let her mother pass without holding her hand and whispering in her ear one more time. Caden would come to the nursing home and meet her there.

John snatched her phone from her fingers.

"Hey!"

He held the button and powered it down, then slid it into his front pocket. Before she could protest, John took a left when he should have taken a right. Ava's heart pounded and her lungs tightened. "Where are you going? What are you doing?"

"Protecting you."

She blinked. "What? John, I need to see my mother. And I need to call Nathan. Give me my phone back, now."

John placed a hand over hers. "Nathan doesn't need to be involved in this."

"Involved—" Dread centered itself in her midsection. It had been him all along? Why hadn't she listened to her instincts? "You have about thirty seconds to explain yourself." Or what? She didn't know, but she'd figure something out. "Where are you taking me?"

"Someplace safe."

"No, no, no. I decided to trust you and you do this?" She wanted to scream. Instead, she pulled in a ragged breath and closed her eyes. "My mother needs me. If you deny me the opportunity to be with her before she dies, I'll never forgive you."

"Your mother is fine. As fine as she can be anyway. I arranged for that call from the facility so I wouldn't have to fight you to get you in the car."

His words finally penetrated, and she stared at him. "Why?" she whispered.

"Because I had to stop you. You're digging into things that need to be left alone."

No, this couldn't be happening. "It was really you all along?"

"What?"

"Trying to kill me. I wondered."

He gaped, then swung his gaze back to the road. "No, I haven't been trying to kill you. Really, Ava? You thought I could be behind—Wow."

She still didn't know what to believe. "You sound very convincing."

"There's a reason for that!"

"But you're as good a liar as I am, John. We both know that."

Again, he let his eyes swing to her, and she noted his pale

face. His fingers spasmed around the wheel. "I don't want you dead, Ava. Quite the contrary."

"And yet, you've taken me against my will."

"Because I'm trying to protect you! And your father."

She gasped, then pulled in a breath and waited to get herself under control. Lashing out wouldn't help. "So, you know he's alive," she said, her voice dull, flat.

"Yes, but when I came to your house, I really thought he was dead."

"So, when did you know?"

"Shortly after he was reported missing, then declared dead. So about seven months ago."

Ava gasped again when her heart lurched and thundered in her ears. "Seven months ago?"

"Yes, but I don't know how to find him, and he hasn't contacted me, Ava. It's been crickets from him. And, of course, I knew he hadn't been in touch with you. But I figure he's got a good reason for it."

"Yeah! Like he's in trouble? Like he's physically unable to reach out for help?"

"No, like he's working on something so covert that he can't come up for air without putting himself—and others—in danger."

"No way. He'd never abandon my mother—leave her to die in a nursing facility—without coming to say goodbye to her." She scoffed. "You know that as well as I do."

Ava clasped her hands in her lap and thought about the phone in his pocket. She'd have to get it somehow.

He frowned and nodded. "I would have thought so, but honestly, I just don't know. He may be putting work ahead of his family once again. He's always done that. You can't deny it."

She couldn't. Maybe. "That wasn't totally his fault. His job demanded it. Which is why I'll never do it."

John shot her a quick look and his jaw tightened. "Never say never."

"Or," she said, ignoring him, her voice soft, "he's really dead after all this time."

"Or that," John agreed, his own words as quiet as hers.

Time clicked past as she struggled to figure out what to do. Try to escape? Or go along with whatever John had in mind. She still didn't know where he was taking her, but at least she wasn't tied up. Yet. "How'd you figure out he was alive?"

He hesitated. "Someone logged into my account at the agency. When I couldn't trace the history to see what the person was looking for, I could think of only one person who would be able to pull that off." He shot her a sideways glance. "Well, two, but I knew you hadn't done it." He sighed. "And then he called me and confirmed it."

"He *called* you?"

"Yes."

Her father had called John, but not her. Ava focused on pushing aside her hurt—and anger—and decided to get as many answers as she could while he was talking. "Did you really go to the high school and get rid of all of my father's pictures in the albums?"

"No. He did that."

"Oh." She sighed. "John, you can't do this. This is kidnapping."

"Not if you go with me willingly."

"Which I'm not doing and you know it. Please, take me back to the hospital."

"I can't." He pressed the gas.

□ □ □

Caden finally had a chance to look at his phone. Daria had located the other two men in the picture and they—and their families—were now on their way to safe houses. He scrolled through his texts and found the one from Ava saying she was going to the nursing home and John was taking her. "She's okay. She's with John." Saying the words out loud didn't help much.

A sensation like he'd never experienced washed over him. John was a man she'd once given consideration to as the person behind the attacks on her. He dialed her number and it went straight to voice mail.

Even more alarmed, he looked up the number to the facility. "Baymont Care."

"This is Caden Denning, I need to get in touch with one of your visitors. Her name is Ava Jackson. She'd be visiting—"

"This is Petra, Caden."

"Oh, hey, is Ava there?"

"No, I haven't seen her."

He'd expected that answer for some reason, but it still sent darts of worry through him. He glanced at his watch. She should be there by now. "How's her mother doing?"

"About the same."

He closed his eyes, searching for strength. "Did anyone call to tell her that her mother was getting ready to die any minute and she needed to get there fast?"

"What! No, of course not. I just checked on Mrs. Jackson not ten minutes ago. She's the same as when Ava was here a few nights ago."

"Thank you, Petra."

"What's going on, Caden? Is Ava all right? I mean, she called to say she was dealing with something that would require her to be gone for a few days, but this sounds pretty serious."

"It's serious."

"Does it have anything to do with the officer who keeps pacing in front of Mrs. Jackson's room?"

The woman was sharp. "Yes. Just let him pace, okay?"

"Of course." She hesitated. "Is anyone here at the facility in danger?"

"No. Not at all. The guard on Mrs. Jackson is just a precaution. I've talked to the director and he knows why the man is there."

"That's good enough for me then. I'll be praying."

"Please do."

He hung up and tried Ava's phone again.

Straight to voice mail. Great.

He went to find Gavin. He found him pacing in front of the vending machines. His friend gave it a light punch, then raked a hand over his beard.

"They don't have your favorite candy bar?" Caden asked.

Gavin jerked to a stop. "Sorry. Just worried and needed a place to vent a little without letting Sarah see."

"Yeah."

Gavin's eyes narrowed. "What's wrong?"

Caden told him. "I'd head over to the facility, but I have a feeling she's won't be there anytime soon."

"But she left with this guy, John?"

"Yeah."

"Let's look at the footage."

Ten minutes later, Caden stood in the hospital security office watching Ava walk out the door with a man he didn't recognize. "Freeze it right there, will you?"

"Sure." The officer complied and Caden pulled out his phone and did a Google search for a picture of the CIA director.

"Well, that's him," he muttered.

"Then maybe he had her turn off her phone so she couldn't be tracked because . . ."

"Because?"

Gavin shook his head. "Sorry, I got nothing."

"Yeah, me neither."

"Let's play it until they're out of sight," Caden told the officer.

He did. "Well," Gavin said when it was done, "we know they're heading south."

"Which means we know nothing." He paused. "But I know someone who might."

"Who?"

"A woman named Julie. I've just got to get her number."

o o o

Ava clutched the seat belt as John took an exit, leaving the highway behind. "Where are we going? At least tell me that."

"To a little place your dad and I used to meet when we didn't want anyone to find us. Where there weren't any lies or fake identities. Just two guys hanging out and enjoying the scenery. Being ourselves without worrying about blown covers or protecting our families."

"John, listen to me. I don't want to be here. I need to find my father."

"No!" He slapped the wheel and she jumped. "No," he said in a lower voice, "you need to stay safe. If Nicolai gets his hands on you, you don't understand the kind of pain and suffering you'll experience before he finally kills you."

Daria's video from the floppy disks flashed in her head and she closed her eyes, swallowing against the nausea. "Yes," she said, "I do know. But it's a risk I'm willing to take. I'm an adult, capable of making my own decisions, and this is kidnapping! Now, take me back!"

He didn't answer, didn't look at her, didn't do anything but drive.

Ava ground her teeth and racked her brain to come up with some way to get away from him. She'd have to, since he wasn't going to listen to reason. And she'd have to find a way to take the car. She'd never been in this area before and wasn't familiar with it, but she'd noted the twists and turns and was fairly confident she could find her way back as long as she was following the route he'd taken.

But first she had to make that happen.

"Hang on," he said.

"What?"

"Someone's behind us. He's been behind us for a while." John gunned the engine and the sedan shot forward.

Ava watched the mirrors and noted the car behind them do the same. John grabbed his phone and handed it to Ava. "Call 911."

"How'd he know where we were? How did he find us?"

"I don't know. Just call." His jaw was tight enough to shatter his teeth and Ava realized just how worried he was.

She punched in the three numbers and hit dial. "He tracked us, didn't he? Followed us from the hospital!"

"Probably."

A hard hit from behind sent the phone flying. Ava cried out, grabbing for it, but the seat belt locked and slammed her back. Pain shot through her still-healing arm. She ignored it and released the seat belt to scramble for the phone.

Another ram sent her back against her seat and the air bag exploding. She bounced into the door and grabbed the handle above the window. The car spun off the road and into a tree before shuddering to a halt. Dust filled the interior and Ava gasped. She released her hold on the handle, pushed aside the air bag material, then reached for John. He had a nasty lump on his head, but his eyes flickered.

"John, come on, wake up."

Panting, she sent up prayers for help and looked out the window to see the SUV that had been following them pull to a stop. "No. Come on, John, please."

He groaned and looked up at her, his eyes finally focusing. "Run, Ava," he rasped and pressed her cell phone into her hand. "Don't let him catch you."

"I can't leave you." She powered up the phone and the screen flickered to life.

"Go. I didn't go to all this trouble to have you land in his hands. Please."

Ava took another look out the window.

Nicolai was already hurrying toward them.

John gripped the pocket of her blazer. "Hurry," he whispered. Blinked and shut his eyes.

A whimper escaped her, then with a low cry she pushed out of the sedan, flashes of being trapped in Caden's truck coming back to haunt her. But the door had opened easily and she rushed toward the trees.

Heavy footsteps pounded behind her.

Harsh breathing pulled closer. She dared a glance back over her shoulder just as his hand shot out and punched her in the head. She went down, stars dancing in her vision. A wet spray hit her in the face. She gasped before she could stop herself and the world tilted.

He leaned over her . . . and smiled.

TWENTY-THREE

Caden hung up the phone for the fifth time, but at least Ava's phone wasn't going straight to voice mail anymore. It was actually ringing four times first. He wasn't sure what was worse—the acute anxiety when it didn't ring, or the crashing letdown when she didn't pick up.

He walked back into the waiting area to find Sarah conversing with their father's doctor. When he got closer, he picked up the last part. ". . . doing as well as can be expected right now, so that's good."

Relief swept over him and his knees went a little weak. He'd been more than worried his father would die. He'd been terrified. "When can we see him?"

"In a few hours."

"Thank you," Sarah said.

The man nodded and headed back down the hall. Caden took a moment to gather his strength, then clasped Sarah's hand.

"What is it? What's wrong?" she asked.

"I think . . . Ava's . . . missing."

Her eyes widened. "Missing? Missing how? What are you talking about?"

"Her friend John came to the hospital to talk to her, but she got a call that her mother was dying and she needed to head to the nursing home. So she left with him. But I've been calling and texting and she's not answering. And she's not with her mom." He raked a hand over his head. "I don't like it. She wouldn't just drop off the radar, knowing how worried I'd be."

"What about her friend? Can you call him?"

"He's not answering either."

"Well, maybe—" She stopped and shook her head. "No, you're right. Ava wouldn't turn off her phone or ignore your calls and texts. Sounds like she might be in trouble."

Her words pierced him. "Yes. Unfortunately, that's the only conclusion I've come up with."

"Do you know where to start looking for her?"

"No."

"Well . . . can you track her phone? Or does that take forever to get permission to do?"

He blinked and held his own device up. "Actually, I can do it from my phone. As long as hers is turned on." He glanced at Sarah, then back to the screen, where he tapped through the sequence that would allow him to see Ava's location. "It's weird. Just a little bit ago, it was going straight to voice mail. Then it started ringing four times before hitting voice mail."

"Like she'd turned it off, then back on?"

"Yes. Exactly."

"You're right. That's weird. First of all, she wouldn't turn her phone off. Second, she wouldn't ignore you." Fear flickered in her eyes. "For some reason, she can't answer, and you need to find out why. Fast."

o o o

Ava blinked, her pounding head pulling her from unconsciousness into a twilight awareness. Nausea swirled and she swallowed hard in order not to lose the contents of her stomach. It was only at that point she noticed she was seated on a hard chair and her wrists bound together. "Ugh."

What had happened? The floor rocked beneath her—a sensation she was intimately familiar with—but it sure didn't help the nausea. She was on a boat. Tied up. And felt wretched. Why?

She shoved aside the need to give in to the rising panic and focused.

John. She swung her head to the left and grimaced. Closed her eyes and took in a few breaths as the darkness threatened to engulf her once more.

No. Stay awake. She needed to . . .

What?

Find her father because he was alive. Right.

So . . .

With her eyes closed, she went through the list again, trying to process.

She was on a boat.

Her hands were tied.

She needed to puke but refused to do so.

And she smelled . . . a combination of body odor and . . . food?

"Ava?"

She blinked and the room came into focus. Somewhat. She squinted, the headache intensifying as the light hit her eyes. Another groan slipped from her and she slammed her eyes shut once more.

"Ava? Time to wake up."

Someone nudged her shoulder.

"Leave her alone."

The low voice jump-started her brain. She knew that voice. "Dad?" she croaked. No, she must still be asleep. Dreaming.

Another nudge. This one harder and more insistent.

Awareness finally hit her, and she remembered John, being hit by the other car, and running. Only she hadn't run fast enough and he'd caught her. Nicolai. The man who'd killed so many. The man who wanted to kill her.

So, why was she still alive?

She kept her eyes closed for the moment.

"Look this way, Ava. Someone wants to see you."

She didn't recognize the voice, but it reminded her of . . . she couldn't place it.

Wait. Yes, she could. It reminded her of the one from the old footage on the floppy disks. The voice that laughed while others screamed their agony.

Terror shot through her, but with effort, she rolled her head to see a man on the bed in the far corner. Cuffs encircled his wrists. Attached to the cuffs were chains that ran the length of the floor to the wall. A dark beard and mustache covered the lower portion of his face, but when his eyes met hers, she stifled a gasp.

"Dad," she whispered.

His eyes drank in the sight of her, his gaze roaming over her from top to bottom. "Ava."

"I found you."

He sighed. "Yes. You did." The sheer agony in his gaze said he knew what they were facing and it was killing him. The bruises on his face and torso said he'd already faced some of it.

"So," Nicolai said, clasping his hands in front of him, "as much as I'd love to watch this little family reunion, we've got a lot to cover before the fun begins." He pulled his phone from his pocket and glanced at the screen. "I've got a few things to take care of and then we'll get started. Feel free to use this time to continue to get reacquainted." He ran a finger down Ava's cheek, and she clenched her jaw, refusing to outwardly react even though she wanted to lose her last meal. She chose to blame it on the residual side effects of whatever he'd knocked her out with, not the sheer terror clawing through her.

He grinned, his face handsome with his high cheekbones and white teeth. But his eyes gave him away. Darkened and dead, reflecting a soul that for much too long had received no nourishment except hatred and bitterness. Even while she was terrified of the man, a strange compassion hit her as well. "Your aunt did this to you," she said, her voice soft. "Her desire for revenge twisted you into the person you are today. I'm sorry."

He stepped back, frowned. Confusion flickered, then faded. He stomped to the door and swung it open. "Business calls," he said, "but soon we'll get to play."

"Caden will find me," she said.

"Why do you think he'll have a clue as to where you are?"

She bit her lip. Her words had been more for herself than for Nicolai. She had no idea if Caden could find her or not. Nicolai reached into his pocket, pulled out her cell phone, and waved it at her. "You think he'll find you by tracking your phone? So sorry. I turned that little 'share my location' feature off while you were sleeping. Fortunately for me, I found it at the dock. Like I said, I'll be back soon."

He left and Ava dragged in a shuddering breath. She looked at the man she'd thought dead and couldn't process the emotions racing through her. She wanted to hug him and yell at him all at the same time. But . . . priorities. "We've got to get out of here. Fast."

"It's impossible."

"Nothing's impossible. You taught me that."

He scoffed. "I've been here three months. You don't think I've gone over every square inch of this place?"

Ava's heart lurched. "Three months?"

"Yes."

"Dad . . ." Tears thickened her voice and she swallowed. "Why?"

"He wants to make me pay."

"For what? What did you do to trigger this kind of hate?"

Her father shook his head and let out a long sigh. "It's a long story."

"Well, while you tell it, can you figure out a way to get my hands free?"

"He's got cameras in here."

"So? It's not like he doesn't expect me to try to get free, right?"

Her father stood and walked over to her. Easily. His movements were fluid and catlike. Exactly as she remembered him.

"You exercise every day, don't you?"

"Not much else to do in here."

"He's not starving you. You get plenty to eat. He's keeping you alive." He'd always kept himself in exceptional shape. Being a captive of a killer hadn't changed that.

"Yes. He has his reasons."

"Which are?"

He gave her a ferocious look that morphed into one of such great sorrow, her lungs spasmed. "I think you know," he said.

Ava swallowed hard. "He wants you to watch him torture me, doesn't he?"

"Yes."

"Why! What did you do to him?"

"I did my job!" His shout tightened her jaw and sent her heart rate into a gallop.

She took a steadying breath. "All right," she said, her voice soft, controlled. "Then we have to figure out how to get out of here before he comes back. And if he's watching and listening, I guess we'll find that out soon enough."

"Ava—"

She stood, cutting him off, and walked into the bathroom. It was a beautiful room with a spa-like feel that she'd normally relish lounging in. Right now, she wanted to rip it apart for something sharp. He followed her into the space. "Does he have cameras in here?" she asked, keeping her voice low.

"No. At least not that I could find."

"Good. Go back out there. We don't want him wondering what we're both doing in here."

With an odd look in his eye, he backed up. At the door, he stopped. "You're zip-tied, Ava."

"But it's not metal. Zip ties can be broken—or cut." Her gaze roamed the area. "He left washrags and towels and soap. How thoughtful."

"No razor, though."

"Go figure."

"Didn't want me cutting my wrists, I guess. That would deprive him of his fun."

The words were sarcastic but held a desperate edge that made her breath hitch. She couldn't help herself. She walked to him, looped her bound hands around his neck, and hugged him. He bent his head and his breath shuddered against her cheek.

"I've missed you, Dad," she whispered.

"I've missed you too. More than I can say."

"All right. We've got to figure this out." She stepped back and pressed her palms to her eyes. She had to think.

"How'd you figure it out?" he asked her. He returned to his seat on the bed.

"A lot of little things." She paused in her perusal of the bathroom toilet and looked at him. "Tell me how you pulled it off," she said. "Faking your death, I mean."

"Tell me what you know."

She drew in a deep breath, wondering how much time she had. She hit the highlights. When she came to the computer password and her confusion at her inability to find the right one, he shook his head.

"I know. I knew I was going to have to play dead for a while, but I wasn't sure how long. So I changed how I created it."

"That's what I figured." She shot him a sour look.

"But you still got in. You got the hints from the puzzle."

"I did. Still don't know what the blueprint was all about."

"I just threw that in there. Thought it was kind of cool."

"Well, that's just awesome, Dad."

"Yeah, I guess that was kind of stupid." He stared at her, his eyes glinting. "But I thought it might throw off anyone else who might get their hands on it." He paused and she studied the hinged toilet seat lid. "I can't believe you figured it all out," he finally said.

"You set it up so I would."

"Not really," he muttered. "I honestly didn't expect you to do it that fast. I kind of thought I'd be dead by the time you put it all together. If you even went looking."

"Thanks for the vote of confidence." She ran her fingers over the hinges, studying the way the seat fastened to the bowl.

"That's not what I meant. I thought I might have made it too hard for *anyone* to put the pieces together. Even you."

"John showed me the video of your 'fall'"—she wiggled her fingers in air quotes—"over the railing of the ferry. Caden spotted Nicolai putting the tracker in your bag just before you went over."

He rubbed a hand over his chin, scratching the beard. "I didn't know he'd followed me. I knew he was looking for me, but I didn't know who he was. I had to find out and I couldn't do that, being constantly on the run."

"So you decided to fake your death?"

"Yeah. Didn't work out quite like I'd hoped. I almost drowned trying to get the backpack off and to the oxygen tanks I had stashed in there."

"But you didn't. You made it to shore. I'm assuming you had a fake passport in the bag and used it to catch a plane home. You landed at JFK. I saw you on security footage. Then what?"

"I grabbed a cab," he said, his rough voice familiar and dear to her heart. "I told him to take me to the worst part of town where I could find things I needed. I'd gone dark and needed to stay hidden. Seemed like a good place to do that. I was fine for a couple of months, discounting the paranoia I constantly felt—which I know now was well-placed. Nicolai was keeping an eye on me, waiting to make his move."

She frowned. "Why do you think it took him so long?"

"He had to regroup, replan. I stayed with a group of homeless folks in New York for about four months. When nothing happened and no one found me, I figured I was in the clear and called John. Told him what was going on and asked him about your mom." His eyes clouded. "How is she, by the way?"

"The same." He nodded and looked at his hands for a moment. "Why John?" she asked. An idea formed, even as she listened to her father fill in the blanks. "Why couldn't you trust me?"

"It wasn't about trust, Ava. I was too afraid of leading him to you." He sighed. "But he found you anyway."

"He did, but not because of you. At least not directly." She told him about the picture as she popped the lid from the toilet. Her heart thudded with the adrenaline crashing through her. "Help me break this. I need something sharp."

Her father walked to the bathroom door and took the lid from her, braced it against one foot, and snapped it in two. "I thought about that ages ago and would have done the same if he'd used zip ties on me. Also thought about slitting his throat with it but couldn't figure out how to get out of the chains once he was dead. I was still thinking about it anyway when you showed up."

She held out her wrists. "Cut this off, please."

He went to work, sawing against the zip tie. His hand slipped and he nicked the soft skin of her inner wrist. She gasped and he froze.

"Keep going," she whispered. "That doesn't hurt nearly as bad as what he's got in mind."

"How do you know what he's got in mind?"

"There were some floppy disks found in Jesse Fields's home. Once one of the analysts found a computer to see what was on them, she sent them to Caden. I was there when he played one of them and saw a video of what someone did to people who crossed the KGB. It wasn't pretty." Her stomach still turned when she thought about it.

He winced. "Yeah, that was Maksim Kuznetsov. He was a nasty one, but he was brilliant and willing to sell his country's secrets. I couldn't pass up helping him defect."

"Well, he's dead if that makes you feel any better."

He glanced up. The plastic parted about halfway and she sucked in a breath. "That's it." She pulled, but it wouldn't release.

The lock pad outside the door beeped, and Ava pushed her father out and shut the bathroom door. Moving quickly, she hid the toilet lid in the bathtub and drew the curtain closed, then turned on the faucet. "I'm almost done, Dad, then you can have it," she called. She shut the water off and opened the door.

A strange whirring sound filled the room and Ava gaped as the chains attached to her father's shackles disappeared into the wall, pulling him toward the porthole, reeling him in like a fish. He didn't fight it, but his eyes blazed.

The door to the room opened and she spun.

Nicolai stood there, that creepy half smile on his face. "It's time."

TWENTY-FOUR

Ava's phone was going straight to voice mail once again. Caden wanted to throw his own device out the window but knew that wouldn't help anything. Unfortunately.

Gavin, Travis, and Asher had volunteered their services and he'd love to have their help as soon as he could figure how they could. They'd all been at the hospital offering their support while he waited for more news about his father. When he'd finished telling Sarah that Ava was missing, she'd called them over and told them to go find her friend. "She needs you much more than my father and I do. Go. You can explain on the way."

And so they'd rushed out the door. And he still didn't have a plan. "I'm making this up as we go, guys, so feel free to throw out something brilliant." He'd call on the Bureau's resources as soon as he could decide which ones he needed. "In the meantime, I'm headed to her last known location."

"Which is where?" Asher asked.

"Back at the bombing. The house on the lake." Caden spun the wheel and took a sharp turn. "I sent an officer out there to take a look as soon as I realized where it was telling me she was. He said he saw nothing out of the ordinary—other than a house in ruins."

"Why would John take her there?" Travis asked.

"No idea. I'm hoping we find out when we get there."

Gavin, in the passenger seat, looked up from his phone. "And you haven't found John?"

"No." Caden seriously suspected the man was dead. He'd called Julie and let her know that John had disappeared off the radar and authorities were looking for him, and if she had connections or favors she could call in, she'd better do it now.

Asher, seated behind him, sighed. "And this Nicolai character doesn't have any other real estate connections?"

"No. Not even a rental agreement. Those were all in his aunt's name. Right down to the little speedboat next to the dock. She bought that too."

Travis frowned. "And she won't tell you anything?"

Caden's fingers curled around the steering wheel. "Not a peep. She's so loyal to Nicolai, it's as admirable as it is infuriating."

"He could be using an alias," Travis said.

"He could be."

"Any idea what name he would use?"

"No."

"So, what you're saying is our only lead is a location that's already been checked out and she's not there."

"Yeah."

"Perfect."

Caden thought so too. But she *had* been there. The question was why. He pressed the gas while praying for Ava's safety and a lead.

Please, Lord, we need a lead.

o o o

The chains held Ava's father almost immobile. "Let her go, Nicolai. Or I swear I'll kill you."

"Like you killed my family?"

261

"I didn't kill your family!" Her father yanked at the cuffs on his wrists, the cords in his neck standing out, a vein pulsing in his forehead. "What happened to them is on your father!"

"If it hadn't been for you, he never would have left." Nicolai simply held a knife to her throat, pressing until she winced.

She refused to cry out, but felt the warm trickle of blood slide down the side of her neck. "Dad, stop!"

"Letting him kill you now might be more merciful," he muttered.

Nicolai eased the pressure and Ava drew in a deep breath. "Dad. Stop. You can't do anything, so stop." She tried to communicate with her eyes that she would be okay, but she doubted he could see her beyond the red rage in his eyes. "Dad!"

Nicolai picked up the remote from the floating shelf next to the door and aimed it at the television. "Don't worry. You'll get to see and hear everything."

"Ava! I'm sorry, baby, I'm so sorry." Tears spilled over his lashes, but Ava's attention was on the screen that had flickered to life.

Her heart shuddered and her stomach twisted into one big nauseous knot at the sight of a torture chamber like the one in the video Daria had pulled from the floppy disks. Her pulse pounded in her ears and she fought to stay calm.

Nicolai grabbed her by the arm and shoved her out the door, then closed it. He pressed a button on the side and the whirring sound of the chains hummed through the area.

"Ava! Nicolai, don't do this!" A heavy thud echoed against the door. "I'm going to kill you!"

Her father's desperate cry nearly sent her to her knees. *Don't panic, don't panic. Breathe, Ava, breathe. And think. Please, God . . .*

Without releasing his grip on her bicep, Nicolai turned slightly and punched in the code to lock her father behind the steel door once again. Four digits. But she couldn't see what they were.

Ava pushed past her fear, ordering her brain to work. *Think!*

"Tell me why you're doing this," she said. "At least let me know why you want me to suffer before I die."

"I'm more than happy to tell you. Your father convinced mine to betray his country." He led her along the deck of the boat as he talked, like they were out for a pleasant stroll, rather than a march to her agonizing death. "He bought my father off, and when the KGB found out, they didn't take kindly to his actions."

Her gaze roamed the very expensive yacht. She thought it might have three levels. "So they killed your family." It was a shot in the dark but seemed to fit.

He snorted. "Killed would have been merciful. After they tortured my mother for a while, making my sisters watch, they then turned to my sisters. Innocent little girls who knew nothing of evil."

"Neither did the children you killed."

"Yes, I know. I regret they had to die, but it's the way it had to happen."

In his twisted mind, she was sure that's what he believed.

"They finally shot my sisters," he said, "then took my mother and did unspeakable things to her, trying to get her to tell them where my father was and who else was spying for the US. But she didn't know. She truly didn't know. If she had known, she would have broken long before then. But do you know why she didn't know?"

"Why, Nicolai?"

"Because my traitorous father didn't tell her he was leaving—and taking his mistress with him. Nope, he kept that all to himself. In the end, after my mother screamed and begged for mercy, for her children's lives, they made her sit on the sofa next to her dead children and shot her. At that point, I'm sure she was grateful it was finally over. And then they burned the house down."

Ava swallowed hard and shuddered.

He must have felt the ripple run through her. "It doesn't sound so fun, does it?"

"No, not at all," she said, her voice soft. "What a horrible thing for them to do. I'm so sorry." And she was. But her compassion wouldn't reach him at this point. He was too lost in his darkness. And she wouldn't deny she was terrified.

He stared at her, his brow wrinkling at her words. Then he shook his head. "I was hiding in a small area in our den that my sisters and I called the box. We used it when we played hide-and-seek. I was in there when they burst into the house, so I saw it all and could do nothing."

"How old were you?"

"Ten. By the time they left, I vowed to get justice for my family. When I went to live with my aunt, over the years she uncovered all the information that would lead me here. As I grew, I trained. And every year, I would visit my mother's and sisters' graves, and every year, I renewed my promise. To make them all suffer as much as I possibly could."

"Starting with your father and his wife."

"Yes." His hand spasmed on her arm as he stopped in front of a door. The door she assumed led to that horrible room. "When I was old enough, my aunt gave me the papers and pictures she'd found in a box my father had left behind. She instructed me to find out as much as possible about the photo of the five men while she worked on tracking down my father. It took years to figure everything out. Years and years and years. Fortunately, my aunt knew many high-ranking people in the KGB and through much effort—and a lot of money—eventually found everything she needed to know about the man who'd helped other high-ranking officials—*and their families*—defect."

"You were the only family left behind, weren't you?"

"Yes."

"So, you decided to kill the other families because . . ."

"They needed to know what it felt like to lose their whole family because of one person's decision. Because of their actions, my family died. Because of my actions, their families died."

"An eye for an eye, huh?"

He shrugged. "My aunt said they had to pay, and I promised to make it happen." He nodded to the room. "I added that after I learned about you. Your father was extremely clever in hiding his family. At first, I was going to just take my pleasure in torturing and killing him, but this has worked out so much better. Now he gets to watch me do to you what they did to my mother. He gets to watch you die knowing that it's all because of him."

Ava clasped her fingers together and brought her hands up, knuckles first, to slam them into his throat. He stumbled backward and hit the rail, gasping, coughing, kicking, as he tried to catch his breath.

She ran.

o o o

The chopper blades cut through the air, sweeping yet another part of the lake. They'd chosen to do an open-door helicopter search. It wasn't the usual way to do things, but it wasn't completely unheard of either, as it allowed him to see more of the ground below.

"What are we looking for, Cade?" Travis asked.

His voice came through the headphones and Caden shook his head. "I'm not entirely sure. I'm hoping I'll know it when I see it."

When they'd arrived at the property, Caden had noticed the absence of the speedboat and called the authorities asking if they'd impounded it. They had not. At that point, he called in a chopper while they searched the area—and found a sedan. "She was here," he told the others. "The boat's missing. I'm willing to take the chance that Nicolai put her in it and headed to whatever location he has set up."

It seemed to take forever, but the chopper had finally arrived just as the crime scene unit pulled up. He and Travis had climbed into the helicopter while Gavin and Asher would keep them updated on the ground activity.

Caden checked his harness again, then leaned out the door as the pilot banked and made another run, following a grid pattern. The sun sank lower and Caden's heart thudded a painful rhythm of desperation. "Where are you?" he whispered. "She has to be on the lake somewhere," he said in a normal volume. "Look for the boat."

"There are several islands out here," Travis said. "Let's check those. You don't need a boat if you have land access to an island. The fact that he left his car tells me he can't get to wherever he is with it."

"Good point."

Caden pulled up the map of the lake and noted four different decent-sized islands. He entered the coordinates of the first one into the GPS and the pilot headed for it.

The water police were standing by, ready to move in when directed, as were other agents.

Nothing caught his attention on a quick tour around the island, and they moved on to the next one.

Caden's phone rang. Asher. "Yeah?"

"I'm here with the crime scene unit and the cops. We found evidence Ava was in the car."

"What evidence?" He and the others hadn't touched it after a brief glance inside, not wanting to disturb any evidence that might have been left behind.

"Strands of dark hair in the back seat and a couple of zip ties. Obviously, we can't be one hundred percent sure that the hair belongs to Ava, but you know it does."

Yes, he knew it did. But where had he taken her?

"What's that?" He pointed.

"Looks like a yacht of some kind," Travis said. "Rich people can rent out their own island and go off-grid for a few days. You know, put their cell phone on airplane mode and only use the internet while they're actually on the yacht."

Caden scoffed. "There's no speedboat there. That's what we're looking for." He showed Travis the picture of the boat that had been tied to the dock.

They circled the island twice. "No speedboat and nowhere to hide one," Travis said. "There's not even a dock."

"Let's try the next one." He nodded to the pilot, who gave him a thumbs-up. "Come on, Ava, where are you?"

TWENTY-FIVE

Ava knelt behind the bar on the third-floor deck, heart racing, her panic barely under control. A fully stocked wine rack hid her from view at the moment, giving her a second to catch her breath—and plan. The pool pump ran with a quiet hum in the background. The cool night air blew across the water and dried the tears she didn't remember shedding.

As soon as she'd been free of Nicolai, she'd found the stairs and headed up, blind panic guiding her, leading her to search for the bridge that would have a radio. Nicolai had guessed her intentions and followed.

But now, she needed to think.

A helicopter passed by overhead and she bit her lip to keep from crying out. There was no way they'd hear her, and she'd just draw Nicolai's attention. *Think! Get a grip on the terror and think! What do I do, God? What do I do? I need a plan.*

She also needed her aching wrists free of the zip tie. While her father had managed to cut halfway through the plastic, she needed it off in order to defend herself and figure out how to deal with Nicolai. The thought of having to kill him made her want to retch, but if it came down to her or him, she'd do what she had to do.

For now, since she couldn't get to the radio, she needed to get to the galley. Galleys had sharp knives, right? Right. But she didn't know the layout of the boat and she couldn't go room to room without risking running into Nicolai. She rested her head on her hands. But galleys were usually positioned aft on the newer crafts. She'd find it, as long as she could avoid Nicolai.

Her punch had taken him by surprise, but once he recovered, she could hear him clearly, stomping after her, threatening to do his worst and make sure she suffered even more than he'd originally planned.

She could *not* let him get his hands on her.

"I'm going to kill him, Ava! Either you show yourself or I'm going to kill him!"

She took a deep breath and pulled at the zip tie by straining her wrists apart. And still it wouldn't give. With a stifled sob, she peered around the edge of the bar.

"Ava!" He was still out of sight but coming up the stairs. "I know you're up here. Come on. Where do you think you're going to go? You're just dragging this out and making me angrier by the second."

The upper deck wrapped around the large boat, and she just needed him off the stairs so she could get down and to the kitchen. He reached the top and looked both ways like he was going to cross a street. Then stalked toward her, although she knew he hadn't spotted her. "I'll kill him! I'll make him suffer! Get out here!"

Ava closed her eyes for a split second and stayed put. He cursed and spun, then walked toward the stern, moving away from her hiding place. *Go, keep going.*

As soon as he was out of sight, she darted around the bar and to the stairs. She pulled the door shut behind her and twisted the deadbolt. It wouldn't keep him out for long, but maybe long enough.

Ava hurried to the middle deck and slipped inside.

A large seating area greeted her, and she kept going until finally she found the galley.

She stepped inside, wishing she could appreciate the grandness. Gorgeous stainless steel appliances, granite countertops, and . . . locking drawers. She released the latch on the first one, then the second.

A harsh cry came from the end of the yacht. A scream of rage and frustration so chilling, she froze for a split second before a shudder rippled through her and she turned back to the drawers. Knives were kept locked up for safety in the event of rough waters. As long as she had time to look, she'd find one eventually.

"Ava!"

And as long as he kept calling out, she'd know where he was.

The top drawer to her left revealed what she'd been looking for. She grabbed the sharpest one in her right hand, worked to flip it so the blade rested against the tie, and pressed upward. The tie fell to the floor and she stooped to pick it up just as he turned the corner into the galley.

In the mirror above the oven, she could see him striding toward her. She positioned herself so that she was out of sight, unable to be seen in the mirror. Crouched in a squat, she watched, her fingers clutching the handle of the knife. He walked toward the counter, and she scuttled backward, doing her best to be silent, but thankful his harsh breathing and mutterings drowned out any slight sounds she might make. If he'd been quiet, he might have heard her. He rounded the corner just as she slipped next to the endcap.

Using the mirror, she let his pace guide hers. He stopped and slammed a fist onto the counter. She flinched and held her breath. For someone who'd been so cool and calm—even methodical—about killing innocent people, he was starting to unravel.

Which was working in her favor at the moment. She whispered silent prayers, keeping her eyes on the man in the mirror. He'd stopped moving, head bent, staring at the counter, his chest heaving with each agitated breath. While he gave the appearance of thinking, Ava held still, hardly daring to breathe. Finally, he walked away from her and out of the galley's second entrance that would take him deeper into the center of the ship.

Heart in her throat, she darted in the opposite direction. Back out the door she'd entered, around the corner to the stairs, and down to the first deck where her father was being held. If she had time, she might be able to figure out the code to get the door open, but then what? She needed something to deal with the chains—and a way to communicate with the outside world.

Ava had lost track of Nicolai's location, but she couldn't stop trying. She wasn't leaving without her father. She noted the speedboat in the dock but had no clue how to release it and get it out of the garage. So for now, she'd concentrate on rescuing her father.

She opened each door she passed until she finally came to the engine room. She shoved inside and shut the door behind her. For a moment, she leaned against it, clutching the knife in one hand, pressing the other to her chest, feeling her heart pound against her palm.

She needed something to get her father's chains off. Something. Anything. The large room was hot, and sweat broke out on her forehead. She drew in a steadying breath and started looking for a tool kit. Surely he kept one somewhere. The engine room made the most sense.

Or maybe it was under the sink in the galley or the hall bath closet. Or a guest stateroom.

Or in the torture room.

No, please, God, don't send me there.

But it would most likely have what she needed, and it would probably be the last place Nicolai would look for her.

She turned and headed for the door.

○ ○ ○

"We've been over this lake twice," Travis said, "and nothing. You want to keep going or look elsewhere?"

Caden didn't know. He wiped a hand across his brow and sent up a prayer for help. For the first time in his career, he didn't know what to do. What choice to make.

"She's out here, Travis. I feel it in my gut. I just don't know how to find her."

"I'll do whatever you guys want me to do," the pilot said. "The weather's good, but it's dark. I can use the spotlight if you don't think that would send him running."

Caden blinked. "Wait a minute. Maybe that's what we need. We need to send him running."

Travis met his gaze, his jaw tight, eyes narrowed. "I think you're right. Turn that spotlight on and let's try this again."

"You got it!"

○ ○ ○

Ava crept down the hallway, her heart in her throat. She thought it might be permanently lodged there at this point. The fact that she could no longer hear Nicolai worried her—for her father's sake. But at least her father was on the same deck as the torture room, so if she could find something to deal with the chains, then—

Footsteps in the hallway alerted her and sent her hurrying to the room she'd run from only a few minutes before—or had it been longer? She wasn't sure how much time had passed, but it didn't matter. The longer she stayed out of Nicolai's clutches, the better her—and her father's—chance of survival. Maybe.

She slipped inside and shut the door. There was a deadbolt on the inside and she twisted it. It could be opened from the outside, but at least if Nicolai decided to do so, the noise of it opening would give her a heads-up.

She leaned her forehead against the cool steel and swallowed hard while her fingers spasmed around the handle of the knife. Her desire not to see what the room held was overshadowed by her desperation to save her father.

With a deep breath, she turned. And saw her father on the television screen mounted on the far wall. He paced his enclosure like a restless lion. When he let out a scream, it echoed through the room and singed her eardrums.

"Dad," she whispered. "Can you hear me?"

He whirled toward the camera, his wild eyes landing on hers. "Ava?" He strode toward the television and reached out a hand as though he could touch her through the screen.

"I'm coming."

"Get off this boat!"

"Get your shoes on and be ready to run."

A mixture of resignation and hope flared in his eyes. "If you make it to the door, the code is 1379. At least that's what Nicolai taunted me with. Said if I could get word to someone where I was, the code to the room was 1379. Told me that over and over."

"Okay. Be ready. I've got to find something to get the chains off."

She turned. He'd lit candles around the table centered in the room and her stomach lurched. She desperately tried not to picture herself strapped to it and at the mercy of a madman. The flames flickered ominously in the dark area, casting shadows on the walls and ceiling.

Focus, Ava. She scanned the tools on the wall behind the table. A saw, hammer, a bucket of nails. A cat-o'-nine-tails and more. "Don't think about what those are for," she whispered, "just find what you need."

And then her eyes landed on the most important thing there—bolt cutters. Keeping her gaze from everything else, she hurried toward the cutters, yanked them from the wall, and strode back to the door.

Only to hear the lock turn.

Ava froze for a split second, then stepped to the hinged side of the door.

Nicolai pushed it open and Ava waited, her blood pounding in her veins. He walked forward and she timed her move according to his footsteps.

Then he paused.

Come on, one more step.

Ava's gaze swung to the television where her father watched with horror stamped on his features. "I'm going to find a way to get to you, Nicolai," he said. "I see Ava got away. I'm next."

"She's still on this boat," Nicolai answered with a sneer in his voice. "I'll find her."

One more step! She shifted the bolt cutters higher.

"Now!" Her father's shout spurred her.

She swept around the edge of the door, swung the cutters, and caught Nicolai on the side of the head.

With a grunt, he staggered back and slammed against the wall. He pushed off and stumbled forward, hands reaching for her. She spun away and he lunged. But he missed and crashed into the table. The candles wobbled, several hit the carpeted floor. Then Nicolai's eyes closed, and he dropped with a thud, blood gushing down his temple to pool on the carpet. She couldn't tell if he was breathing or not. Was he faking?

"Get out of the room, Ava! Go!"

The flames licked along the carpet quickly and were too much for her to try to put out at this point. She had nothing to use. She started to turn but caught a glimpse of Nicolai's chest rising.

She raised the cutters to hit the man who had terrorized and murdered so many one more time, but hesitated.

"Ava!" Her father's strangled cry swung her gaze up. He gave a slow shake of his head.

But she didn't need his silent protest. She couldn't do it. Not with Nicolai unconscious and no longer a threat. It would feel too much like murder.

And besides, death would be too easy for him. She leaned over and poked him in the arm, and got no reaction. "Leave him, Ava!"

"I'm going." She started to rise, and Nicolai's hand clamped hard around her wrist.

"Ava!" Her father's shout echoed in her ears. She kicked out, caught Nicolai in the stomach, and yanked out of his grip. She spun and raced to the door.

"You'll pay for this!"

She glanced back. Nicolai had pushed himself to his feet and stood there swaying, blood dripping off his chin, while the flames reached toward the wall with the tools. He tried to walk, only to fall to his knees, his hand raised to his head. She almost went back for him but couldn't take the chance that he'd manage to overpower her. With one last look at the man, she snagged the knob and pulled the door shut.

Bolt cutters in hand, she ran to her father's room-slash-prison and punched in the numbers. 1379. *Please, please work.*

The beeps echoed through the hallway.

Smoke seeped under the torture room door to swirl around her.

She ignored it and pulled her father's door open. He stood

as close as he could get to the entrance, hands held out in front of him. "Hurry."

Ava ran to cut the chains shackling him to the wall first. Once he was free, she grabbed one hand and turned to lead him out of the room. Flames were already eating up the carpet in the hallway, and the thick smoke blinded her for a moment.

"We'll get those others off as soon as we can," she shouted over the roar of the fire.

"I'm good. Let's get out of here."

Together they raced for the stairs.

A gunshot sounded behind them and Ava ducked. Her father shoved her ahead of him. "Go!"

Ava bolted up the stairs, still clutching the cutters.

Another shot pinged off the ceiling in front of her. At the top, she spun away from the stairwell and her father did the same. Two more bullets whipped past.

Her father gripped her hand. "Into the water!"

TWENTY-SIX

"This isn't working." Caden raked a hand through his hair and dejection set in.

"We're not done yet," the pilot said. "We've still got the part of the lake on the other side of that island."

"We've been covering the same territory for the last hour."

"This is a big lake, Caden," Travis said. "Lots of little islands. Several big ones. Water patrol has started going island to island."

"Which is going to take forever. That's why we have the chopper." He pressed his palms to burning eyes. "What if he came out here and hooked up the boat and hauled it off and this is all for nothing?" He hated to ask that out loud, but he had to face the possibility that he was wrong. *God, we need some help here. Please, please let us find her.*

The prayers had gone up nonstop, and he knew Sarah and the others were adding their prayers to the mix as well. But . . . no Ava.

"What if I was wrong?" he asked.

Travis glanced up from his study of the lake as the spotlight illuminated yet another land mass in the middle of the water.

"Sorry, buddy. Maybe—" He frowned. "Hey, is that smoke?" he asked. "Hey, Roger, keep the light on that smoke, will you?"

"Yeah," the pilot said, "passing around to see where it's coming from."

Caden looked out the door. "It's that yacht. The one we saw earlier. Get lower! I think someone just jumped off the deck!"

The helicopter swooped lower, causing the water to churn. "It's Ava! And someone's with her!"

A flash sparked from the yacht and something solid hit the windshield with a thud. Caden jerked back. "They're shooting at us!" Another bullet pinged on Caden's side.

"Gotta get out of here," Roger said.

"No way! I'm not leaving Ava with an active shooter!" Caden ripped off his Kevlar vest that would sink him like a rock. "I'm jumping. Get me close enough." Then he pulled his headset off so he didn't have to hear the protests coming from the others.

Travis shoved a life jacket into his hands and grabbed one for himself. "Guess I'm coming too. Send the water police to the right island!"

"Go!" Roger motioned for them to bail just as a huge fireball headed toward them. "It's a flare!"

Caden jumped, feet straight out below him. Travis followed and he heard the chopper whine off just as he hit the water with a hard *whoosh* and lost his grip on the life jacket.

He kicked, pushing himself back up toward the surface. He broke through and looked around for Travis. He spotted him about ten feet away. "You okay?" Caden called. The life jacket floated nearby and he grabbed it.

"Yeah. You?"

"Peachy."

"Then let's go get Ava." Travis struck out in the direction they'd seen Ava go in. More gunshots bit the water in that same area, spurring Caden to stroke faster. The water was cold and his clothes weighed him down, but Ava was in trouble.

At least she was alive. Relief made him want to go weak, but he pressed on. He hadn't realized how terrified he'd been that he would be too late. If he was even able to find her at all. But he'd seen her. Even though he'd lost her for the moment, she was alive.

He caught up to Travis. "Swim for the island. That's where they'll have to go."

The gunshots had ceased.

Guided by the burning yacht, fighting the weight of his clothing and his desperate fear for Ava, he swam, his senses tuned to the scene in front of him.

Finally, his feet hit the bottom of the lake and he pushed through to the shore, feeling the fatigue in his muscles but the adrenaline flowing through his veins.

Travis joined him on the sandy beach, and together they raced for the tree line in case the shooter was still looking for a target.

The yacht still burned, a bright spot amidst the inky blackness. "How long do you think it'll take the water police to get here?"

"Shouldn't be long. My concern is whether or not Nicolai made it off the boat. If he didn't, then we should be good."

A shot rang out beyond the trees and Caden hit the ground. Travis did the same a second later. "That wasn't aimed at us, was it?"

"No," Caden said, "but I guess that answers our question."

"Yeah. Nicolai's out there and so are Ava and maybe her father."

□ □ □

The bullet screamed past Ava's ear and she ducked back behind the tree trunk. Her blood pulsed and she fought the fear that wanted to suck her under. She had no idea where they were or how they'd gotten there. Her father pressed a hand to his bloodied side and groaned. "Ava, get down."

"I'm down, but I need to know where he is."

"The bullet came from your left. I think he was running from the direction of the yacht when he fired."

"And I think it was a shot in the dark. I don't think he knows where we are." Unfortunately, he wasn't the only one.

When they'd jumped from the deck and hit the water, Ava had managed to grab her father and pull him to the surface. But he'd been hit by one of Nicolai's bullets and had a hard time using the arm to swim—not to mention he still wore the shackles on his wrists. She'd had to drop the bolt cutters to pull him through the water. Now, exhaustion swept over her and her muscles trembled. But somehow, someway, they were going to survive this. She needed to tell Caden she loved him. And she wanted to go out on a date with him. No, she wanted to go out on *many* dates with him. And she wanted to kiss him. And she wanted to see her mom again, then hug her brother and tell him she would do better as a sister. She refused to cry as the thoughts pressed in.

"It's not too bad, I don't think," her dad said, looking at the wound in his bicep and bringing her back to reality. "I think it might have nicked the bone, but it's not broken. Just painful." He looked up. "Guess we might have matching scars."

"Lovely."

She could only pray he was right because she had no idea how she was going to signal their location and bring help. The burning yacht should alert the water police for the need to investigate, but she was going to have to warn them—or anyone else drawn to the flames—about Nicolai. "Stay here, Dad. I've got to watch for help. If anyone comes close, Nicolai's going to shoot them and take their boat to escape."

"What are you going to do?"

"Make sure he doesn't have a chance to kill anyone else."

He caught her hand. "Ava, you can't—"

She covered his mouth. "Stop. There's no other choice. If we want to get to safety and make sure no one else dies in the process, I've got to do something."

He groaned and leaned his head back against the tree. "Please don't get yourself killed."

"That's the plan." She planted a kiss on his forehead. Then hesitated. She grabbed a sturdy tree branch and snapped off a portion of it, creating a sharp point. "Send this through his heart if you have to."

"Not sure that man has a heart, but this is good. Better than nothing, for sure." He shifted with a low grunt and nodded. "Okay, I'm set. Let's go."

"You're not coming."

"I sure am."

"You'll make too much noise, Dad. Your breathing alone will alert Nicolai to our location. You sit here, get your breathing under control—and trust that you and the Navy trained me well enough to do what I need to do."

He studied her for a brief moment. It was dark, but the moon filtered through the trees, allowing her to see his face. Finally, he nodded. "You're right. Do what you've got to do."

She turned and raced back the way she'd come, heading for the beach area. At the tree line, she stopped and scanned the beach. Two figures, backlit by the moon, moved along the shoreline, and she squinted, trying to figure out who they were.

"Well, Ava, I guess it's just you and me now."

That hated voice came from behind her. Somehow she'd passed him, alerting him. Then the smell hit her. A nauseating combination of singed flesh and a coppery metallic scent that turned her stomach. She stood frozen as a dozen responses flickered through her brain.

Slowly, she turned and her gaze collided with his. He held the gun on her, and she took in his appearance. The left half of his face had been charred beyond recognition. She swallowed. He limped as he moved closer—he had to be in horrible pain. But the hand that held the gun was steady.

Ava backed up, placing one foot carefully behind the other. "Stop."

"No," she said. "If you plan to shoot me, then go for it."

Sirens cut through the night. Helicopter blades pounded the air, drawing closer with each second.

"You ruined it," he said, his breath hitching. "You ruined it all. It wasn't supposed . . . to go like . . . this."

"Put the gun down, Nicolai. It's over."

He hesitated, swaying, his breathing growing more ragged by the second. "You're right. It's over. But if you don't die, then I will have broken . . . my . . . promise. And I can't . . . do that. I . . . prom—" His hand twitched.

A gunshot sounded and Ava flinched, waiting for the pain to hit. Instead, blood foamed from Nicolai's mouth and he went to his knees as two more shots caught him center mass. His weapon dropped from his fingers to the sand.

He fell face forward and was still, the tree branch protruding from his back. Ava's father stood beyond him. She spun. "Caden! Travis!"

Caden held his weapon on Nicolai. He'd shot it at the same time her father had launched his homemade spear with surprising accuracy.

Ava ran to Caden and threw her arms around his neck. He pulled cuffs from his belt and tossed them to Travis. Then he hugged her close, burying his face in her hair, his breath rasping against her ear. "I was scared to death I wouldn't be in time. You're okay? You're not hurt? You need an ambu—"

She turned his face toward her and settled his lips over hers.

And clung. She was so happy to see him that she wanted to cry. But kissing him came first. Once he got over his surprise, he responded most enthusiastically, wrapping his fingers in her hair while his kiss conveyed his sheer relief that she was in his arms.

She wasn't sure how long the embrace lasted, but when Caden finally lifted his head, she caught Travis doing his best to hide a snicker while he sat next to the cuffed dead man. Her father had a similar look of bemusement, before he winced and clenched his jaw in pain.

Because of his gunshot wound.

She gasped. "Dad." She ran to him and gripped his arm, then looked back at Caden. "We need to get him to a hospital."

"The water police are here. Let's get him loaded on the boat. They can call an ambulance to meet us back at shore."

"Thank you."

Officers swarmed the sandy beach, and two of them took over helping to get her father on board.

One of the others wrapped a blanket around her shoulders and did the same for Travis and Caden.

Once they were in the boat with her father stretched out on the floor between the seats, she held his hand and looked at Caden. "It's over now, right?"

"It's over."

Ava's tears released and she sniffed, trying to hold them back and failing. Caden slid over next to her and wrapped an arm around her. "It's all going to be okay now."

"I want to go see my mom," she whispered.

"Sure thing."

"And John, I want to know how John is."

Caden asked one of the officers if they could borrow his phone. The man handed it back to them and Ava dialed Julie's number.

The woman answered on the first ring. "Hello?"

"It's Ava."

"Ava!" Julie's screech had Ava yanking the phone from her ear. "Are you okay?"

"Yes, yes, I'm all right. Is John okay?"

"We're at the hospital and he's recovering. Hold on a minute. He wants to talk to you."

"Ava?"

His deep voice brought tears to her eyes. As irritated as she'd been with him, she hadn't wanted him dead. "John, I'm so glad you're okay." The words came out of a suddenly tight throat.

"I'm sorry, Ava. I only wanted to protect you and Paul, and I . . . messed up. I acted without thinking everything through and that was a disaster. If you'd been killed—"

"But I wasn't. And Dad's okay too." She looked at her father's pale face and prayed her words were true. "We'll be at the hospital soon and I'll fill you in."

She hung up and swiped the tears from her cheeks once more. She handed the phone back to the officer and leaned into Caden, not caring that he was soaking wet. He kissed her head and she smiled. "Thank you."

"You're welcome." He fell silent, then cleared his throat. "So . . . where do you want to go for our third date?"

She sat up, recognizing what he was doing in the attempt to cope with the horror they'd just survived. "What?" she asked. "Third date? We haven't had the first one yet."

"Of course we did."

She blinked. "What'd I miss?"

"Actually, now that I think about it, we've had a bunch of dates."

Ava shifted so she could see him. "Explain yourself, Caden Denning."

"All those times I came to the nursing home to see you. We did puzzles, played board games and cards, and talked about nearly every topic you can think of. Those were lots of dates."

"Those weren't dates. Those were just . . . hanging out and eating and talking."

He tilted his head. "So, how is that different from a date?"

"It's not," her father murmured.

"No one asked you, Dad," she said.

"Thank you, sir," Caden said at the same time.

Travis snorted.

"And then there was the night that Petra sent us out to eat."

"That wasn't a date, that was . . . forced proximity."

A choking sound came from her father. Travis turned his back, but his shaking shoulders gave him away. Ava found herself fighting her own smile. How could she smile?

Because she was alive. *Thank you, God, for life.* And she wanted to relish the feeling.

"Actually," Caden said, "we've already had our third date. I cooked steaks for you, remember?"

"Yeah. Those were really good."

"Thank you." He paused. "So, was that a date?"

"That was . . ."

"It was a date," the officer said as they pulled to the dock.

"There was no kissing," Ava said. "It wasn't a date."

"But you'll go out with me on a real date?"

"Yes! Yes, I'll go out with you."

"Thank God," her father rasped.

Caden leaned over and planted his lips on hers, kissing her in such a way that left her breathless. Again. When he released her, she blinked. "What was that for?"

"According to you, kissing is what makes it officially a date, so that's our second. You just said you'll go out with me and that will be our third official date because there will be kissing involved." He shot her a smug smile. "Told you I'd get a third one."

"You never told me that."

He frowned. "I didn't?" His face cleared. "Oh yeah, I told myself I would. So, that's all that matters."

Ava let loose the laughter that she'd been choking back. Giggle after giggle pealed from her, and it was from more than just the inane conversation. It was a release of the terror, the gratitude that she'd just lived through a nightmare—and the excitement that Caden wanted to date her. And kiss her.

Yes, she had much to process, but at least she got to do so with the man at her side.

Once everyone was off the boat and she and Caden were encased in the back of a cruiser, she reached for his hand and squeezed. "You saved my life, Caden. Thank you. And, truthfully, I'm looking forward to our third official date."

He hugged her one more time, then the officer climbed into the driver's seat and they headed to the hospital, following the ambulance carrying her father.

Away from death and destruction and toward a future filled with hope and love.

TWENTY-SEVEN

Ava held Caden's hand as they walked into the hospital and headed for the maternity ward. "How'd the talk with your dad go?"

"Good," she said. "Really good. He answered a lot of questions I've had for years."

"The biggest one involving the intruder that night when you were fifteen. What'd he say?"

"The man was Maksim Kuznetsov. He'd just learned about his former wife's and children's deaths and came to ask my father how he'd let that happen. He went crazy and attacked my father because Dad had promised they'd be safe. And the truth was, Dad had arranged to get them out of Moscow that very week, but the KGB found out and acted. My dad said after I left, Max completely broke down. He sent the man on his way and never heard from him again." She shook her head as they rounded a corner toward the elevator. "Okay, change of subject. I can't believe she's finally here." Brooke had given birth six hours ago and had texted them to come meet the baby.

Caden smiled. "Asher said Brooke was ready about two months ago."

"He's going to be a great dad."

"He's already wrapped. That little girl is going to cause many sleepless nights."

"She's a newborn. That's what babies do."

He laughed. "True. So do sixteen-year-olds, from what I've heard."

They waited for the elevator and he took her hand. "When we leave here, we'll get the flowers for your mother's grave, then head over to put them in the vase. Does that work?"

She nodded. "Thank you." Her mother had passed away four weeks ago, and she, her father, Caden, and Nathan had been at her side. It had been peaceful and fast after they'd received the call that her mother probably had only hours to live. And while Ava missed her terribly, she rested in the promise that since her mother was a believer, she'd see her again one day.

Nathan now knew the truth about his father and Ava and was processing it but, thankfully, seemed to be handling it okay. Like Ava, he was just glad for the miraculous return of the man. He'd shaken his head at the end of the long story. "You realize I can never tell anyone about this. I'd be laughed out of medical school and branded a liar."

"You're not mad or hurt or . . . something . . . that we didn't tell you?" Ava had asked him.

"Are you kidding? No way. I didn't need that kind of stress." He'd glanced at his father. "You're retired now, right?"

"Uh . . . well . . ."

Nathan waved a hand. "Never mind. I don't want to know. Let me enjoy my ignorance."

He'd returned to school and would graduate with honors in December, and Ava had stopped "helicoptering." As much as possible anyway. He *was* still her little brother.

"Room 227, right?" Caden asked.

"Yeah."

They stepped into the elevator, and Caden pulled her into a hug and kissed her, a light peck that spoke of comfort in their relationship. "I just want you to know this has been the best six weeks of my life. Discounting your mother's death, of course."

Ava smiled. "I feel the same. And Mom was ready to go. I'm glad she's not suffering anymore."

"Any nightmares last night?"

"A few, but I'm certain they'll get better. Talking to Brooke has helped. What about you?"

"Just the same one."

That she'd jumped off the deck of the yacht, only to have Nicolai catch her and drown her. She squeezed his fingers. "They'll pass."

The doors slid open and they walked down the hall to room 227 to find a crowded room and Brooke sitting in the bed looking radiant. Ava blinked. "You have makeup on. Like you literally could go pose for a family portrait or something."

Brooke laughed. "I gave birth. I'm not sick."

Ava shook her head and held out her arms to Asher, who couldn't seem to take his eyes off his new daughter. The besotted look on his face made her smile.

He hesitated, then passed her to Ava.

"What's her name?" Caden asked.

Brooke shot a look at Asher, who grinned. "Ashlynn Christine."

"I love it."

"The A stands for Ava," Brooke said, "the S is for Sarah, and the H is for Heather. The Lynn and Christine are just because we like them."

Ava's breath caught and she met the eyes of her other two best friends. "I'm so honored."

Sarah and Heather nodded and swiped tears. Gavin and Travis reached for the tissue box at the same time. Gavin snagged it and passed it to Sarah, who pulled a tissue from it.

The ring on her left hand winked at Ava about the same time Heather saw it. "Hey, what's that?"

"What?" Sarah asked, her innocent expression not fooling Ava. Or Heather. Heather stepped over to look at Sarah's hand, then up to meet her gaze. "You didn't."

"Well . . ."

"We did," Gavin said.

"When? Why?" Brooke asked.

Sarah shrugged. "We weren't sure my dad was going to make it there for a while. So, two days after Caden and Ava managed to escape that psycho, Gavin and I decided we didn't want to wait anymore. And we got married at my dad's side."

Brooke raised her eyebrows at Sarah. "So that's why you said you postponed the wedding." She turned those brows on Ava. "I'm impressed. You kept this a secret."

Ava shrugged. "It was hard, but it wasn't my news to share."

"But we want to celebrate with everyone," Sarah said, "so just as soon as things calm down, we're going to have a party and everyone's invited."

"Well, that makes me feel slightly better," Brooke muttered.

Sarah bit her lip and scanned the room. "You're not upset with us, are you? It's not that we didn't want you there, I promise."

Heather pouted. "I'll get over it."

"Maybe," Brooke said.

Ava passed Ashlynn back to her father, and Travis wrapped an arm around Heather's shoulders to whisper something in her ear. She flushed and shook her head. Ava thought she said, "Not yet."

"So," Ava said, "what's going on with you two? You have something to share?"

Travis grinned. "We didn't want to steal anyone's spotlight."

"Tell us," Sarah demanded.

"Heather said yes."

Ava gasped. "What? That's so wonderful! Congratulations! I know Ryker has to be over-the-moon excited." Ryker was the young man Travis had taken in to live with him after his homelife imploded. He'd also saved Heather's life during the time she'd had a killer after her.

"Ryker takes credit for it, actually," Heather said.

Sarah stood. "Well, as much as I hate to break up the party, I guess we'd better go. Dad is expecting us for dinner." She looked at Caden. "Are you coming?"

"Of course. After we go put flowers on Ava's mother's grave."

"Good." She and Gavin said their goodbyes and left.

Heather and Travis did the same, leaving Brooke and Asher alone with Ava and Caden.

Brooke studied him. "Have you made your peace with your dad?"

Ava squeezed his hand and he nodded. "Yeah, I think I have. Almost losing him was a big eye-opener. I don't agree with him a lot, but he's my father and I love him."

"Good, I'm glad." Brooke's eyes drooped and Ava pulled Caden backward.

"I think it's time for us to leave too. Your daughter is beautiful, Brooke. Thank you for letting her have a piece of my name. I'm touched and thrilled."

Brooke smiled. "Of course. And you get to keep her so Asher and I can have a date night sometime soon."

"That works for us," Caden said. "Just so you know, Ava and I have our sixteenth official date tonight. Dinner with my dad, but . . ."

"You're counting?" Brooke's amusement shone in her eyes.

"Absolutely. For a guy whose goal was to get through the third date, I'm quite proud of myself."

Ava groaned. "You're such an overachiever. Come on. I think your dad invited my dad to come tonight too, so we may be dodging all kinds of crazy."

Caden's groan matched hers and Ava smiled. Never in a million years would she have pictured this as her future. Her father alive, her falling in love with Caden—surpassing the second date. She almost laughed. It just went to prove that whatever she prayed for, if God said no, it was because he had something better in mind for her.

And she was okay with that.

She and Caden said their goodbyes and left. He slid an arm around her shoulder and tucked her next to him.

"So . . . ," he said.

"Yes?"

"If I asked, would you say yes?"

Her heart thudded. "Depends on what you're asking."

"We made it past the third date."

"We did." He guided her left when they should have gone right. "Cade?"

He pushed through a set of stained-glass double doors into the hospital chapel and a calm certainty settled over her. He walked her down to the front and turned her to face him while they stood in front of the cross.

Clasping her hands, he smiled at her. His hands trembled slightly, and she squeezed them. "When Nicolai came after you," he said, "I was terrified and I prayed that God would spare you so that I could tell you how much you mean to me. And he answered that prayer."

Ava swallowed and her heart thudded in her ears. "I was doing a lot of praying myself. Very similar to yours."

"Ava, I love you. I'm at the point where I know with one hundred percent certainty that I want to spend the rest of my life with you, but I know you've had tons of upheaval in the last few weeks with moving and your new job—and everything. If you need more time, I'll wait for you to let me know when you're ready."

"I'm ready."

He paused and his eyes narrowed. "That was fast."

"I knew it before the third date, Caden. I probably knew it when I was sixteen years old with a big fat crush on you. But I'm not that giddy teenager anymore. What I feel for you is an adult-sized love." She paused. "Otherwise you never would have made it through the third date."

He laughed, and she said, "I can't believe this is happening. I always said I'd never marry. Not that you've asked yet," she rushed to add.

"I'm asking, but I'm willing to take it slow too. Although, when you think about it, you said 'never' to quite a few things that you're now saying yes to. It's funny how life can throw you a curve ball when you least expect it—or how God can change your perspective."

"No kidding. Are you sure you're all right with God's latest curve ball?" she asked.

"I'm fine with it. In fact, I'm very proud of you. And I've already been approved for the transfer, so it's pretty much a done deal. But we'll work hard at this because we both want it. And as long as we make sure there aren't any lies between us, we'll be okay."

She drew in a deep breath. "There's just one more thing."

"What?"

"I don't know that I'll ever want children. I mean, I do. I would love to have children, but . . . not yet. And I don't know if that will change."

"I kind of suspected that would be the case when we discussed you taking this job. I'm willing to wait and see how

God works that out too." He smiled. "In the meantime, we'll just borrow little Ashlynn if we need a kid fix."

She threw her arms around him. "Oh, how I love you. Then in answer to your question, yes, I would say yes."

"Then I'll ask again. Better this time." He dropped to one knee and kept his gaze on hers. "Will you marry me, Ava Marie Jackson?"

"I will, Caden Lewis Denning."

He rose and kissed her. A long kiss that held only a fraction of the passion she knew he was capable of.

The ringing of her phone interrupted them and she pulled away to glance at the screen. "It's John."

Caden nodded and she put it on speaker. "Hi, John."

"Glad I caught you, Ava. How are you feeling?"

"Like I'm on cloud nine. Caden and I just got engaged."

"Congratulations." He really did sound thrilled for them. "I hate to cut the engagement festivities short, but I've got a question for you."

"Okay."

"All of your paperwork has been processed, your housing is ready, and everything is in place. Are you ready for your first assignment?"

She looked at Caden. "We're ready."

Turn the Page for a Special Sneak Peek of

LYNETTE EASON'S **NEWEST SUSPENSE SERIES**

COMING JANUARY 2022

CHAPTER

ONE

FRIDAY
NOVEMBER
4:45PM

Today was not going to be the day they died—not if she had anything to say about it. EMS helicopter pilot Penny Carlton tightened her grip on the throttle of the Messerschmitt-Bölkow-Blohm Bo 105 chopper and prayed the wind would calm down long enough to get their patient to Mercy Mission Hospital just on the other side of the mountain.

Flying in bad weather was nothing new and Penny often did it without hesitation, knowing it was a life-or-death situation. But today was exceptionally bad, with rain and ice slashing the windshield, and requiring all of her concentration to keep them on course. Not to mention in the air.

"Come on, Betty Sue, you can do this. We've come this far, we're gonna make it, right?" Penny talked to the chopper on occasion—mostly when she was worried.

She'd protested the flight to her supervisor, and he'd ordered her to do it or find another job. With only the brief thought that she should walk away, her mind went to the person in jeopardy. At the time, the weather hadn't been nearly as violent as it was now, so she'd ignored the weather warnings and agreed, praying they could beat the storm long enough to get in, get the patient, and get out.

Unfortunately, things hadn't worked out that way and now she battled the weather while fifteen-year-old Claire Gentry fought to live.

Claire had been hiking with friends along one of Mount Mitchell's most rugged trails when a gust of harsh wind had blown her off balance and over the side of the mountain onto a ledge below. Once the rescue team had gotten her back up, it had been her turn to make sure Claire lived to see sixteen. "How's she doing back there?"

"Not good," Holly Cooper said into her mic. A nurse practitioner, Holly could handle just about any medical emergency that came up. However, controlling the weather was out of their hands. "Raina, hand me that morphine," Holly said. "She's hurting. And get pressure back on her side. She's bleeding again."

Raina Price, the critical care transport paramedic, moved to obey. The three of them had been saving lives together for the past twenty months.

Thunder boomed and lightning lit up the sky way too close to her for comfort. Penny tuned out the familiar beep and whine of the machines behind her, knowing the best way she could help Claire was to get her to the hospital.

A hard slam against the left side of the chopper knocked the cyclical control stick from her grip, sending them sideways. Yells from Raina and Holly echoed in her ears. "Hold on!" Penny grabbed the stick, righted the chopper, and pushed the left antitorque pedal, the helicopter sluggish in response to her attempts to turn it into the wind.

"Penny! What's happening?"

"We got hit with something! I think it's the tail rotor. I'm going to have to land it."

"You can't." Holly's calm words helped settle her racing pulse. A fraction. "Claire's most likely going to die if we don't get her to the hospital."

The wind sent them into a rapid descent, sending Penny's stomach with it. The chopper wasn't spinning so the tail rotor wasn't completely damaged, but something was definitely— desperately—wrong. "I don't have a choice!" They were *all* going to die if she didn't do something now. She keyed her microphone and advised air traffic control of the emergency and their approximate location.

". . . breaking up . . . please repeat."

Penny did and got silence for her efforts. "Mayday! Mayday. Anyone there?"

Nothing. She was out of time.

The instrument panel flashed and went dark. "No, don't do that. You're not supposed to do that."

"Do what?" Holly yelled.

Penny ignored her and got a grip on her fear while she tried to make out the fast-approaching ground. A flash of lightning allowed her to spot a small neighborhood with a row of houses farther down the side of the mountain—at least she thought she did. It was dark and the storm was now raging, visibility practically nil.

She was going to have to go by the memory of the brief glance. The top of the mountain was flat with a bare area where she thought she could safely land. Or at least not crash into trees—or homes.

The throttle was set, controlled by the governor. Now all she had to do was point the nose of the chopper downward to keep them from entering an out-of-control spin. "Come on, girl, you can do this," she muttered. "We can do this. Just a little farther." The trees were somewhere straight ahead. The loose watch on her left wrist bounced against her skin in time with the movement of the chopper.

"Penny!" Holly's tightly held fear bled through her voice. "Tell me what we're doing."

"Just focus on your patient and I'll get us on the ground. We're going to be fine." *Please, God, let us be okay. Please.* She'd trained for this. Over and over, she'd practice what to do if she lost a tail rotor or had engine issues or whatever. The engine was still good. For now. For a brief moment, her panel flickered to life and she quickly checked her altitude and airspeed. So far so good.

"I can do this," she whispered. "Come on, Betty Sue, please don't quit on me now." She'd trained for this very situation.

They'd *all* trained for this. Mostly, focusing on how to keep the patient stable in the midst of an emergency landing. *Landing, please. Not a crash.*

When her panel fluttered then went dark once more, she groaned and squinted through the glass. More thunder shook the air around them, but the nonstop lightning was going to be what saved them.

The landing spot she'd picked out wasn't perfect, but it was going to have to do. At least it was mostly flat—and big. "Brace yourselves," she said. "It's going to be a rough landing, but we *are* going to walk away from this. *All* of us."

The tops of the trees were closer than she'd like, but the small opening just beyond them was within reach. "Almost there!" A gust of wind whipped hard against her and debris crashed into the windshield spreading the cracks. Penny let out a screech but kept her grip steady. "Come on, come on." She maneuvered the controls, keeping an eye on the trees through the cracked windshield. Okay, the tail rotor was responding somewhat. That would help. "We're going to have a hard bounce! Be ready."

She whooshed past the trees, their tips scraping the under-belly of the chopper, but she cleared them. Her heart pounded in her ears. Down, down . . .

The helicopter tilted, the right landing skid hitting first and sliding across the rocky ground. A scream came from the back and supplies flew through the cabin. Something slammed into the side of Penny's helmet and she flinched even as she pushed hard on the collective, desperate to get both skids on the ground while whispering prayers beneath her breath. They bounced, rocked, then settled on the skids. Upright and still breathing.

She'd done it. She was alive. *They* were alive. With shaking hands, she shut down the engine and took off her headphones. *Thank you, Jesus.*

She turned to see Raina and Holly unbuckling their safety harnesses. Holly dropped to her knees next to the patient while Raina dabbed at a cut on her forehead. "You okay?"

"Yeah. This is minor compared to what it could have been."

"How's Claire?" Penny asked.

"Hanging in there," Holly said. She pulled the stethoscope from her ears. "Where are we?"

"I don't know, but there's a rescue team on the way. I hope." If they could get through. Even now, the rain and wind whipped at the chopper body. "We just need to stay put until someone comes."

Raina met her eyes. "You did good, Pen. I don't know how you did it, but you did."

Penny wasn't sure either. "God did it. I was praying the whole time, so that's the only explanation I've got."

"Yeah."

She needed to check the chopper and see what the damage was. Not that she could fix it, but . . .

She glanced upward. "Thank you," she whispered.

Holly shot her a quick look. "What?"

301

"Nothing." Penny eyed the teen and didn't like what she was seeing. She snagged the radio and called it in, then waited. No reply. With another glance at her passengers, she tried one more time, all the while knowing it was useless. "Mayday, Mayday, Mayday. This is Medevac 2646 advising of an emergency landing somewhere on top of Mount Mitchell. Requesting immediate extraction. Four passengers. One critical. Over."

No response.

"Okay, that's not good," she muttered. She snagged her cell phone from her pocket. One bar. She dialed 911 and waited. The call dropped. She tried again with the same result. If she had a sat phone, she could use that, but she didn't. And she didn't have time to be angry over the reason why.

Think, Penny, think. She turned back to the others who were monitoring Claire. "Holly, I can't get a signal and nothing's happening with the radio. I'm going to have to try and walk until I get something."

Raina scowled. "Stupid mountains."

"All right, here's the deal," Penny said. "I have no idea if anyone heard my Mayday—or anything else. You guys keep Claire stable. I'll be back as soon as I can get word to someone where to find us. I saw a few houses scattered in the area. I just need to find a road and follow it. Hopefully, the closer I get to a neighborhood or house, I'll pick up a cell phone signal."

"Can't they track the ELT?" Holly asked.

The emergency locater transmitter. "They should be able to, but I don't know that I want to take a chance on it malfunctioning. Something's going on with the electrical. The instrument panel keeps flickering, and the radio's not working."

"You can't go out in this," Raina said. "This weather is too dangerous."

"If Claire wasn't in such bad shape, I'd sit it out with you guys, but I've got to try—and as soon as we get back, we're having a fundraiser for a satellite phone." She was going to have it out with her supervisor as soon as she saw him face to face. Thanks to his budget cutting, they could very well die out here. If she had a sat phone, she could—

Nope. Not going to think about that.

Penny grabbed the poncho from the bin next to the stretcher. "If I'm not back and help arrives, you get Claire to the hospital. I can wait for the next ride."

"But Pen—" Holly started to protest, but Penny was already shaking her head.

"I mean it," she said. "You know you can't wait on me to get back."

"Fine," Raina said. "But if you're not back in an hour, I'm coming looking for you."

"Don't you dare. Holly needs your help with Claire. I'll be fine. If I can survive juvie, this little storm is child's play."

"Juvie?" Holly asked. "Why is this the first I've heard of that?"

"Long boring story. I was a bad girl, they sent me to juvie, and I got my head on straight. End of story."

"Right."

Penny pulled four protein bars and two bottles of water from the small pack she carried on every flight. "Just in case you guys get hungry." She slid the pack with the remaining protein bars and bottles of water over her shoulder and grabbed the emergency flashlight from the box, then opened the door. The rain had slacked off slightly—at least she thought so. She pulled the poncho over her and the pack and hopped to the ground. "Keep her alive! I'll be back!"

Penny shut the door behind her and turned. With her cell phone clutched in her left hand, she darted into the woods.

□ □ □

FBI Special Agent Holton Satterfield jerked his feet from the desktop and slammed them to the floor even while he pressed the phone to his ear. He hadn't thought the day could get any worse. First his conversation with his sister Rachel about their older sibling Zoe had gone so far south, it was probably north at this point. And now this. "I know you didn't just tell me that."

"Unfortunately, I did," Gerald Long said. The Special Supervisory Agent didn't sound any happier than Holt. "But Darius Rabor is armed and on the run."

"How?"

"He had help. His loyal girlfriend, Shondra Miller, disguised herself as a nurse and walked right in with a key to the cuffs." Gerald's disgust echoed through the line.

Holt wasn't going to bother asking how she managed to bypass all the security and ID checks to get to the patient. That was someone else's responsibility to investigate, but it had happened and now he needed to deal with the fallout.

"When?" After Darius Rabor, also known as the Lothario Killer, had killed a federal judge, the FBI had joined the hunt for him. Holt had been lead on the task force that had put Rabor away two years ago. He'd been on death row, his execution date coming up next month.

"Two hours ago," Gerald said. "Darius was in the hospital for emergency gall bladder surgery. Killed a nurse and the two transport officers. One of the hospital security guards is in surgery. I'm reconvening the original task force as everyone is already familiar with this guy. I need you and Sands in Asheville, North Carolina, yesterday."

"Asheville. Of course, he'd go back there," Holt muttered. "He knows those mountains well and he has family and friends there." Holt was in the Columbia, South Carolina, field office and Darius had been incarcerated at the Broad River Correctional Institution just a few miles away.

Where his sister was also an inmate. He grimaced at the unwanted thought. But there was nothing he could do about Zoe. He had a killer to capture again before anyone else died by his hand.

"Yep. He had surgery yesterday. This afternoon, he was in his room, cuffed to the bed. The next time someone checked on him, he was coming out of the bathroom, dressed in street clothes. Before the guard had a chance to pull his weapon, Rabor used a knife to stab the guy three times."

"That's his weapon of choice. A knife slipped to him by his girlfriend along with the key?"

"No doubt. And the clothes to allow him to blend in. After he killed the guard, he took the man's weapon and, in the ensuing chaos, shot his way out. The two then stole a car from the valet parking attendant and headed out of town with police after him. He made it to Asheville, then crashed at the bottom of Mount Mitchell. He and Shondra took off on foot going up. I'm sending you the coordinates. Police chased them up the mountain and put out an alert for residents to lock their homes and report anything suspicious. Asheville RA is expecting you and will be offering support." He paused. "On the ground anyway. Air support is iffy at this point with the storms getting ready to unleash their worst on the area. But you're going to have to take a chopper to get there. It's standing by. When you land, there'll be a car waiting for you."

Great. "We're on the way." He hung up, took a moment to gather his thoughts and emotions, then shot to his feet.

His partner, Martin Sands, looked up. "What now? More stuff with Zoe?"

Marty was the one person Holt felt comfortable venting to about his sister and her confession to killing her husband two years ago—and the fact that he believed she did it. He ignored the shame that tried to creep in every time he thought about her. He should be turning over every rock to find evidence to the contrary, but the truth was, he believed his sister guilty of murder. Why work to prove her innocence when all the evidence and her own words said the effort would be a waste of time?

"No, she's on the back burner for now. The Lothario Killer and his girlfriend are on the loose. You and I are now officially back on the task force to recapture him."

"What? You're kidding me. How?"

"I'll explain on the way."

Martin followed him out the door, muttering his displeasure. Holt let him vent while he concentrated on how best to catch the man. Again. It hadn't been easy the first time.

Darius would be even smarter—and he had his girlfriend helping him this time. However, he was one day out of surgery. How far could he get? Then again, the fact that he'd managed to kill three people in spite of being on drugs and, most likely, in pain, sent dread coursing through him. Holt knew better than anyone just how resourceful the killer was, and he had the scar to prove it. His hand went to the area just below the edge of his vest on his left side, but he didn't need to touch the place to know what was there. The nightmares reminded him most nights.

They headed for the chopper while thunder boomed in the distance. It wasn't raining yet, but it was ready to start at any moment. The pilot nodded to them and soon they were in the air headed toward the mountain. Thirty minutes later, he slid into the driver's seat of the Bureau's waiting sedan and checked the weather app on his phone. "This is going to be a fun drive. It's cold and icy and storm warnings are everywhere."

"We've driven through worse. Right?"

True, but he didn't like it any more than Marty did—and Marty *really* hated bad weather. Holt's phone dinged again. "Command center is on the way, too. We'll meet them there."

They drove through the blowing wind and rain with Holt fighting to keep the vehicle on the road. Across the street, at the base of the mountain, the mobile command center had already been set up in the elementary school parking lot. Holt ducked into the customized motorhome and shook the water out of his hair. Marty entered behind him. Seated in front of the first computer to Holt's left was Julianna Jameson. "Jules? What brings you here? He hasn't taken any hostages, has he?"

"Not yet."

Julianna was one of the Bureau's most skilled negotiators with the Crisis Negotiation Unit. She was also one of his favorite people with her quick wit and dry humor. However, she usually didn't go into the field unless the situation called for it.

"I was in the area doing some training. When I got word about the situation, I hightailed it over here. I'm here as a precaution," she said. "Local cops are swarming the area in spite of the weather. There are six small neighborhoods spaced out along the road that leads to the top of the mountain. There are two cop cars assigned to each one. One at the entrance and one that's driving a constant loop."

"What about the houses that don't have neighborhoods or fences or alarm systems?"

"We've activated the reverse 911 and officers are going door to door and asking residents to phone everyone they can think of to warn them, but it's definitely possible someone will be missed."

"Yeah."

"That's not all. We've gotten word that a Medevac chopper made an emergency landing about an hour ago in a clearing on top of the mountain and Gerald asked me to be on site just in case Darius manages to get there first."

"Oh no." He took a seat opposite her.

She studied him. "It's Penny and her crew, Holt. They've got a fifteen-year-old patient in pretty serious shape."

Holt raked a hand through his hair. Penny, Holly, and Raina had been the ones to save his life eighteen months ago. He and Penny had hit it off and had gone out a few times after he'd recovered. While their relationship was only at a friendship-but-could-possibly-be-more stage—and had been for longer than he liked—their schedules hadn't allowed more than brief dinners and short conversations on the phone. But he cared about Penny. A lot.

Penny and Julianna were tight friends, sharing a past that he still didn't know all the details of. "All right, then we need to head that way and get them down off that mountain. If Rabor or Shondra run into them . . ."

"Yeah. And unfortunately, they're not answering the attempts to contact them. The emergency locator beacon is the only thing they have to go on right now."

"That doesn't sound good."

"This storm is only going to get worse in the next little while," Julianna said. "Hopefully, we can get up there and get to them before too much longer."

"We?" Julianna wouldn't normally do something like that, but since it was Penny . . .

"I'm going with you." She narrowed her eyes. "There's a killer up there. And so are Penny and the others. If he manages to grab one of them . . ."

"Yeah."

"I need to be there."

"I agree," Holt said. "Rabor knows we're on his tail and is going to be looking for someone he can use as leverage. I don't want to give him that opportunity."

She nodded. "Exactly."

With practiced movements, they gathered their gear, satellite phones, and rain ponchos and headed back out into the storm.

Acknowledgments

Writing a book is never a solitary event. I often get asked how I come up with my stories, and while they *all* come from my imagination, I always have help creating them. I have a group of brainstormers who are amazing and talented people. Whenever I need help figuring out the plot, the characterization, the *whatever*, I can simply send out an email, asking for help. You know who you are, and I am forever indebted to you.

Speaking of being forever indebted . . . I can't thank former FBI Special Agents Wayne Smith and Dru Wells for all of your input into my stories. I learn so much from you EVERY SINGLE TIME. It's often overwhelming, all of the information that could go into the books, so thank you for keeping it accurate and yet manageable at the same time. You guys are simply amazing.

I need to give a shout-out to Officer Jason Fort, who is always my "go to" for hospital security. You've helped me in several books, and I thank you for your willingness to take the time out of your busy schedule to answer my questions.

Thank you to the Revell team. You guys are phenomenal, and I consider it an honor to work with you all—from cover designers to beta readers. But most especially Barb and her tireless efforts to find all of my mistakes. :) I definitely couldn't do this without you. So, remember, you're not allowed to retire until I do!

I'm sending a big hug and thanks to my amazing and brilliant agent, Tamela Hancock Murray of the Steve Laube Agency. You've become a wonderful friend and I love you dearly. Thank you for all your hard work on my behalf.

I must say thank you as well to all the faithful readers. Thank you for buying the books. It allows me to keep doing the job I love.

And as always, a special shout-out to my family. Thank you for supporting and loving me and putting up with me! Thank you for learning to cook. I know it was a means of survival, and you all do it so well now. And thanks, Mom and Dad, for always encouraging me to follow my dreams. I love y'all to the moon and back.

And last, but never least, thank you to my Savior, Jesus Christ. Thank you for allowing me to do what I do, and thank you for the lives the stories touch. Thank you for your grace when I whine about being tired or brain dead. Thank you for loving and redeeming a sinner like me.

Lynette Eason is the bestselling author of *Collateral Damage* and *Acceptable Risk*, as well as *Protecting Tanner Hollow* and the Blue Justice, Women of Justice, Deadly Reunions, Hidden Identity, Elite Guardians, and Danger Never Sleeps series. She is the winner of three ACFW Carol Awards, the Selah Award, and the Inspirational Reader's Choice Award, among others. She is a graduate of the University of South Carolina and has a master's degree in education from Converse College. Eason lives in South Carolina with her husband and two children. Learn more at www.lynetteeason.com.

Also from Lynette Eason:
The **WOMEN OF JUSTICE** Series

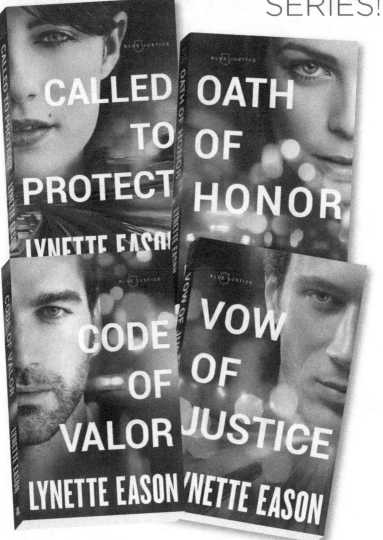

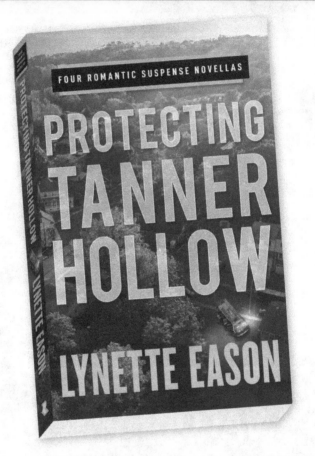

You are not alone.

Popular speaker Jack Eason unpacks the loneliness that plagues us,
shows us how to find and nurture deep relationships and true community,
and inspires us with stories of the power of doing things together.

Connect with
LYNETTE

Sign up for Lynette Eason's newsletter to stay in touch on new books, giveaways, and writing conferences.

LYNETTEEASON.COM

 Lynette Eason | LynetteEason